1

The rhythmic stomping of the crowd shook the entire arena. Feet pounded the bleachers in unison while people cheered and whistled. Blasting out of a loudspeaker, electronic music thumped down the stairway of the creaky old ice-rink and along the narrow hall beneath the stands.

Inside the Kingsford Crushers' dressing room, Sixteen-year-old Mitch Mythic scrambled about in his full uniform, searching under equipment and looking behind doors.

"Has anybody seen my lucky stick? It's a black and green Dryden," Mitch shouted out before he ran his hands through his dark brown hair in frustration, but all of his teammates looked around and shrugged. The coach's head popped in the door and shouted at the players.

"Ok boys, let's go. Mitch, you take 'em out. You're the captain and all."

The team pushed out of the dressing room, forcing Mitch to take the lead, empty-handed. As the lights dimmed above the ice, a booming voice came over the speaker.

"Ladies and Gentlemen, and kids of all ages, here they are - the pride of the north - your very own Kingsford Crushers!"

The Crushers' team anthem pumped through the speakers while a kaleidoscope of spinning lights flooded the ice, causing everyone in the packed arena to leap to their feet and cheer with wild enthusiasm.

Mitch stood in front of his teammates as the gates to the ice opened. He still hadn't found his stick, and he cringed at the thought of entering the ice without it, but the other players shoved him forward while they rushed out. In a vain attempt to flee, he spun around to find the Crushers' enormous goaltender, Gareth "Double-Cheese" Lishinski, barreling down upon him. Mitch leaped away, but Double-Cheese knocked him backward and he tumbled out onto the ice. A roar of laughter erupted in the stands as everybody watched Mitch collect himself near the center of the rink.

"Way to go, Mythic," he heard from behind the players' bench before he got to his feet. "What a mythical entrance."

The taunting or the fall didn't bother him as much as his missing stick. The thought of playing the final match of the season against the Crushers most hated rivals, The Vanderton Thunder, without his lucky stick, filled him with dread.

The Thunder players were already out and warming up. He could feel the cold stares from the other team at the opposite end of the rink. While he searched the bench for his missing stick, he heard skates on the ice behind him. Eric Archibald, the Captain of the Thunder, circled around nearby the Crushers' bench.

"Hey Mitch, what kind of mythical performance will we see from you tonight?" Eric shouted. "If it's anything like your entrance, I'm sure it will be a sight to behold. See you on the ice, Mythical Mitch!"

Ignoring Eric's comments, Mitch searched the Crushers' bench while the panic in his guts grew to a boil, but the horn sounded, signaling the start of the game. Biting down on his tongue, Mitch fought back the urge to scream in frustration.

Mitch's father, Mike Mythic, coached the Crushers, and he spoke with a commanding tone as the players gathered around.

"Men, this is the final game of the season. Whoever wins tonight will claim the league championship. We've worked hard to get here, and we don't want to let those dirtbags from Vanderton take away our glory on home ice. Everybody came here to see you do us proud. Don't disappoint them."

"Hey, Mythic, you planning on showing up today?" Sage Rhinus said before he leaped over the boards onto the ice. Tall, lean, and muscular, Sage played right wing on Mitch's line and together they were a force to be reckoned with, but over the course of the season, their relationship had chafed due to Mitch being made captain.

Groaning under his breath, Mitch rifled through a pile of sticks behind the bench. He found a right-handed blade with minimal damage and skated to the center of the rink.

"Well, looky looky, here comes the grand and glorious Mitch Mythic. How mythical it is to be in your presence," Eric jeered as Mitch approached. Mitch didn't respond.

The linesman entered the circle, and the two players came forward to the dot. The puck dropped, and Mitch swiped at it only to catch Eric's elbow to the back of his head. Face-planting onto the ice, Mitch came up quickly and looked around in disbelief for the referee.

"No penalty?" he cried out, but the referee ignored him while the other players raced away.

"Get going, Mitch," his father screamed from the bench. Groaning again, he skated towards his own goal while Eric lined up for a shot. Before Mitch knew what happened, all the Thunder players were congratulating Eric for scoring the opening goal.

"Nice going, Mythic," Sage said as he skated by while Mitch's father beckoned him over to the bench.

"Get your head in the game, Mitch," he screamed after Mitch sat down in a huff amidst his teammates.

Needless to say, the rest of the game did not go well for Mitch. The Crushers, however, managed to battle back, and with time almost out in the third period, the score remained locked at two goals apiece. The horn ended regulation play, and the referee indicated that the game would go into sudden death overtime.

"Your team mates are looking for some leadership, Mitch" his father said from behind the bench. "It's only the most important game of the season. We might need our captain to show us how it's done."

As the overtime period lurched to a start, Mitch knew he needed to do something, but the excellent defense of the thunder smothered him at every turn. Although both teams battled ferociously during the overtime period, neither side managed to score. While the final seconds of extra time ticked down to zero, everybody knew a shootout would decide the game.

The referee came to the bench and told the coaches each team would get three shots.

"I want Sage first, followed by Darren. Mitch, you shoot last." Mitch's father said. Mitch sighed under his breath, and he felt the hot stares from his teammates burning through the back of his helmet.

The first shooter for the Thunder skated to the center ice dot. Pointing at the puck, the referee blew his whistle. The Thunder player paused for a moment before skating toward the net. Moving to his left, he tried to deke out the Crusher's big goaltender, but Double-Cheese steered it aside with ease. The crowd roared in approval.

Sage went next. Skating quickly toward the goaltender, he blasted a shot to the top left corner of the net. The crowd went wild.

The next Thunder shooter prepared himself at center ice. As he closed in on the net, he faked left, then right, sending Double-Cheese sprawling onto the ice. Stepping past the goaltender, he slipped the puck into the net.

Darren Francis from the Crushers came forward. Lanky and easygoing, he saluted the audience while he came to a stop at center ice. Pausing for a moment, he lined himself up before striding forward under the roar of the crowd. As he neared the goal, he tried to fake, but the goaltender poked the puck away. The crowd murmured their disappointment.

"Ready to be embarrassed on home ice, Mythical?" Eric sneered while making his way past the Crushers bench. Without hesitating, he skated directly at the net. He wound up to shoot as Double-Cheese rushed out to cut off the angle, but Eric faked and spun around the big goaltender before smashing the puck into the back of the goal and giving the Thunder a commanding two goals to one lead with one shooter remaining.

Mitch stepped onto the ice. The entire season rested firmly on his shoulders. The fear and dread boiled in his stomach and he gagged as he skated toward the referee. No, not now, hold it back, he thought to himself. Before he reached the puck, he heard a voice cry out from the bench.

"Hey Mitch, wait." Jason, the team's equipment manager, shouted. "Is this your stick?"

The elusive lucky stick sat in Jason's hand. Its carbon shaft gleaming in the overhead lights. Skating back to the bench, Mitch snatched the stick from the Jason. "Thank you so much. You are a lifesaver."

The stick felt light and agile in his hands. Filled with strength and purpose, he returned to the puck and took a deep breath before looking toward the Thunders' goaltender.

"It all comes down to this, folks," the announcer said over the loudspeaker. "Mitch Mythic must score now, or the Thunder will win the game."

"You can do this," he whispered to himself before driving toward the net. As he neared, he leaned into his stick, faking right before pulling to his left. The goaltender fell for his deke, and he lunged to the right again. Only Empty ice, white and clean, sat before him and the open goal.

Mitch reached forward with his stick to slide the puck into the net, but out of nowhere came the leg of the sprawling goaltender. The pad caught the puck and Mitch's lucky stick at the same time before slamming into the post. Going full force, Mitch watched in horror as his stick jammed into the goalie's pad and simultaneously speared him in the crotch, causing immediate and immense pain. With the stick planted firmly in his groin, Mitch, in agony, pole-vaulted above the goaltender and over the net. He fell to the ice behind the goal in a crumpled heap, only to hear the referee blow his whistle. Looking up, he watched the official wave his hands from side to side, indicating a stopped puck.

All the Thunder players rushed onto the ice and piled on top of the goaltender. The game was over. The fans filed out of the arena, while the Thunder celebrated. To his right, Mitch saw the lucky stick, snapped in half, lying on the ice beside him.

2

A few months had passed since the Kingsford Crushers' shocking loss to the Vanderton Thunder on home ice. The game marked the end of the season, but it took a few more months for winter's firm grip upon the northland to give way to kinder weather. Warm rays of sun melted the giant piles of snow blanketing the ground, and the evergreens shed their icy beards to welcome the spring.

Everybody in Kingsford eventually moved on from the defeat at the hands of the Thunder, all except for Mitch Mythic. Devastated by the loss, and he couldn't help but blame himself. To make matters worse, the ubiquitous and ever-present Internet behemoth known as MindHIve featured his video through their streaming service, spreading the incident far and wide across the web.

A massive social media and technology company, MindHIve dominated the industry in every way. Through one of the tech giant's interconnected applications, any SNS function could be completed with ease. From texts and games to video and beyond, MindHIve was ever-present and unavoidable. Mitch had a strong following on MindHIve, and he actively cultivated his presence on the platform. However, after his epic fail went viral, the video of the incident racked up millions of views on MindTv, the video extension of MindHIve, in a matter of weeks.

Mitch watched in shock as the dark forces of the web dragged his carefully crafted persona into the bowels of internet humor. A crueler place had never been imagined, and all that found themselves drawn into this horror rarely returned unscathed. Mitch had often been amused by the never-ending stream of gifs and memes MindHIve offered up on his feed. He and his friends shared them amongst each other for their amusement, but Mitch never imagined he would become the "joke."

"#Epiccrotchshot," as the incident became known, trended heavily across all platforms after the local news team posted the video to their website. Reposted all over the Internet, the video caught the attention of every single comedian in the country. After a short while, #Epiccrotchshot transformed into a buzzword throughout the world, and for months it slotted into the punch line of any joke imaginable. Mitch, like most kids, always thought being famous would be amazing, but he never imagined it would turn out like this.

To make matters worse, his IRL social life absolutely disintegrated in tandem with the rise of his online celebrity status. After the loss, his teammates slowly turned their backs on him. He felt the cold shoulders during the season while he bore the burden of being the team captain, but in the aftermath of the game and his newfound fame, it seemed like the entire community ghosted him.

Photos of his 'friends' posing together in any manner of circumstances littered his news feed. Weeks after the final game, Sage posted a photo titled: 'the guys.' In the photo, all of his friends and teammates were gathered around a table in Sage's backyard having a BBQ. Mitch felt the pangs of anxiety knot in his gut as he realized he hadn't been invited. He texted Sage after he saw the post.

"Hey, what's up? You having a party?"

He waited by his phone in anticipation of a response from Sage, but nothing came. Switching back to MindHIve, he saw another post by Sage. This time, "the guys" were posing like gangsters and making gestures with their hands. Mitch texted Sage again, only to watch in horror as his message went unread.

While spring turned into summer, Mitch found himself more and more cut off from his own community. Sitting at home alone one Friday night, Mitch opened his MindHIve feed and saw a red banner notification that read: "Sage Rhinus has started a live video, click here to catch the feed."

Hesitating at first, he clicked the link. He was immediately redirected to a streaming video of his friends dancing around a fire at the Kingsford gravel pit. Screaming and shouting at the camera, a large group of people stood next to a raging fire while music pumped in the background before Sage turned the camera to face himself.

"Yeah, what up? What up? We off the chain tonight! I'm here with my tightest homies, and we are gettin' into it!"

A screeching voice cut through the distorted music before the crowd parted to reveal an enraged woman.

"Sage Alister Rhinus, what is the meaning of this?" the voice demanded.

"Mom, what are you doing here? This is a live video feed," Sage shouted at his mother.

"I don't care if you are on the phone with the President. You shut it down this instant! You are out way past your bedtime and are you drinking beer?" Sage's mother shouted.

"Shut up, Mom. I can do whatever I want. I'm 16 now," Sage shouted back.

"Not while you are living in my house!" His mother screeched.

Fighting back the urge to laugh, Mitch watched in amazement as Sage and his mother wrestled for the phone. In the background, several kids laughed and cheered at the spectacle before the video went black.

Everybody at Kingsford Senior High had seen the #epiccrotchshot video, and it seemed like hardly a moment could pass without it being brought up. As Mitch walked through the halls of his school on his way to class or during breaks, he overheard the snickering behind his back and the blatant taunts echoing off the concrete walls of the school.

His friends, having ghosted him online, were no different at school. He once sat at the cool table in the cafeteria, but he soon found himself relegated to the outer edges of the social order into no-man's-land. A big school in a small town, Kingsford boasted an omnipresent social pecking order. The only place Mitch could find a space to sit now was way in the back near the doors to the rear garbage depository, or the stink pit, as it had been aptly named. Sitting near the stink pit meant one's social status sat at the bottom rung. In order to reach the stink pit, he needed to make his way past every table in the cafeteria, turning the entire ordeal into a daily walk of shame for Mitch Mythic.

After grabbing his lunch on the last Monday in May, he pretended not to notice the table filled with his teammates and walked toward the back of the cafeteria while pondering the contents of the soup. It appeared to be a tomato broth with what looked like carrots. He heard the catcalls begin as he attempted to trudge to the stink pit unnoticed. As he walked by, a leg shot out from the side of a table and caught his foot. Tripping over the outstretched limb, he stumbled across the floor, and launched the entire contents of his lunch over the crowded tables of the cafeteria.

Governed by Candace McAllister, the pretty girls of Kingsford High always sat together. As the captain of the Kingsford High Volleyball team, Candace ruled her squad with an iron fist, and she didn't hesitate to take offense to anything she considered out of line. She held court in the cafeteria at the third table from the right with her back to the wall. As usual, her posse flanked her on both sides, each dressed in well-fitting brand name stretch lycra.

Unfortunately for Mitch, his soup chose this table, filled with the prettiest girls in school, as its final destination on its journey across the cafeteria. Reaching the apex of its climb, the bowl inverted and let loose its payload, bombing the entire group of girls before coming down with a hard clang in the middle of the table.

For a moment, the cafeteria went silent. The girls sat motionless while tomato soup dripped from their hair and soaked into their clothes. Candace happened to be wearing a full sleeve white yoga top she paired with a matching white hairband. She appeared to have taken the brunt of the soup, and a bright red splash sliced diagonally across her clean white top. In an instant, her face turned to the same shade of red as the tomato soup. Without warning, she let loose a scream strong enough to shake the windows above the table.

"You ruined my top, you giant tool!" she screeched at Mitch.

Climbing to his feet, Mitch attempted to comprehend the surrounding chaos, but from behind him, he heard the voice of Sage Rhinus.

"What an epic fail! Mitch Mythic, everybody, Mitch Mythic! King of the fails," he said from the table filled with his friends. Candace and her gaggle of girls got up, gathered their designer bags and charged out of the cafeteria toward the girls' bathroom.

"You'll pay for this, Mitch!" she snarled while she walked away.

"It, it, it ... it was an accident," Mitch stammered. The troupe of distressed girls marched by, and each one glared at him in anger as she passed.

"Did anybody get that on camera? It'll go viral for sure!" Sage said, loud enough for everyone to hear. Hopping over the table, he paused to fix his spiky black hair.

"Mitch, you've got quite the talent, don't you? Mitch Mythic: Fail Master," he sneered, and the entire cafeteria lit up with laughter.

Mitch, having sat on his emotions for too long, felt a fiery rage take hold of him. Turning toward Sage, he charged forward and tackled him in the midsection. Mitch came up on top and pummeled Sage with his fists. The anger brewing in his guts gushed out, and he hammered his rage into Sage's face and body.

Every student in the cafeteria chanted "Fight, Fight," while the spectacle played out before them. Sage tried to get back to his feet, but Vice Principal O'Hare grabbed Mitch from behind after charging into the cafeteria.

"You're coming with me, Mythic." Mister O'Hare growled as he dragged Mitch through a set of double doors.

"This isn't over, Mitch," Sage shouted after he got back to his feet and wiped off his Kingsford High Hockey Jacket.

3

Vice Principal O'Hare dragged Mitch out of the cafeteria and down the hallway towards the principal's office. The sound of kids hollering in the cafeteria rattled through the doors while Mitch followed after the hefty school administrator. He looked down, and his hands were shaking as adrenaline pumped through his body.

"What were you thinking, Mitch?" Mr. O'Hare asked while holding Mitch in an arm-bar.

"It wasn't my fault," Mitch half-shouted.

"It doesn't matter whose fault it was. Violence doesn't solve anybody's problem. It just makes things worse. You're in a lot of trouble, young man." Mr. O'Hare said.

"I know," Mitch groaned.

Striking Sage was crossing a line and not just the school's zero violence policy. He could now consider himself fully ostracized from Kingsford High's elite social community. Even worse, the people he once thought of as his friends were most likely plotting against him while he rushed to meet his fate in the principal's office.

Mr. O'Hare banged open the office door with his shoulder and dragged Mitch into a square waiting room with chairs lining two walls. He sat Mitch down in a chair, still holding him in an arm bar.

"Mitch, I'm going to let you go now. Don't take any swings at me. I don't want to have to send you off to a youth detention camp," Mr. O'Hare said as he eased his grip on Mitch's arm and stepped away. "Ok, you sit here and cool off, Mitch. I'm going to reheat my meatloaf. I've got to eat too. We'll discuss this when I finish my lunch."

The vice principal closed the door and left Mitch in the room. Dropping his head into his hands, he stared down at his shoes. A bit of blood dripped on the floor. He touched his nose and saw blood on his hand. Wiping it with his sleeve, he sighed before looking up at the ceiling.

"Kind of makes you want revenge," a voice growled.

In the corner of the room sat a dark figure wearing a gray hoodie. The hood was drawn over their head, concealing their identity.

"Revenge," the voice growled again. "Don't you want it?"

"What do you know?" Mitch snapped back. "Why don't you mind your own business? I don't need any more trouble today. Things are bad enough as it is."

"You trend well," the figure half chuckled as he spoke.

"What's that supposed to mean?" Mitch snapped back. "You think that's funny, huh? You think I haven't heard it all, already?"

"Careful, we are being watched." The figure looked up and made eyes towards the ceiling.

The CCTV camera sat in an upper corner of the room, monitoring their activities. Vice principal O'Hare was no doubt watching while he scarfed down his meatloaf. For the first time, Mitch saw the face of the person sitting across from him. The boy had dark skin, and his long black hair spilled out of his hoodie in dreadlocks. He appeared to be around the same age as Mitch, but there was something about his demeanor that made him seem years older.

"Well, just keep quiet. I'm not in the mood for any more incidents," Mitch said.

"What if I told you I can help?" the boy replied. He toyed with a ring on his finger as he sat with his left leg crossed over his right. Mitch could detect a strange accent in the boy's voice. He couldn't recall ever seeing him in school before. The boy emitted a quiet cool, and while aloof, he seemed to be watching Mitch's every move.

"What are you gonna do? Go shoot up the school? I don't want to be involved in any mass murder," Mitch said.

"Mass shootings are crude and pointless," the boy said before a grin flashed across his lips. "For any real impact to be felt, a certain sense of style must be imposed."

"Are you some kind of terrorist?" Mitch asked.

"Depends on what you think terror is," the boy replied. Mitch tried to pinpoint his accent, but he couldn't place it. In any case, he definitely was not from Kingsford.

"You've got a lot going for you, Mitch," the boy continued.

"Yeah, right," Mitch scoffed. "I thought I told you to be quiet."

"Over 150 million views the last time I checked. That's a heavy footprint," the boy said.

"Heavy footprint? I'm not talking about this with you right now. I don't even know who you are," Mitch said and turned away.

"Let's just say we have mutual interests." The boy half growled.

"I don't think so. I don't want anything to do with you. Just be quiet," Mitch snapped.

"I could keep quiet, but then you won't know what I offer," the boy said.

"Not interested, and once again, shut up," Mitch said.

"Ok, but I can help with the situation," the boy said.

"My situation? Why am I even talking to you? We're done. No more interaction. Understand?" Mitch said while he looked away.

"Ha, that's funny, you don't have a lot of allies at the moment. Turn me down and you are all alone in your struggle," the boy said.

"Well, maybe that's what I want right now, to be left alone. Can't you take a hint?" Mitch said.

"I can take a hint. But maybe you should also take a hint and listen to what I offer: help," the boy said.

"You can help me? Are you some kind of magician? Can you turn back time?" Mitch said with a laugh.

"Ha, that's funny. A magician, I am not, but I have skills that could be of use. The internet is a strange place filled with all types of hidden danger," the boy said.

"Oh, you're a hacker. Look, I don't know what you're after here, but like I said, I'm not looking for any more trouble. I also don't want to wind up on some blacklist for hacking nuclear codes," Mitch said.

"I am not interested in nuclear codes," the boy said.

"This is nuts. Why am I still talking to you?" Mitch snapped back.

Just then, the door opened. Mitch expected Mr. O'Hare to walk into the room. Instead, it was the school's elderly administrative assistant, Mrs. Peachers. She always wore long flowery dresses, and she enjoyed dying her hair in various exotic colors. Today, she sported a long purple dress dotted with white tulips. Cat faces hid behind the flowers, and sparkly silver shone from their eyes. She whirled into the room and peered around.

"Drakon, Drakon Trendago? Are you in here?" Mrs. Peachers asked.

"I'm here, Mrs. Peachers, and I thought I told you to call me Drak," the boy replied, changing his tone. As he Rose to his feet, he flung off his hood in a dramatic fashion. Stretching up to his full height, he towered over the diminutive secretary as his long limbs hung loose at his side.

"Drak, please come with me. Agent Reynolds is ready to speak with you now. What are you doing in the detention room? I thought I told you to go to the meeting room. The immigration officer arrived 10 minutes ago, and he's been waiting for you." Mrs. Peachers said as she walked out of the door.

"I'll be so happy to get my permanent residency. I'm grateful to stay in this country," Drak responded while he walked toward the door.

"We be in touch, Mitch Mythic," he said as he walked by.

After the pair left the waiting area, Mitch peered out of the room and down the hallway. Mrs. Peachers showed Drak into a well-lit office. A pudgy man in a blue suit stood and greeted the tall, gangly boy.

Who is this guy, Mitch thought to himself while he sat alone in the room, but he didn't have much time to ponder. Mr. O'Hare's heavy footsteps plodded down the hall. The vice principal had finished his meatloaf and was now ready to talk.

"All cooled off, Mitch?" Mr. O'Hare inquired.

"Maybe," Mitch responded, trying to keep his emotions in check.

"Well, come with me. Let's go to my office and discuss this situation."

Walking sullenly behind Mr. O'Hare, he watched the vice principal's bulky torso lumber down the hall in front of him. His large brown loafers thudded on the green linoleum lining the hallway.

Nearing the end of the hall, Mitch almost puked as the vice principal opened his office door. The stench of the meatloaf Mr. O'Hare hastily consumed only moments before still hung in the air.

"Mitch, I'm going to be blunt. This is not good," Mr. O'Hare said after he sat down behind his desk and gestured to a chair. "As you know, the school has a no violence policy and any fight will result in an immediate suspension. Now, I know how this could look on your record, and I understand you've been having a tough time lately, but boy is that video funny. I couldn't imagine having that happen to me, let alone in front of everybody I know. In all honesty, I'm surprised you didn't snap earlier."

"Me too," Mitch half mumbled under his breath.

"So son, in light of all that has happened to you, I'm putting you on an in-school suspension for a week. You will spend the next five school days in the computer lab. There, you will write an essay explaining what happened and why you feel bad about what you did." Mr. O'Hare said before he got to his feet. "This suspension will take place immediately. We'll head over to the lab now so you can start working on your essay. I've notified your father about the fight, and he said he will discuss it with you when you get home. Are you listening, Mitch?" Mr. O'Hare asked.

"Yes. Fine, let's go," Mitch grumbled and got to his feet.

"It's this way, Mitch," Mr. O'Hare directed Mitch down the hall.

"I know where it is," Mitch said.

"Well, you don't have to get testy with me, Mitch. I'm trying to help you out here," Mr. O'Hare snapped back.

On the way out of the office, they walked past Mrs. Peachers while she typed into an aging computer console.

"I'm taking Mitch down to the computer lab for his suspension. You remember Mitch Mythic, Mrs. Peachers?" Mr. O'Hare asked.

"Oh, of course, I don't think I've ever laughed so hard after seeing such a video. It's really quite amazing," Mrs. Peachers snorted.

4

Mr. O'Hare swung open the door, revealing a room filled with flickering monitors from a bygone era. Established over 15 years ago, the school's computer lab received widespread applause from the local community when it opened.

"Now the students at Kingsford High can participate in this new digital age," one local politician had announced during the unveiling of the lab, amidst a throng of reporters. A photo of that celebration still hung on the wall.

Those days of glory had long since passed. Years of abuse and neglect left the lab in a grim state. Most of the computers were embedded with viruses. Their ancient operating systems displayed archaic applications encouraging students to reach out and surf the Worldwide Web.

Mr. O'Hare sat Mitch down at a computer and patted him on the shoulder.

"I know it's been tough, but take this time to gather yourself. The computer lab monitor will be here shortly, and he'll get you sorted," Mr. O'Hare said.

"Mr. O'Hare, always great to see you. How can I be of service?" A familiar voice said from the door.

"Drak, good to see you as well. It's really exciting that you might get your residency permit. I hope it all turns out for you," Mr. O'Hare said as he shook hands with the strange-looking kid Mitch had met minutes earlier in the office.

"We'll see how all turns out. I just hope that I can contribute to the greater good of this country," Drak said.

"That's a mighty wise and selfless outlook to have. I wish I was as wise as you when I was your age. Drak, I'm sure that you know Mitch Mythic," Mr. O'Hare said.

"Of course, I know Mitch Mythic. How could I not? He is perhaps the most famous person in all of Kingsford at the moment," Drak said while he flashed a knowing grin at Mitch. "Everybody all over the world has seen the video. It's quite incredible."

"I know," Mr. O'Hare said. "The first time I saw it, I almost had a heart attack. I laughed so hard."

"It is hysterical," Drak said, agreeing with Mr. O'Hare. Mitch fumed.

"Ah, good times. Anyway, Mitch made a mistake in the cafeteria, and he's going to be spending some time here for the next week working on an essay for regarding what took place. Could you find Mitch the disciplinary essay document and get him started? I've got to get back to the office. Somebody has been stealing canned cheese from the cafeteria, and I'm going to track down some suspects," Mr. O'Hare said before he made his way to the door. "Mitch, hang in there, OK. Things are going to improve for you. I mean, I can't see how they could get any worse. You're in good hands with Drak. He is a computer wizard."

As Mr. O'Hare left, an awkward silence filled the room. All that could be heard was the whirring of the obsolete computers.

"Ugh," Drak said, breaking the silence. "I have no idea how you put up with this for so long. You are an immensely well-composed individual. This is also reflected in the data."

"What data? Why am I still talking to you? Who are you?" Mitch shouted.

"All in good time, my friend. I will reveal many things to you as we work together. It may shock or scare, but you need to know the truth in order to accomplish our goal," Drak said while he walked toward the front of the computer lab.

"This is insane. I'm not working with you on anything. I don't even know you, and I already know I don't want anything to do with you. Can you just shut up and leave me alone? You sound completely nuts, and I don't think I need any more insanity in my life at the moment," Mitch said.

"I know you are suffering," Drak replied, locking eyes with Mitch from across the room. "But I am about to show you that your suffering is not in vain," Drak said while turning on a bank of computers. "Although your circumstances are trying, you have a larger part to play here. What befell you in the past will be a boon to our cause in the future."

"Just leave me alone," Mitch said. "I don't know who you are or what you want, but this is totally nuts."

"I'll tell you what I am. I am a refugee. I fled to this place from my home to escape persecution and imprisonment. I alone escaped, leaving my family far behind. As we speak, they are confined to a place filled with torment and horror." Drak's eyes grew distant as he spoke, and he fell into a deep silence. After what felt like an eternity, he turned and looked at Mitch. "It could always be worse, Mitch. Now, if you don't mind, I will help you now."

"Well, that's a sad story," Mitch said. "But I don't know why you think I can help you. I'm not some commando warrior or something."

"I am not asking you to free my people. I have skills that can help you. Allowing me to help you will help me," Drak replied.

"I still have no idea what you are talking about," Mitch said.

"Let me have access to your MindHIve account. I will relieve your social distress."

"You want me to let you into my account. I don't think so. Look, I've got to write this stupid essay for Mr. O'Heavybutt, so could you leave me alone? I'm just not in the mood for this right now."

"Perhaps you need a better understanding of my skill set. Allow me to demonstrate a few of my abilities."

"What? Whatever, man, just, oh well, fine, show me what you can do. Just go away afterward, OK?"

"You need to write an essay, yes?" Drak asked. "I'll make it easy on you. Let me apply the algorithm to problem."

Dropping himself into the chair next to Mitch, Drak bypassed the ancient operating system of the computer with ease before he hammered streams of code into a black screen with skill and precision. After a few moments, he paused and hit the return key. A stream of numbers and symbols shot across the black screen. Without warning, the screen went blank, and the room fell back into silence.

"What did you do?" Mitch asked.

"It's there on the desktop," Drak said.

"Where? What's on what desktop?" Mitch replied.

"Open the file on the computer," Drak said.

Peering at the screen in front of him, Mitch saw a file called

"Disciplinary Essay by Mitch Mythic."

"What is this?" Mitch asked again.

"Just open it," Drak said.

"Did you just yank this off of the internet? Anybody can do that!" Mitch said while he clicked on the file.

"I'd never participate in an act of plagiarism," Drak stated. "I have, however, applied a special algorithm to the word processor. By assigning a few key tasks, the computer wrote an essay for you based upon readily available information. Authoritarian rulers often wish to impose 'busy work' upon subjects to maintain a dominant position. By using the tools Mr. O'Hare left available, we have freed you from this injustice. I have much experience dealing with injustice."

Mitch looked over the essay and was immediately blown away by what he read. The essay outlined the situation with accuracy. It mentioned the fight, and the people involved. It also went into detail about Mitch's actions and how he felt remorse for what he did.

"How did you do this?" Mitch asked with astonishment.

"With the right tools, any task can be accomplished. It's how one applies the algorithm," Drak said.

"What is this algorithm you're talking about?" Mitch demanded to know.

"It not important right now. Just think it as a tool that produces things you want. I gave it the available information, including the feelings and emotions of the people involved, and told the program what the outcome should be. The algorithm did the rest," Drak said.

"So I don't need to write an easy for O'Hefty?" Mitch asked.

"Not unless you feel a need for penance," Drak replied. "Now, if you are satisfied with my abilities, will you please allow me to show you some of my other skills?"

"Uh, what is it that you're trying to do?" Mitch asked.

"To put it simply, you are much more powerful than you think. I intend to allow you to be the star of the content you so much despise. Seize control of the message," Drak said, leaning back in his chair.

"What is that supposed to mean?" Mitch said.

"Mitch Mythic, you must open your mind. You have made yourself the victim in this situation, but you need to realize that you are the hero of the story. Once you see it that way, you will be able to climb out of this pit of misery and become the master of your destiny."

"Whoa, stalk much, dude? How is it that you know so much about me? That's a really inspiring speech, but just show me what you want to do."

"In order for you to take control of the message, we need to put your face at the forefront of the story. In the video, you are merely a body sent flying. We must attach your identity to the video," Drak explained.

"That is the last thing I want to do," Mitch said.

"But it is the one thing you need to do. We cannot control outside circumstances, but we can control how we react to them. So far, you've been a passive actor in this drama. By coming out and saying to the world - 'I am #epiccrotchshot boy. I am proud to be me, and I not ashamed of it' - you will have stepped into the spotlight and placed yourself in the story. That is you in the video, no one else."

"Once again, that's a great speech, but how do you intend to take control of the video? It's already got millions of views, and there are so many reposts already. Somebody even made a cat version."

"I will use the same algorithm I used to produce the essay. Do some magic. Just allow me to access your account."

"How am I supposed to trust you?"

"That's up to you. But look around, I don't see anyone else trying to help you."

"Ughhh, fine, just don't do anything nuts."

"Oh, don't worry. What I'm going to do will be more than nuts," Drak said, and he flashed another mysterious grin. "All I need you to do is look in the camera and say: 'My name is Mitch Mythic, and I am epiccrotchshot boy."

"What? That's insane! Why would I say that?"

"Because it is totally insane to say. If you want people to notice, you must do crazy things. Saying I am #epiccrotchshot boy is a crazy thing."

Mitch had a tough time arguing with Drak's logic. Thanks to MindHIve's own content algorithm, to get the attention of the public, one had to engage in an escalating cavalcade of one-upmanship. Mitch was also keenly aware of the fact that he had bottomed out. Aside from going to prison, things couldn't get any worse.

He also knew he might have committed a crime. Hitting a person was considered an assault, and he hit Sage really hard, several times. Perhaps Sage had already contacted his father, a prominent lawyer in Kingsford, and they were preparing a lawsuit against him for aggravated assault. As far as Mitch could tell, he didn't have a lot of options.

"Do you really think you can help me?" Mitch asked.

"I do not doubt it for a moment," Drak replied.

"Fine. How do you want to do this? Do you have a camera, or should I use my phone?"

"Your phone will be fine," Drak said. Mitch noticed the slightest hint of a smile cross Drak's face.

"Hmm, all right. So just look into the camera, and say it? That's all you need me to do?" Mitch asked again, looking to Drak for reassurance.

"You just need to say: My name is Mitch Mythic, and I am #epiccrotchshot boy."

"I can't believe I'm doing this," Mitch said before he picked up his phone and opened the camera app. Pausing for a moment, he closed his eyes and took a big breath. His thumb pressed the video record button on the camera before a red light flashed. He looked into the camera and said: "My name is Mitch Mythic, and I am #epiccrotchshot boy."

5

After being released from the computer lab by Mister O'Hare, Mitch spent the walk home from school reeling between emotions. In one moment, he would grimace at the thought of being abandoned by his friends, and then in the next, he found himself elated for having stood up to the people who had disrespected him.

The route home from Kingsford High to Mitch's house led through a sprawl of suburban homes known as Dream Acres. The neighborhood comprised a massive property development in Kingsford, and all the homes had been built following a pattern. Each house boasted a beautiful front entrance lined with pillars, and on both sides of the door sat two large bay windows. Through the windows of every house, a large television spouted an endless stream of news and drama.

A pathway through a greenbelt provided a shortcut to Mitch's street, and it also offered a break from the monotony of the well-cured lawns and aluminum paneled houses that were the signature style of the Dream Acres Property development.

The trail followed a water drainage that led to the massive Franklin River nearby. Gushing with the spring runoff, the stream pooled around a culvert before disappearing under the road. As birds chattered in the trees and the warm rays of light cast off by the afternoon sun crept in through the branches of the soaring pine trees that called the ravine home, a feeling of peace ebbed up Mitch's spine, and he let go a deep exhale while he walked through the forest.

He couldn't help but feel relieved after speaking into the camera at Drak's request. The shame he had felt over the last few months had been tremendous. By simply admitting it was him in the video, he felt a gigantic release of stress and frustration. There was nothing he could do to change the past, but he wasn't going to be a victim. It didn't matter to him if Sage wanted to turn everybody against him, or if everybody thought he was some kind of joke. He didn't care what they thought, and he didn't care about hockey.

Coming around a corner, Mitch came to a fork in the road. One way led uphill, and the other continued following the stream. Mitch took the uphill path which led to a neighborhood park and Mitch's street. Walled in by slopes on both sides, the pathway cut into the hill at a steep angle. Mitch heard something moving behind him. As he turned, he could see three boys approaching him from the other direction. He recognized them immediately, for they were his teammates or his former teammates. They sneered when they saw him. Mitch turned to run, and then he saw Sage standing at the top of the path flanked by two boys on either side.

"Where are you going, Mitch Mythic? We've got some unfinished business, you and I," Sage said while the other boys snickered beside him. "Grab him, Donnie, before he runs."

Bigger than the others in both size and stature, Donnie grabbed Mitch by the arm from behind. Mitch tried to break free, but Greg Curtis caught him by the other arm. Mitch wasn't afraid of Sage on his own, but he knew he didn't stand a chance now. He stopped struggling and raised his head in defiance.

"You think you got the best of me in the cafeteria, Mitch? Let me show you I mean business. Let him go, boys," Sage said. Donnie and Greg shoved Mitch from behind as they released their grips. Stumbling forward, he landed on his knees. As he tried to get to his feet, Sage hit him hard in the chin, and he went down again. Mitch tried to lift himself up, but Sage kicked him hard in the ribs.

"That's for blowing the game. And this is for hitting me today." Sage yelled while white flashes of pain ripped through Mitch's body.

As Mitch took the beating, a strange whistling filled the air.

"Whooo-heee Whoo," echoed through the forest causing Sage to give pause.

A gangly kid wearing a grey hoodie over his head walked down the path toward the crowd gathered over Mitch. Drak's strange body type was unmistakable. His long arms swung casually at his side as he strolled up to the group of boys.

"Good afternoon, fellow students. I am walking in the woods for pleasure. It seems you are having pleasure with Mitch," Drak said while flashing a grin.

"What do you want, freak? Get out of here before we take care of you too," Sage snarled. "Wait a minute, are you friends with this weirdo, Mitch? Ha, seems right; you two losers should be friends. Grab him, Donnie. When I'm finished with Mitch, I'll deal with him next."

Donnie reached out to grab Drak, but he stepped aside and grabbed him by the arm before flipping him on to his back in one swift movement. Donnie's big body came crashing down, and he groaned as the wind left his chest. Everybody stood motionless for a second, astonished by what they had just witnessed.

"Oh look, we got Bruce Lee on our hands. Get him," Sage said.

The remaining assailants turned and moved towards Drak, who crept backward cat-like. His face calm and relaxed while his long arms hung by his side. Greg swung at him, but Drak knocked back the blow, and at the same time, grabbed his attacker by the collar. Drak pulled Greg down and effortlessly flipped him over onto his back before slamming him into the ground. The same fate met all the other would-be attackers. Drak tossed them all aside again and again until they were all exhausted.

"Let's go," Drak mouthed after he stepped away from his final victim. Scrambling to his feet, Mitch made his way up the steep path to the park as Drak followed close behind.

"You'll never play on our team again. I don't care if your dad's the coach. We're done," Sage yelled, stalking up the opposite path.

Mitch ran all the way through the park, past the merry-go-round and the swings, and up the hill until he reached the sidewalk. Turning around, he grabbed his knees to catch his breath as Drak jogged up the hill behind him.

"What are you a ninja too? Do you know how bad you've made this whole thing now? All those guys are going to want to kill me, thanks to you," Mitch said.

"What they think does not matter. Soon this situation will be forgotten. There are much bigger problems on the horizon," Drak said.

"Oh, I know. I might have gotten myself into this, but you just made it worse. I was doing fine there on my own. Now those guys are going to come back even harder than before. And another thing, are you following me? What's wrong with you, dude? Don't tell me you are some kinda stalker. My life is already messed up as it is. I don't need some psycho making everything worse," Mitch said.

"A friend needed help, so I helped," Drak said. "Why are you angry?"

"I'm angry because... ahh... look, it doesn't matter. Listen, I just want to go home and forget all of this happened. I know you're trying to help, but you're just making things worse. You might get sued after what you did to those guys."

"They attacked. I hit back. No one got hurt. They started the fight. I finished it. I don't know why you care what they think. They wanted to hurt you. They are enemies. You fight back. This is the way."

"It's not the way. Oh, you just don't understand how things work around here."

"I understand very well. Social hierarchy is very important in your culture. Don't worry. Go home. Rest. Things will be different tomorrow."

"Oh, things will be different tomorrow, for sure. Thanks for all the help, Drak," Mitch said and walked away. After a few seconds, he looked back. The park was empty, and Drak had vanished.

6

A big living room window sat next to the front entrance of Mitch's house, and could see his mother standing in the living room with her hands on her hips, watching him walk up the driveway. She had, no doubt, heard about what happened at school, and a long and infuriating lecture awaited him inside.

Mitch walked through the side entrance into the garage. His mother's small gray sedan sat to the left of the interior door. It looked like his mother had just arrived home from shopping. Mindy Mythic loved a bargain, and she always brought back all kinds of strange and interesting items she found on sale. Picking his way past an assortment of boxes cluttering the entrance, he took off his shoes before walking inside. His mother stood on the stairs leading to a landing in the kitchen. Her jaw quivered as he stood at the door.

"Your father told me there was an incident at school," his mother said before Mitch sighed and sat on the couch.

"What's happening with you, Mitch? It looks like you are letting this family down. Your father and I have a good reputation in this town, and we won't let our son go around, giving our name a black eye. There is talk all over town that you've been fighting with your teammates. It looks like nobody is going to press charges, but we can't have you clobbering on anybody you like. The world isn't a hockey rink, Mitch. Despite what you think, your father and I aren't rich people. I don't want some lawsuit ruining my retirement plan."

"Thanks for understanding, Mom. It's all about you, isn't it? I just had a brutal day, and this is what I get. Nobody is on my side here," Mitch shouted at his mother. He got to his feet, grabbed his backpack, and went down to his room in the basement.

"You can't just walk away from me," his mother shouted back. "Your father will be home soon, and he'll want to talk to you too."

Mitch slammed the door to his room and threw his bag down in disgust. Flinging himself on his bed, he closed his eyes in an attempt to block out the outside world.

Next to his bed sat a battered dresser and a cluttered desk. An old couch Mitch had taken from upstairs before his mother threw it away after purchasing a new set of DIY Swedish furniture to decorate the house slotted into the corner beside the closet. The floor was littered with old clothes and spare change. Mitch had covered the walls with posters of sports stars, bands, and old movies. On the desk, his computer gaming computer stared back at him, its blank screen awaiting commands.

Sitting up, he moved to the edge of the bed and spotted his reflection on the computer. Even in the grayed-out monitor, Mitch could see how disheveled he looked. He picked a leaf out of his hair that must've gotten in there when he was shoved to the ground by Greg and Donnie. Staring at the leaf for a second, he tossed it on the floor before he got up and turned on his computer.

He laid his head down on the desk and listened to the sounds of the computer booting up. Although Mitch loved playing sports, he also loved playing video games. Mitch's computer wasn't the best computer in the world, but he had set it up with all the right hardware for online gaming. The most popular game at the moment was "Deathworld," an online open-world RPG that allowed players to build custom characters and join quests or battle alongside other players online. Mitch had been building his character for months, and he had recently upgraded his armor to snake level after defeating an evil wizard. Gaming had been Mitch's way to escape the horrors of his everyday life since #epiccrotchshot went viral. It was the only way he could turn off the outside world and cease to be himself, if only for a short time.

DeathWorld, however, was a product of MindHIve, so Mitch's gaming profile connected to his MindHIve account. MindHIve made sure all of their products infiltrated the user's daily life, and DeathWorld was no exception. While tracking down and killing enemies, the player was constantly bombarded with notifications and player interactions. Mitch had been able to mask his identity by using the handle "Legend23," but he could not stop MindHIve from sending push notifications through the game's HUD. Synchronized across multiple platforms, DeathWorld allowed anyone with an Internet connection could access the same world as anybody else. Although it wasn't the first of its kind, DeathWorld was very good at integrating itself into the user's daily life. It was addictive and endless, and it provided Mitch with enough distraction to forget about his problems.

As his computer finished booting up he logged into his MindHIve account without thinking. For a moment, the screen was white and the company's logo - a simple interlaced MH - flashed on the screen. Watching his profile load, he sat in stunned silence for a moment before he pressed the reload button in disbelief.

"That can't be right," Mitch said to himself out loud. Once the screen loaded again, Mitch stared aghast at his profile. His picture had changed to a screenshot taken from the #epiccrotchshot video. It showed him in mid-air being flung over the top of the net. Next to the profile photo in the banner read the statement he had said to Drak earlier in the day: "My Name is Mitch Mythic, and I am #epiccrotchshot boy." Below the letters, a gif of the video played on an endless loop.

"What has that crazy maniac done?" Mitch said aloud before something else caught his eye. There were three things that mattered most in the world of MindHIve users: likes, comments, and most importantly, connects. A connect was someone that had hit the connection button on any given account, linking them together. How many connects a user had determined their status, so obviously, more connects meant a higher rank. In the morning, Mitch had 1723 connects. He had more than most kids he knew, but like everybody else, he wanted more. Shocked by what he saw, he reloaded the page again and stared in disbelief. There were 23,472 new connects since his last login, an unbelievable gain. His likes and comments had exploded as well. Thousands of people had posted on his feed. Mitch was certain he was being trolled, but, as he read the comments, he struggled to comprehend what he saw.

Cher45 wrote: @epiccrotchshotboy you are my hero.

Drontheeagle wrote: @epiccrotchshotboy incredible!

Hockeyhead wrote: This guy is awesome!

The comments rolled on and on. He couldn't understand what had happened, but he knew Drak had everything to do with it.

7

Robert Chapman stood behind the curtains to the left of the stage, waiting. Packed to the rafters, the auditorium buzzed with anticipation. To the right of Robert, his assistant, Allan, clutched a clipboard while holding his finger to a slim earpiece. Any moment now, the engineers would signal that all was ready for Robert's entrance.

Among his peers and the general public, Robert Chapman was considered the greatest innovator in the IT world. As the founder of MindHIve, the largest technology firm in the industry, he had achieved the status of "grand wizard" among the disciples of digital information. Credited with a multitude of earth shattering tech creations, he possessed the inmate ability to craft gadgetry that defied any expectation. It was he who had introduced "Untouch" commands. Untouch had changed the game. While touchable screens had brought handheld devices to the forefront of the tech world, MindHIve's Untouch technology had altered the playing field. These days, Untouch had been implemented into almost every single piece of technology available. From cars to fridges, everything was using Untouch, and Robert had been lavished with praise for his extraordinary achievement.

The board of directors and all the top executives of MindHIve, along with a mass of shareholders, assembled in the grand and glorious MindHIve auditorium for Robert Chapman's latest development. As the lights dimmed, the sound of booming drums and synthesizers filled the room.

"Ladies and Gentleman, are you ready to be a part of history? Please put your hands together for the CEO of MindHIve Robert Chapman," a voice said over a loudspeaker.

A spotlight appeared on the stage, and a huge shadow of a man filled up the background. The crowd roared with approval as Robert took the stage. Beaming in the spotlight, he bowed several times before reaching out to the front row to shake hands with some people. Turning away, he walked to center stage and raised his hands in the air. The audience hushed, and the room grew silent. In the background, on a massive screen, the MindHIve logo spun slowly, animated green static electricity shooting through matte gray letters.

"It's been a long journey to come to this point, ladies and gentlemen, but I have never been more excited to stand on this stage before you. Are you ready for the future?" Robert boomed before another wave of cheers filled the air. "The world has changed, and the technology must change with it. We here at MindHIve believe in one thing before anything else - adapt or die. It's well known that the ingenuity of humans and our technological developments are what dragged our Stone Age relatives out of their caves and into the future. From fire to the wheel to the internet - Bold and innovative ideas have driven humanity into this amazing age. Since its inception, MindHIve has continued to lead the world in innovative technology, and our incredible growth allows us to invest in new ideas. We have made some amazing products, and we have also been able to make a lot of money. Our great success is owed to hard-working people and their ingenious concepts, but let us not forget the technology that failed."

Robert paused and looked out at the audience for dramatic effect.

"Why should we consider things that have failed, you may wonder? Well, as the adage goes: 'If we don't consider what has failed, then we cannot learn from others' mistakes.' Let's look at some technology from recent years that was said to change our world but fell short, shall we?" Robert asked again, and the audience agreed.

On the screen behind Robert, an earpiece appeared.

"Remember these things?" Robert asked. "It was a great idea, hands-free technology. Answer your phone and talk all without touching anything. The only problem is nobody wanted to wear them. Why would that be? It's because you look like an idiot if you wear one of these things. Who wants to go around talking to themselves? We've all seen these guys: 'Hey, what are doing? Oh, I'm just getting some pizza. I think I need to go to the bathroom.' And when it was all said and done, the technology failed," Robert said and looked out at the audience.

"Sometimes good ideas fail because they don't integrate well into people's lives. Technology is as much of a status symbol as it is a useful device," Robert said, and the audience nodded along with him.

"Let's see another one," Robert said. Behind him appeared a pair of glasses.

"We all remember these things: Glasses that allow you to interact with the Internet using your eyes. Billions of dollars got pumped into this tech, but nobody wanted to wear them. They said it would change everything, but the tech geeks didn't realize they have no fashion sense. Again, this technology died. Not because it didn't work, but because it wasn't cool," Robert said, and the crowd laughed.

"What have we learned from all of this? People don't want to look stupid. Even if it's good tech, nobody wants to be bothered with something that isn't cool," Robert said. "Even though we in the biz think something is cool, it doesn't mean people will think it's cool. This is a big problem for us. How do we allow people to use our amazing technology and keep buying our products if they don't think it's cool? What did I say earlier? Adapt or die."

The crowd jumped to their feet again and cheered.

"What we have learned is people like to touch things and use their hands, but they don't want these things to make them stand out or look foolish. How do we create technology that integrates into people's lives yet doesn't burden them with more devices? Well, it just so happens that we have been working on something that will blow your minds," Robert said as he reached into his pocket. The crowd hushed in anticipation.

"Ladies and gentlemen, I give you MindHIve's greatest achievement. A product so innovative, you will not know how you lived without it," Robert stated.

The audience hung to edge of their seats. Reaching into his pocket, he pulled out an ordinary-looking smartphone and held it up in front of him. Everybody sat back in their chairs, unimpressed.

"Ah, you're not amazed, are you? Well, why should you be? This is only the Hive 5, our latest phone. Why would that blow your minds? Our devices have been the pinnacle of our success, and they have driven stock prices through the roof, making all of our shareholders very rich. What is impressive about that?" Robert chuckled, and the crowd laughed and agreed with him.

"People, this little phone is no ordinary device. Along with the greatest operating system on the planet and the fastest internet access one could ask for lies the most important advancement in our modern lives," Robert boomed. The crowd came forward, intrigued, yet not convinced.

Returning the phone to his pocket, he stood in silence. Nobody blinked. After a few breathless moments, Robert reached out with his right hand Turning his hand palm up, he made a fist. Without warning, an opaque sphere engulfed his body The crowd gasped.

After pausing to let the crowd take in the spectacle, he reached out with his finger and drew a circle. An access panel appeared in front of him, and he made a gesture with his hand. The clicking sound of a photo being taken echoed through the room. Grabbing the air with his hand, he placed over a slot on the sphere. A whoosh sound echoed through the auditorium before the MindHIve homepage appeared on the massive screen behind him. A selfie of Robert standing on the stage sat at the top of the feed.

"People, what you are seeing is the first selfie taken with MindHIve's very own technology, which we call: inReal," Robert boomed out to the crowd. Everybody jumped to their feet and cheered. "This is the very first wearable tech you don't have to wear," Robert continued. He reached out again with his hand and made a fist. The sphere around him disappeared. The crowd gasped in astonishment. Robert bowed once more and held out his hand. Turning his hand palm up again, he made a fist and the sphere returned.

"With this technology, you can access anything and everything you want. Maps, health stats, music, social media - it's all here, and it's all inReal," Robert said to the crowd.

Stepping to the edge of the stage, he demonstrated the functions available with inReal. He made music play, and he wrote emails. He edited photos. He found directions. He created a greeting card, and he made a blog entry. The crowd was in a fervor.

"Now, you may be wondering when this new technology will be made available to the public. While we are still in beta testing, we will have full prototypes ready for demonstrations at this year's MindHIve tech convention coming up next month. As you all know, only the most elite, emerging talent around the world is invited to our annual convention, but this year, I believe, is going to be something special. Each attendant will be able to use our inReal technology while they participate in the convention and awards and prizes will be granted to those who best apply the inReal technology to their work," Robert stated. The crowd roared.

"People, we have great work yet to do. I look forward to seeing all of you at the tech convention next month. Now let's go out and make history," he said and bowed in front of the crowd. Everybody rose to their feet and applauded. Robert stepped off the stage, shaking hands as he made his way up the aisle. Reaching the exit of the auditorium, two security guards opened the door to let him pass. He waved to the crowd once more before walking away as the security guards closed the door behind him while the crowd buzzed beyond the door.

8

"You killed it in there, sir," Allan said while trying to keep up with Robert as he strode down the hall.

"I know," Robert said.

He walked to the elevator entrance and waited for Allan to push the button. Standing motionless, he stared forward at the unopened doors. He had killed it in there. He always did. Robert knew how to play the role, and he played it well. The elevator doors opened, and the pair stepped in. Allan made sure he kept just behind Robert and a little to his right, as he had been instructed on several occasions.

Robert glanced to his right and noticed Allan's clipboard. "Are the prototypes ready for inspection?"

"Not quite, sir. The engineers are still adjusting some settings."

"Those eggheads never stop tinkering. Don't they know too much stirring will ruin the broth?" Robert said. "I may just have to pay them a visit."

"I'll let them know you plan on stopping by," Allan said as he reached for his phone.

"Don't inform them. A little surprise will keep them on their toes," Roberts said. "But I'll deal with them later. I have a call to make."

"I don't see it on the schedule."

"It's not on the schedule."

"Oh, I see."

"Yes, you should. Remember, your job is all about discretion. Let's not forget the non-disclosure agreement you signed before taking this job."

"Yes, sir. I understand," Allan said and gulped.

Reaching the top floor, the elevator doors opened to a marble hallway leading to a large oak double door with gold trim. A secretary sat at a desk to the left of the door, and she rose to her feet as Robert strode toward her.

"Good morning, Mr. Chapman. Your speech was wonderful, and your face is all over the news at the moment. Everyone is talking about inReal and the tech convention," the secretary said.

"Good morning to you too, Melanie. Of course they are talking about me. What else could they possibly be talking about?" Robert said. "I'm going into my office now, and I do not want to be disturbed for any reason. If a nuke is about to go off, or if terrorists are attacking, it doesn't matter. Don't even think about buzzing in. Allan, sit on the couch. If I need you, I'll let you know," Robert ordered his underling.

Allan made his way to a long leather couch adjacent to the door.

"Allan, open the door," Robert demanded.

"But you said to sit on the couch?" Allan asked.

"Open the door and then sit on the couch. Do I have to tell you everything?" Robert snapped.

"Yes, sir." Allan jumped up and pressed a button on the wall. The gold-trimmed doors opened, revealing an office that stood in stark contrast to the modern facilities at MindHIve headquarters.

Before a large arched window sat an enormous oak desk. Rays of sunshine streamed in through the window and cut across the office. The walls were wood paneled with gold trim, and several immense bookshelves filled with classic literature sat at regular intervals long both sides of the room. A long red rug lined the way up to the desk.

Stepping into the cavernous office, he turned to look out at his minions through the open doors.

"One more time, just to be clear. Nobody disturb me. Nobody. If anybody even touches this door, I'll have you executed in front of your friends and family," Robert said as he walked away. "Close the door, Allan."

"But, you said don't touch it," Allan said from the couch.
"Oh Allan, stop being such a baby. Close the door and then don't touch it." Robert said while glaring at his assistant.

As Allan pressed the button, the doors closed without a sound. An audible hush filled the room as the lock clicked shut, shrouding the office in silence, a vast womb against the clamor of the outside world. Walking to the center of the large red carpet before the desk, Robert got down on his knees. He took out the smartphone he used during the presentation and placed it on the floor. For a few moments, he hardly seemed to move.

Bringing his hands together in prayer form, he raised his arms over his head. A light burst out of the phone, and a large orange orb appeared in the room. The lights dimmed, and the globe rotated to its left at a slow rate. Still on his knees, Robert bowed low and placed his hands flat on the ground. He waited silently in this position for a moment until a fluttering specter appeared within the orb. Without warning, a giant face came into focus within the sphere. Humanoid, it had large bulbous eyes and bumpy metallic ridges along its forehead and the bridge of its nose. The face looked around snake-like to assess its surroundings before settling on Robert.

"Rise, my loyal servant," the voice commanded.

"As you wish, my master. I am once again humbled by your presence, Grand Commander Holrathu. Glory to Emperor and Empress," Robert said while bowing low before the giant head within the sphere.

"My dear, sweet Robert. Your devotion to the Masters makes our Emperor smile. It is this dedication you and your cohorts display for our supreme leader that allows our reign to flourish. You, lovely Robert, serve our purpose well, and in time, you will be rewarded for your enduring efforts. I presume our agreed upon schedule is being fulfilled?" the voice inquired.

"We have had some trouble, but we are persevering," Robert said. "We don't want any errors to interfere with the process."

"Very well, precise execution is necessary to ensure the success of our conquest. We can't have any of our subjects slipping under the net," Commander Holrathu said. "Your grandfather and father both served our cause well. And now you, Robert, are following the example your forefathers made. Your commitment to our plan has been recognized by the Master's Council. This devotion will not go unnoticed by the Emperor. Those that have served us well will be rewarded. We have placed great faith in you, Robert. The plan must be carried out with the greatest care and devotion."

"Yes, my master. The people will willingly take their yokes and place them around their necks when the time is right. Our marketing department has taken care of that. My announcement this morning was brilliantly delivered. The people are frothing at the mouth to get their hands on the device. It will take some time to dispense, however. Our trouble has been in securing enough material for production, but once we have distributed a sufficient volume of units, the transfer should prove seamless."

"I see you are applying foresight. This is an ability that is in short supply among your species, hence your current troubles, but we will assist you as best we can. This project is of the utmost importance to his Majesty, the Supreme Emperor, and Her Royal Majesty, the Empress. Anything but complete success will not be tolerated," the head hissed. "Do you still recall the terms of our arrangement? I wouldn't want you to suffer any consequences. His Royal Highness, as you know, is severe in his punishments."

"Of course, my master, have I ever failed you? My family has humbly served at the behest of our Supreme Rulers for generations. We owe all of our success to the Emperor, and we wouldn't dream of disappointing him. The complete symbiosis of our earthly domain with the realm of the Divine Masters is in the best interest of my family and humanity itself," Robert said.

"We are here to take care of this planet and your species. Your shortcomings are what have put this world in peril. As you know, this particular planet and its capacity for life is an incredibly rare and important domain, and we are not going to let your backward species devastate it with these barbaric ways. You need us now, and we will provide you with the guidance you require. In time, the humans will appreciate all we have done for them. Unfortunately, we'll have to be a little rough in the beginning. All beasts of burden fight the reigns at first, but over time they come to accept their circumstances and begin to thrive," Commander Holrathu said.

"We are honored and grateful for the assistance of the Grand Masters. Your wisdom and knowledge are beyond compare," Robert said while bowing his head.

"You are as astute as you are obedient, my loyal subject. When will you begin testing your devices on the population? We are anxious to see if you have been able to fully immerse our technology within the confines of this particular extent."

"We have plans to begin implementing the devices at our annual technology gathering. Everything should be ready at that time. After we have successfully tested the devices on a live, uncontrolled population, we will begin disseminating the devices globally."

"You seem convinced you have the technology under control. Do you think you will be able to secure the domain?"

"Some, I'm sure, will resist. But, as has been discussed, our goal is to control a fraction of the population and eradicate the rest. Those able to acquire the device within the window will be spared, and all others will be disposed of. It is possible we will meet resistance, but any insurrections will be dealt with," Roberts said before the floating metallic head.

"Yes, I'm sure we shall meet some resistance," The Commander said. "Our Great and Glorious Emperor only allows the most pious of his servants to be granted access to his weaponized devices. Robert, I am pleased to inform you the Emperor has selected you to be a recipient of His Royal Majesty's 'Ray of Divine Light,'" Holrathu said.

Robert fell to his knees and bowed to the ground.

"I am not worthy of the Emperor's most blessed gift," he said with his face buried in the red carpet.

"Worthy or not, you are a necessary part of this operation, and we are certain you are the human capable of getting the job done. As we speak, the 'Ray of Divine Light' is being transferred to your device. After the download is complete, the device will be weaponized. Crossing your arms in front of you will activate the weapons mode. The device will accentuate any gesture you make. Furthermore, you will be able to maneuver through space using the instruments levitation abilities. I'm sure you will be pleased with the results of this upgrade. However, I do suggest you find a safe place to test out your new abilities."

"I am honored to serve your noble cause. This humble human is forever indebted to the Grand Masters."

"Now that you have the correct tools, you will be capable of completing your task. His Supreme Excellency, The Divine Emperor, is counting on you to secure this domain in his name," the head said. "But there is one more matter that still needs discussing. I take it the fugitive is still at large?"

"We have been unable to pinpoint the culprit, but there is good news. Our tech sensors picked up some algorithms in the network that match the signature, yet their origins remain unclear. We believe this may be the clue that will lead us to your fugitive."

"He must be apprehended. Although one individual seems rather insignificant, any resistance must be handled with full force. We cannot have anything compromising the plan," the giant head of Commander Holrathu said.

"I will not disappoint the Emperor. We are certain that the algorithm has infiltrated our network, and we have allowed it to continue operating in order to monitor its activity. Once we have located the fugitive, we will apprehend him immediately," Robert said while bowing low again.

"Do not underestimate the danger this fugitive poses. They possess a device that has compromised our technology. If they were to gain access to the system, all could be lost. It is unfortunate this task has been thrust upon you at such an inconvenient time, but should you apprehend the fugitive and deliver him to us, the Emperor will be most grateful," Commander Holrathu said.

"It is my great honor to serve his Royal Highness. The fugitive will be apprehended, and we will not tire until he is," Roberts said.

"Very well, it is of the utmost importance this problem is contained. We shall be watching as you make progress towards your goal. We will not tolerate anything less than success," the giant head said while eyeing Robert.

"Glory to the Grand Masters! your servant bows before you," Robert said while getting on his knees again.

"Until next time, Robert. Remember, we will be watching," the giant head said before it vanished. The room fell into a deafening silence. Robert once again raised his hands over his head before he lowered his arms over the device and made two fists. Bumping his hands together, the sphere collapsed into the device before he placed it into his pocket.

He stood up and reached his hands out in front of him and crossed his arms in an X across his chest as Commander Holrathu had instructed him. A strange orange glow covered his body. Making a fist, a ball of energy appeared around his hand. He flicked his fingers in shock, and the ball spun across the room. Crashing into the bookshelf, his classic literature burst into flames.

A smile spread across Robert's lips before he made another fist and threw a ball of energy at the opposite wall. More books were incinerated. Laughing out loud, he brought his two hands together and a large blade of energy extended out before him. He looked at the blade for a moment before turning toward his immense oak desk. Raising his arms, he brought the blade down across the oak desk, splitting it in half.

As his desk crumbled to the ground, he laughed out loud, and he brought his hands to his side. Crouching down, he inhaled and shot into the air. Expecting impact, he brought his hands to his face, but he stopped a few inches short of the baroque painting of himself he had commissioned to cover the ceiling. He pushed off of the picture and coasted back down to the ground. Crossing his arms again, the energy field around him disappeared.

"Oh, this is going to be fun," he said as he sat down in his chair and picked up the telephone console strewn across the floor. Placing the phone in his lap, he pressed a button on the console.

"Allan, get in here. We're going to need someone to clean this up," he said into the intercom. The door swung open, and Allan stood there with his mouth open.

"Well, don't just stand there, gawking, Allan. Get maintenance on the phone. We need to clean this up. I've got work to do," Robert snapped before he leaned back in his chair and put his feet on the broken desk.

9

Mitch sat in his room alone. His father hadn't returned home, even though it was after ten. Usually, Mike Mythic returned home at 6pm sharp for dinner. Mitch tried to play DeathWorld to kill some time before the inevitable showdown with his father, but notifications from MindHIve, indicating new likes and connects, made playing the game unbearable. Upset his account was getting that much activity, Mitch knew it was only a matter of time before the system disabled his account.

MindHIve had been battling hackers and spammers for some time, and they employed sentinel bots to track down infractions. He hoped his account wouldn't become fully disabled like so many other spam accounts out there.

The more he thought about it, the angrier he became. He regretted giving Drak access to his account, but he was a little afraid to confront him on it, considering what he had witnessed earlier in the greenbelt. The guy was weird and dangerous. Mitch knew he shouldn't have trusted him, but the damage had already been done.

A heavy knock disrupted the stream of worry pouring through his head before the door swung open to reveal his father standing in the door frame. Mike Mythic was a hulk of a man, and he took up the entire doorway. A big belly filled up his blue polo-style shirt and spilled over the top of his brown pleated pants. He stood in silence for a moment, scratching his balding head before looking his son in the eye.

"You've really stuck your foot in it this time, Mitch," he said. Mitch didn't respond. He just stared at the ground. "I talked with some other parents, and we've all decided you need to apologize to your teammates publicly, so we can put this behind us and get ready for the next season. It's all for the good of the team. You're the leader, and we need you to start showing some leadership."

As a palpable tension filled the room, Mitch surpassed the urge to scream and shout at his father. The whole thing was his fault. If his father hadn't made him captain and hadn't made him take that shot, none of this would've happened.

"Look. I know you've been through a lot, but you're going to have to get over it. It's really easy to be unhappy. Anybody can do it. Right now, by moping around like this and getting angry, you are giving in and giving up. You're a winner Mitch, and even though you lost, you still need to act like a winner, cause I won't tolerate you going around acting like a sore loser. Are you going to rise to the challenge, or are you just going to take it all laying down?"

"How am I going to apologize to everybody? Are you calling a town meeting?"

"As a matter of fact, I am. We're going to get all the players and their families together at the arena, and you are going to apologize in front of everybody for what happened. I heard you, and some weird punk beat up some of the guys in the park earlier today too. You think I didn't know about that, did you? Sage said a friend of yours attacked them. Are you starting to run with another crowd? Don't even think of turning your back on the team we've built together. You're going to apologize, and we are going to put this team back together, so we can go out next season and win like the champions we are,"

"Fine, but can you just leave me alone, please Dad?" Mitch said.

"I know it is a burden to carry the name Mythic. Believe me. I have lived with it. But in my playing days, I never let the name define me. I became the name. I'm not sure if I ever told you this story, but when your great-grandfather came to this country, so many years ago, nobody could pronounce his name. Vaeleskin Mykaveisckaya was a little too difficult for folks around here to say, so he went to a dictionary and looked up words that began with M. He liked the sound of 'Mythic,' so he chose it, and he became Vic Mythic. There is no meaning to it, Mitch. It's just a name. Don't let your circumstances define you. Take me, for example. Do you think people judge me by my name or for what I've done?"

Mitch sighed again. Everybody knew about Mike Mythic in Kingsford. He was the hometown hero - the biggest thing ever to come out of Kingsford. He had been a star player for the Kingsford Crushers years before Mitch was born. Under Mike Mythic, the Crushers won three league championships. When he came of age, he had blazed into the professional hockey world and lit it on fire. He had a sensational rookie season, and his name was splashed everywhere. Known for his lightning speed and his tremendous slap shot, he was the most exciting new player to come into the league in years. Playing for the Longdale Legends, he had been a perfect fit. He played alongside great players like Eddie Olzylthong and Geoff Boukenal and together they won a championship in his first season.

"A new myth has arrived in the land of the legends," a local paper had written.

The media and advertisers had gobbled up everything Mike Mythic did, and the Mythic's home was covered with old cutouts of Mike Mythic's name in newspapers: "Mythic performance from the young rookie from Kingsford," "Is it a 'Myth'? No! It's Mike Mythic!" read another headline. There were also old endorsements he had done, including cereal boxes and bobbleheads.

The Mythic's entire home was a shrine to Mike's hockey career. Everywhere you looked, there was an old piece of memorabilia. It was under this shroud of greatness that Mitch had been brought up.

Mike Mythic was a sensation, but a string of injuries ended up cutting the young kid from Kingsford's career short before he could really make a name for himself. He returned to his hometown heartbroken but still standing and set about rebuilding himself. Marrying his high school sweetheart, Mindy Saunders, they didn't waste any time starting a family. When Mitch was born, Mike couldn't wait to get him on the ice. Mitch had pictures of himself clutching a hockey stick as a newborn while being held by a beaming Mike Mythic.

Around that same time, Mike and Mindy started a sporting goods store. They called it Mythic Sporting Goods, and Mike's reputation ensured everybody in town came to his store. It was a success right away, and it soon became an institution in Kingsford. If you needed anything to do with sports, it was the place to go. Mike had made sure he was well celebrated at the store as well. There were more memorabilia there than at the Mythic's home.

Along with the store, Mike poured everything into Mitch's hockey career. Mitch was enrolled in minor hockey as soon as possible, and he always had the best gear in town. From the beginning, Mitch had shown promise. He was fast and determined, and he spent hours practicing his shot out in front of his house or at the local outdoor rink. He could seemingly score at will, and he was fulfilling his father's expectations. Mythic Sporting Goods sponsored the Crushers, and when old coach Campbell retired, Mike Mythic was an obvious replacement. He gladly took the job and knew he would do his best to see his boy go all the way.

Mitch had big shoes to fill, though. His father's reputation preceded him in every situation. Where ever he went, people would tell him things like: "You're gonna be just like your dad. He was so good."

Although Mitch had a lot of talent, it was difficult for him to live up to the hype. The pressure on him to perform was always there, and when he didn't do well, people would often say: "I wish he played more like his dad. That guy was amazing."

It was this unceasing pressure that caused Mitch to keep his feelings deep inside. Over the last few months he had kept things bottled up so much he was bound to snap. He regretted hitting Sage, but the guy was such a jerk, and he had turned everybody against him. When he needed his teammates the most, he was all alone, and now he had to go and apologize to everybody. Mitch was so angry he wanted to scream, but like always, he pushed his feelings down.

"Mitch, it's going to be alright. We'll fix this together. Go out there and show these folks you know you made a mistake, and you didn't mean to disappoint everybody. Do that, and we'll all be able to move past this. You're a great leader and a great player. You can't let the little things get you down," Mr. Mythic said. Mitch rolled his eyes. He couldn't believe what he was hearing.

How could his father think that way? It wasn't a little thing. It was the worst moment of his entire life and after that came months of embarrassment. He had been cut off from the people he thought were his friends, and he had suffered in isolation the entire time. Now he was the one that had to go out and make things right. Where were all the people that were supposed to have his back? Why didn't anybody care about him, Mitch thought to himself.

"I already said I'll do it. Now just leave me alone," Mitch snapped at his father.

"Look, you don't have to get angry, Mitch. I'm trying to help you out here," Mitch's father said while trying not to get angry. "One day, you're going to look back on these days and realize this was the best time of your life."

"I don't know about that," Mitch said under his breath.

"What did you say? Are you talking back to me, boy? Don't waste this opportunity, Mitch. I'll leave you alone if that's what you want, but everybody is counting on you to do what is best for the team," Mike Mythic said while closing the door.

Mitch listened to his father's heavy footsteps plodding up the basement stairs. Rolling over on his back, he looked up at the ceiling. Taped above Mitch's bed, a Poster of Geoff Boukenal stared back at him.. He was Mitch's favorite hockey player of all time and a good friend of his father. "To Mitch, Be the best you that you can be, Geoff Boukenal," Geoff Boukenal wrote before he handed Mitch the poster several years ago.

"I don't know about that, Geoff," Mitch muttered as he rolled over and looked at his computer monitor. The notifications and comments continued to pour in. He groaned and got out of bed. Without looking at the screen, he reached down and held the power button until the computer shut off. Standing up, he sighed once more before turning off the lights in his room. He crawled into bed, dreading what the next day would bring.

10

"Play it again, Andrew," Robert said. The MindHIve executive board room was empty save for Robert and a few engineers. Sitting in a swivel chair, Robert scratched the top of his head while he waited for his head engineer to restart the video.

"Are you ready, sir?" Andrew inquired.

"Andrew, of course I'm ready. Just play the thing already," Robert snapped.

"Uh y-y-yes sir, right away," Andrew stammered.

"You know Andrew, for a genius you really are as sharp as a hammer sometimes," Robert said, swinging around to look at the screen.

Beamed onto the massive white screen that dominated the western wall of the MindHIve executive boardroom, the best possible production of the #epiccrotchshot video played at a fraction of the actual speed before an audience of one. Re-rendered to bring out the very best video quality the MindHIve engineering department could muster, Mitch Mythic flew over the goal, larger than life, and in glorious HD quality. The technicians zoomed in on the video so the only thing that could be seen was Mitch's body as it reached its apex before descending to the ice behind the net.

"You're sure about this?" Robert asked his engineering department.

"Yes, sir," Andrew piped up. "We've been able to isolate the algorithm's most recent activity, and it seems to be fixated on this particular video and others like it. The algorithm has somehow sidestepped our governor protocols, allowing these videos to flood the network. We cannot prove the video or the system has been hacked, but we are certain the algorithm is affecting it in some way. The scary thing is: nothing is violating our 'terms of service' agreement. We even had the lawyers go over it several times. But anything to do with these types of videos is funneled back to this kid's account."

"This kid is it? Really? This kid is the one we've been looking for the whole time. Somehow, I just don't believe it," Robert said.

The slow motion descent of Mitch's body was now fully underway. His face turned from shock to horror as he realized what was about to happen.

"We also agree it seems unlikely he is the culprit. I mean, look at him. That's got to be the most embarrassing thing that could happen to anybody, right? I imagine his whole family watched this happen. Why would he go to great lengths to promote it? So yes, we are a little confused by that. It is possible a third party is using the algorithm to influence the system, but why exactly, we're not sure. We are certain the source of the algorithm's activity can be traced to local networks around the community of Kingsford, which also happens to be the subject of #epiccrotchshot boys hometown." Andrew said.

Slowed down to 1/50th of its actual speed, his face contorted in slow motion as Mitch pummeled into the ice.

"Who is this kid?" Robert asked while scratching his head.

"His name is Mitch Mythic. An ordinary teenager from the small community of Kingsford. Other than this unfortunate accident, which just happens to be really amusing, there is nothing particularly special about him, making the presence of the algorithm in this context somewhat puzzling," Andrew said. "He has been a MindHIve user for a few years, but he mainly just posts selfies and watches fail videos like most teenagers. He is also an avid DeathWorld player."

"Are we missing something here?" Robert asked. "Why this video? What does it mean? Is there some kind of subversive message here? What is being said in the comments? Have we had the linguistic department examine the language? Are there any phrases people are repeating? Look over everything. There must be something we're not seeing. Thank you for bringing this to my attention and thank you for all your hard work. Get back to the lab and make sure my prototypes are ready. The tech convention is only a month away."

"Yes, sir," Andrew said as the technicians disassembled the equipment.

"Gerald, what do you make of all this?" A tall black man with a bald head rose from a chair in the corner and stalked across the boardroom toward Robert.

As the head of MindHIve's security, Gerald Tobero proved time and again to be an indispensable tool in Robert Chapman's arsenal. He had come through big time during MindHIve's largest data breach a few years ago. It was Gerald's hunch that the hack was coming from within MindHIve's headquarters that lead to the apprehension of O'Dell Grimes, the leader of the hacktivist group known as "The Cell."

The group had placed operatives inside the main complex in an attempt to free MindHIve's encrypted data. Gerald Tobero had been the man responsible for interrogating employees, and he was able to crack a junior engineer that had been lured into The Cell's network.

A former military operative with experience in several theaters of war, Gerald specialized in subversive militant online terrorism, and he held a top position within the intelligence community before Robert lured him to MindHIve with the promise of a lucrative salary and bonuses galore.

"It's a puzzling situation, sir," Gerald said.

"Although this child seems unlikely to be a terrorist, he may have been compromised in some way."

"Compromised? In what way?"

"There are some aspects of the situation I find a little too convenient. If the fugitive is in possession of such dangerous technology, why would he use it in this way? Furthermore, why would he be so reckless with the algorithm's footprint? We are either dealing with someone who is very stupid or very smart. In this instance, I would choose the latter, due to the elegant use of the algorithm to sidestep our terms of service and our immense security measures. It seems highly irregular that such care would be taken to elude our protective measures only to allow the location of the implementing device to be revealed."

"Well, that's a very astute analysis, but if this guy is so smart, why would he do it?"

"As peculiar as it may sound, it appears you are being called out, so to speak"

"Called out? Like a challenge? You mean whoever the hell is behind all this is calling me out?"

"Precisely, sir. First, he shows you what he is capable of with something so benign, and then he lets you know where he is. It appears that he is saying: Here I am, Come and get me. I've seen other terror groups act this way in the hopes that they will be engaged on their terms."

"Well, if that's the case, let's go get this little jerk. Contact Homeland

Security, and we'll haul this kid into a black site and waterboard it out of him."

"That is exactly what your culprit wants you to do. In my professional opinion, the entire situation feels like a trap."

"That's why I hired you, Gerald. It's this kind of thinking that keeps our company on track and gets you those bonuses I know you're after. If this is a trap, then how do we handle it?"

"The best way to beat a trap is to lay a trap of our own."

"I'm listening."

"In order to apprehend the fugitive, you will need to draw them out into the open. To do so, you will need some type of bait. What is it you believe the fugitive is after?"

"I happen to know he wants to bring our system down from within. He's an anarchist and a dangerous revolutionary."

"In that case, what better bait than access to MindHIve's core network? If we were to allow the perpetrator to believe they could breach our security system locally, then it's possible they could be enticed to step out of the shadows. We will need the fugitive to believe we have fallen for their trap and open our doors to them. Once they have revealed themselves, we'll be able to apprehend the subject. I've run several operations similar to this before."

"You want to give him access to our system. Are you kidding me? Who knows what kind of damage he could do before we get hold of him?"

"We don't give him any access. We just need him to think he can get access at a certain place. If we set up an outpost in a region where we believe he wants us to engage him, and reveal our phony access point, we may be able to lure him out and catch him red-handed."

"The tech convention!" Robert shouted out. "It's perfect. We'll invite this stupid kid to the tech disrupt. If he's a patsy, as you say he is, whoever is setting him up will surely come along for the ride. The tech convention is a testing ground for our new tech, anyway. It's the perfect situation. We'll be able to monitor everything this 'Mitch Mythic' does, and we'll make it seem like the system is accessible from the inside. If things are as you say they are, our fugitive will undoubtedly show himself. This little, butthole town - what's it called again?"

"Kingsford, sir."

"Yes, Kingsford. A small town like this is the perfect. A remote location with a small population is an ideal setting for inReal's first contact with a live population. We've already linked the satellite system, so honing in on any location will not be a problem," Robert said, as a dangerous glow lit up his eyes. "Allan, get in here."

Allan bolted in at the sound of his name and approached Robert like an obedient puppy.

"What can I do for you, sir?" Allan asked.

"Get the board of directors on the phone. We've got a change of plans. I'll need to schedule some TV appearances, and you'd better tell Tracy in Logistics to pack her bags. This year, the MindHIve tech convention will be in a remote location," Robert said.

"What do you mean, sir?" Allan asked.

"Allan, we're going to Kingsford," Robert said.

"Where is Kingsford?" Allan asked again.

"I have no idea, Allan. I hire people like you to figure out things like this for me. Now get the board on the phone. We've got to make a massive pivot, and I need to move quickly."

"Right away, sir," Allan said, scuttling to the exit.

"Gerald, I leave it in your hands to make all the necessary arrangements. Your team will have all the access it needs to see this through. Keep me updated regularly. I'll ensure all goes well with the board."

"Of course, sir," Gerald replied. "I'm certain we'll be able to apprehend our man using this technique. I've seen it used in the field before. In fact, it was this tactic that allowed me to capture Alhaim al Habib in Afghanistan."

"That sounds great, Gerald, but I don't have any time for war stories at the moment. You can regale me with your exploits another time. Right now, I only care about results."

"Understood, sir. I won't disappoint you."

"Only if you don't want that beach house I'm dangling out in front of you," Robert said. "Now get out of here. I've got to convince the board to allow us to move the tech convention. It should be easy, though. Those boobs let me do anything,"

"Good afternoon, Mr. Chapman," several voices chimed in. Gathered on the big screen behind Robert, sat each member of the board as they reported in through video chat.

"Ah, the members of the board. I was just discussing some security concerns with Mr. Tobero. Allan was supposed to let me KNOW when everything was ready, but he seems to have forgotten his protocols. I will have to deal with him later," Robert said while glaring at Allan, who stood in the doorway staring at his shoes.

"Thank you, Mr. Tobero. Everything we discussed is fully confidential," Robert said with a smile. Gerald nodded before making his way to the exit.

"And now board members, let me tell you of what I have planned next. Who here has heard of a small town called Kingsford?" Robert asked while grinning from ear to ear.

11

Mitch's head jerked up as he snapped out of sleep. Sunlight streamed through his bedroom window, lighting up the room. The remnants of lucid dreams clung to his tattered psyche, shadows lurking in the dark.

Rolling over, he placed his feet on the floor. His digital alarm clock, a Christmas gift from ancient history, read 8:07. Putting on his jeans and a clean t-shirt, he loped upstairs to the kitchen to discover an empty house.

He spotted a note scribbled on a pink stationary pad in the middle of the round kitchen table.

"Had to leave early to take Toby to the clinic. We'll see you tonight. Team meeting at the arena at 7:00 pm. Mom & Dad."

Mitch groaned as his fresh feeling melted away. The whole meeting felt like something his mother planned. She most likely texted every single parent on the team with a message filled with hopeful optimism. There was no way out of it. He would have to stand up in front of everyone tonight and say he was sorry.

Eating a bowl of cereal, he fiddled with the phone in his pocket. Without a doubt, MindHIve shut his count down over the night. Either that they blocked access for violating some kind of service agreement, his name added to a list of likely terrorists. It was only a matter of time before a black van pulled up in front of his house and hauled him off to a remote location in the mountains. Government goons would waterboard him until he coughed up the answers they sought.

After several moments of hesitation, he grabbed the phone and opened it up. Across the home screen were several red banners signaling notifications. As he opened his MindHIve account, his jaw dropped. He had gone from just over a thousand connects to over one-hundred thousand in one night, an unbelievable gain. Unbeknownst to him, his account had uploaded a video sometime in the night: a dubtech remix of him saying "I am Mitch Mythic and I am #epiccrotchshot boy" mixed in with shots of him flying over the net.

The video received hundreds of thousands of views in a matter of hours. He knew Drak had everything to do with it, but he couldn't figure out how he did it all in one night.

Glancing at the clock at the top of his phone, it read 8:35. He had to get to school. Mr. O'Hare would be waiting for him, and he didn't want to get into any more trouble. Throwing the bowl into the sink, he headed to the door. He grabbed his backpack and shuffled his feet into his shoes.

It was a fifteen-minute walk to school. Mitch took the shortcut back through the greenbelt where he had been confronted by Sage and all of his former friends. The scuffle marks from the fight were still visible as Mitch jogged past the T intersection. He shook his head in amazement at what had transpired in the last twenty-four hours.

Sure enough, Mr. O'Hare sat waiting for Mitch at the main entrance of Kingsford High. He wore a short-sleeved, white button-down shirt and a blue tie, sweat stains growing under his armpits in the May heat.

"Good Morning, Mr. Mythic. Prompt as usual. Let's see you keep it up. I wouldn't want to add any more time to your in-school suspension. You'll attend your morning classes and then report to the computer lab for lunch break. The same follows for the afternoon. Go to class and then head to the lab until 5pm. Understood?"

"Got it, sir," Mitch said through the veneer of a fake smile.

"You'd better hurry up. You're going to be late for class. We'll see you at lunchtime," Mr. O'Hare said while Mitch walked by.

The morning went smoothly enough, and he almost felt relaxed after his first two classes went by without incident.

He walked into his third period social studies class and grabbed a seat next to the wall while Ms. Pitchford addressed the class.

In her class, students were expected to debate, and she tried her best to incorporate social media into her lessons as much as possible.

That morning, Ms. Pitchford wore a maroon polo shirt tucked into her beige khaki pants; her hair tied back into a neat bun. A relatively new teacher, she didn't take any guff from the unruly high school students forced to attend her class. Mitch strolled in a minute late getting to the class, and Ms. Pitchford let him know it as he eased into his seat.

"Glad to see you decided to join us this morning, Mr. Mythic," she said before returning her attention to the class. "Ladies and Gentleman, today is a special day. I'm sure all of you are aware of the recent tech developments from MindHIve. I watched the presentation yesterday. This inReal stuff they have developed is quite incredible. My newsfeed has just informed me the CEO of MindHIve will be making a special announcement this morning regarding their tech convention next month. It starts in a couple of minutes. Let's watch it together and then, after the announcement, we'll discuss MindHIve's new technology and its implications on society."

Picking up a remote control from her desk, she turned on the large TV embedded into the front wall of the class. The TV was set to the 24-hour news channel, New News Now, or NNN. The familiar face of Cassandra Lang greeted the class from behind the news desk.

"We're just moments away from the next big announcement from MindHIve CEO Robert Chapman. It will be hard for him to top yesterday's news, but Mr. Chapman never fails to keep everybody excited. Let's find out what MindHIve is up to now. We're joined live via satellite by Trisha Yamaki, who is at MindHIve's headquarters in Los Altos, California, for the big announcement."

The camera switched to a live feed at MindHIve headquarters. Trisha Yamaki stood before a crowd of reporters. An empty podium emblazoned with the MindHIve logo sat loaded with microphones.

"This is Trisha Yamaki, and I am reporting live from MindHIve's corporate HeadQuarters here in Los Altos. I've just been told that MindHIve CEO Robert Chapman will be taking the stage in just a moment."

"What is the mood like over there now?"

"It's fever pitch at the moment. The whole world is thronging for inReal, so anything Robert Chapman says or does is going to get a lot of attention. Uh, it looks like Mr. Chapman is taking the stage now. Let's all see what he has to say," the reporter said while stepping away from the camera.

Robert Chapman walked in from the right side of the stage. The camera zoomed into the podium as the CEO readied himself to speak.

"Greetings again to you all. I know it was only yesterday we announced our latest technological development, but I am very pleased to bring you an update regarding MindHIve's technology convention. As you know, we usually host the event at these very headquarters, but this year we are going to be doing something a little different - actually a lot different. Along with the unveiling of our new technology, for the first time ever, MindHIve's tech convention will take place at a remote location. I'll reveal the location in just a moment, but let me tell you why we chose to set our event outside of our headquarters," Robert paused before carrying on.

"We chose to set our event at a remote location for a few reasons. First, we need to test the capabilities of our technology outside of our control grid here at MindHIve headquarters. We also need to be able to contain that location, so we chose a small remote town to host the event. This way, we will be able to put our devices in the field and see how they interact with the community at large without too much disruption. We will have the ability to track and monitor all activity effectively, and we will have the power to control the area down to the nearest millimeter with our MindHIve tracking applications. It is a unique opportunity, and the lucky participants in the tech convention will all be awarded with their very own inReal devices they can keep after the event is over," Robert halted for a moment to let the impact of what he just said sink in.

"We could choose any community we want. There is no question of logistics because the entire operation will be carried out in the cloud, so to speak, using MindHIve's very own satellite monitoring system. But we wanted to choose a town that ultimately sums up the values of this country. A small town with a big heart. A place any one of us could call home. We spent hours poring over the data to find the right community to host such an extraordinary event, and after a long and careful consideration we have chosen the community of Kingsford, Colorado to host this year's MindHIve tech convention."

There was an audible gasp in the classroom as the students realized their town had been chosen by MindHIve.

"A lot of people will be wondering why we chose Kingsford over any other town. This wasn't an easy decision. There were a lot of towns that fit the description, but we chose Kingsford over every other location because of its unique setting. It is remote enough that we can have direct control over the network without compromising its security. Interference, both intentional and unintentional, are risk factors we need to consider. Kingsford is far enough from the main grid, and it is small enough we can easily contain the environment without causing too much havoc on the network. I know a lot of people are going to come out and say we are trying to control people's lives or bring in some kind of dystopian electronic monitoring system, but that is not the case. Our goal with this project is to ensure the user experience allows for the highest degree of mobility, coupled with our client's freedom to integrate the inReal system into their daily lives. MindHIve has always been about the user experience, and the inReal technology will provide the greatest user experience in human history. We intend to prove this at our test demo in Kingsford next month," Roberts said with confidence and bravado.

The students in Ms. Pitchford's class were stunned. The largest tech firm in the world chose their hometown to be the testing ground of one of the most significant new technologies ever invented. In a flash, everybody pulled their phones out to post on MindHIve and send messages through MindCHat while Robert Chapman spoke. Mitch, on the other hand, could not ignore the uneasy feeling creeping up his spine.

"As everybody knows," Robert said, resuming his speech after taking a sip of water. "The MindHIve tech convention is all about bringing new ideas into contact with our latest developments. We always strive to find the best and brightest innovators throughout the world and invite them to our convention. This year will be no different. We will bring the brightest new talents in the industry to this year's convention, and I am delighted to inform you of about some of the new stars in the tech field we have chosen to invite," Robert said.

"This year's convention will be centered on the use of the inReal technology, and we have chosen our participants based upon the developments they achieved and how the potential ways inReal could impact their research. While it is too difficult to list every single participant at the tech convention during this press briefing, I would like to mention a few notable people that will be attending this year's event and the stellar work they are doing."

Robert turned his attention to the large screen behind him. The MindHIve logo flashed briefly before an image of the globe appeared.

"The tech world is constantly in flux, and one of our greatest obstacles to overcome is what to do with all the old technology and devices that we have produced. There is a young Lady named SoHee Moon from South Korea that has been doing groundbreaking research in the strange and wonderful world of micro-bacteria and its ability to devour certain particles. This young lady has been able to manipulate the enzymes present in a particular type of bacteria, enabling it to consume and repurpose any type of material it comes into contact with. What an incredible development. This type of research will greatly reduce the ecological footprint of modern technology. We are pleased to have Ms. Moon SoHee attend our convention," Robert said amidst an enthusiastic applause.

"I would also like to announce a very special guest at this year's tech convention. Our users are our most valued resource. MindHIve wouldn't exist without the normal, everyday individuals that have made our platform home. Although there are countless people using MindHIve applications in extraordinary ways, there are a few people out there that show us just how much value users bring to the MindHIve community," Robert said while scanning the room.

"User-driven phenomenons have changed the way we interact with each other. The meme, the emoji, and the gif, just to name a few, altered the way we communicate in ways we are still comprehending. Some people are unwittingly made the subject of these viral segments, as we like to call them. It is difficult to comprehend for most folks, but the highs and lows of going viral are a reality for a select few among us. Internet culture has a mind of its own, and we can't possibly predict what will be the next hot content. One viral video this year has become as ubiquitous as it is funny. All of us laughed out loud at this incredible clip." Robert said as the clip for #epiccrotchshot appeared on the screen. Mitch all but melted into the floor. Everyone in the class erupted in laughter and dismay.

"Yes, this clip is incredibly funny, but what most of you don't know is the reason why this particular video has made its way into almost all of our news feeds. The young man who happens to be the star of this video is also the very same person who has allowed us to view it so many times. As difficult as it is to imagine, this young man decided on his own that he would not take this humiliation lying down. In fact, his ingenious online activity allowed this video to go viral," Robert said while every pair of eyes in Ms. Pitchford's class focused on Mitch Mythic.

"There is also one other factor that has influenced our decision to invite this young man to our convention. His home town is Kingsford! Ladies and Gentlemen, I am beyond excited to announce that we will be extending an invitation to Kingsford's very own #epiccrotchshot boy - Mitch Mythic." The classroom fell silent for a brief moment before every student in the class surrounded him and patted him on his shoulders while chanting 'Ep-ic-Crotch-Shot,' as Ms. Pitchford tried to calm the class down.

12

"Have you made arrangements for my next call?" Robert asked Allan as he exited the briefing room after the press conference.

"Yes sir, the President had cleared his schedule and will be available whenever you contact him. His aides have ensured me of this," Allan said, following after Robert, a little to the right.

"Excellent, Allan," Robert said before stepping onto the elevator. "For such a small-minded person, you sure are a good worker. Much like the President, it is useful idiots like you that allow the world to keep spinning."

"Thank you, sir," Allan replied while the doors opened.

"Everything has been prepared for your call, sir. The President is standing by," Melanie said as Robert strode down the hall after stepping off of the elevator.

"Excellent. Once again, I am not to be disturbed during this call. If you value your life, do not open this door," Robert said. "Allan, open the door."

"But sir, you just said not to open the door," Allan said.

"After I'm inside, you thick-headed runt. Use your head, Allan. You're already on thin ice with me after that board room incident. You better get your act together, or I'll send you back to the sorting room where I found you," Robert snapped at his assistant.

Allan gulped again and hit the button on the wall. The doors swung open to reveal a stark and bare room. Gone were the bookshelves and the oak and gold furniture. Instead, Several large steel pillars arranged into two distinct columns led to a metallic desk set before a concrete wall.

"Please keep up all of your hard work, my minions," Robert said.

He stood there with his hands on his hips while back at his underlings. "Allan, close the door already."

Allan jumped up again and hit the button. As soon as the doors closed, Robert crossed his arms over his chest to activate his weapons system and an orange glow came over his body. Dropping his arms to his side, he made his hands into fists and levitated into the air. As he pushed forward with his right hand, he maneuvered around the pillars before coming to a resting position in the center of his office. He put his left hand out in front of him, with the palm facing up, and gestured with his fingers. Upon doing so, several holographic soldiers appeared in the room. Robert made two fists at his side while the holographic soldiers took defensive positions behind the pillars. Flicking his wrist at one of the pillars, a beam of energy rocketed out of his hand. The holographic soldier fell over and disappeared. Another soldier fired at Robert. He made a shield gesture, and a sphere appeared along his arm. Deflecting the shot, he fired back, and the holograph disintegrated. Robert made short work of the other holographs before lowering himself to the ground. Crossing his arms again, the opaque glow vanished, and he walked towards his desk.

"I think I'm getting the hang of this thing," he said while he sat down. "Now, let's sort out this idiot."

A red light flashed on the console in the center of his desk. As he reached out and pressed a button, the window behind Robert turned opaque, and a large circle spun in its center. After a brief moment, the face of an older man appeared on the screen, peering at Robert through large glasses.

"Is that you, Robert? It's really dark in that room," the man asked.

"Of course it's me, Mr. President," Robert said while getting to his feet.

"Ah, now I can see you. How are you, my friend?"

"Since you asked, I'm pretty pissed off. You told me you'd get those regulators off my back and now I'm being told I can't access my own satellites because I don't have the security clearance. This company sold the government those satellites, and it is this company that provides the network that supports its security protocols. You gave me your word we wouldn't have any problems executing this plan."

"I understand the situation, but it's not like I can just wave my hand and make everything right. I'm only the President. I can't force Congress to pass any legislation at the drop of a hat."

"Well, sign an executive memo or some damned thing. If I don't have my security clearance, then I won't be able to test the system. The whole reason you are sitting in that chair is because we put you there. This is on you. You need to get it done, or I'll find somebody else who can."

"I don't think you understand what I'm up against. Congress doesn't work that way."

"You think I don't know how Congress works? Half of those morons are on my payroll. They work for us. They do our bidding. I will not have this operation go off the rails because some do-gooder wants things to go by the rules. Just tell whatever lackey you installed over at the communications bureau to lift the security clearance. By the time anybody finds out what happened, we'll be in stage two already, and nothing will matter anymore."

"I'll see what I can do."

"You'll see what you can do? You'll get it done, and that's that. Do not forget the oath you swore. We are in the final stages of a plan generations in the making. I will not have all of this effort squandered by a technical snag. Do you hear me?"

"Yes, I understand."

"You better if you know what's good for you. Now go get it done. I don't want to hear from you until my security clearances have been authorized. Goodbye, Mr. President," Robert said and disconnected the call.

"What a tool," he said before he stood up from the desk and walked to the center of the room. "And now I get to talk to another one."

Reaching into his pocket, he pulled out his phone and placed it on the ground. He raised his hands and made two fists, summoning the giant orange sphere. After a few moments, the head of Commander Holrathu appeared before Robert.

"If it isn't my loyal Earthling Servant. I hear you've been a busy boy. Do you have more news of the fugitive?" the Commander asked.

"I do, sir," Robert said while bowing low.

"Very good. Is he in your custody?" Commander Holrathu asked.

"We haven't apprehended the fugitive yet, but we have been able to find his approximate location. We believe we will have him in our custody very soon."

"Yes, your status report was well-received. After analyzing the data, we understand why the fugitive would appear in this particular location. The surrounding area is ripe with the energy required to open a gateway. This location you provided is an excellent place to establish the portal. We wish for you to build our gateway there. Have you completed the construction of the generator?"

"We are in the final stages of producing the generator. I have been a little distracted with the fugitive and the preparations for our convention, but my engineers tell me progress is being made at a rapid pace."

"That is excellent news. But do not take the fugitive lightly. He must be apprehended as soon as possible. You do realize this individual is the only thing that could stand in the way of our end goal. He happens to be carrying some of our most advanced technology. You will have to use all the powers of your device to contain him once he has been located. I understand you have been working hard to master your new abilities. You will need to prepare others to use these devices. On your own you are powerful, but just one man is not enough."

"As we speak, I am preparing our first security force to be equipped with armed devices. We will be doing our first trial run at the tech convention in one earth month. All will be ready by then."

"You have always served us well, Robert. This is why we have blessed you with the finest technology we have to offer. The stakes are high now. We cannot afford any mistakes at this point. The fugitive must be apprehended, or the plan is in grave danger of being compromised. You must focus all of your efforts into bringing him to us."

"I understand the gravity of the situation. We are currently preparing a trap the fugitive will be unable to resist."

"I have read your proposal and we approves of your approach. Using your convention as a cover, you will be able to contain our problem and begin phase two of our project - a permanent gateway to our new Domain. We shall use the transfer of the prisoner as the first test of your developments. We have placed a great deal of trust in you and your abilities. Do not disappoint the Emperor," Commander Holrathu said while glaring down at Robert.

"The Emperor will not be disappointed. It is my solemn duty to serve his Excellency, and I will fulfill my obligation," Robert said before bowing low.

"You better, for your sake, Robert. The Emperor is a shrewd ruler, and he is swift and merciless with his punishments. Please keep us informed of any further developments."

"Yes, sir. I will bid you farewell now, Commander Holrathu. In the service of the Emperor," Robert said as he bowed again.

"May he reign forever," Commander Holrathu said before the orange orb disappeared, leaving Robert alone once again.

13

"Well, Mr. Mythic, it looks like the world has made some lemonade for you. I couldn't imagine a better way to redeem yourself than representing this community at the tech convention. It's a great honor you've been given," Mr. O'Hare said while patting Mitch on the back as he walked into the computer lab at lunchtime.

"I'll try not to let you down," Mitch said, faking a smile.

"It doesn't look like Drak is here, but you know your way around. Find a spot and eat your lunch. After that, I want you to continue working on your essay. You'll need to have it done by the end of the week if you want your suspension lifted," Mr. O'Hare said while making his way to the door. "I've got some beef Stroganoff heating up in the microwave right now. I like to eat it nice and hot. Congratulations Mitch."

Alone in the lab, he felt the comfort of an empty room, quiet, save for the soft whirring of the computer fans. The tattered Venetian blinds sat half shut, allowing light from the warm spring day to spill into the room. Mitch plopped himself into the computer station he chose the day before and placed his bag on the ground. Taking out a brown paper bag containing his lunch, he put it on the desk in front of him, and pulled out a sandwich.

Bumping the computer's mouse with his elbow by accident, he brought the ancient machine out of sleep mode. He glanced at the screen as the desktop became visible on the archaic monitor. An old chat sat open in the middle of the screen, the cursor flashing in a slow, rhythmic fashion. As he took a bite of his sandwich, a text bubble appeared in the chat program.

"Mitch, are you in the lab? - Drak."

"Where are you? We need to talk," Mitch typed into the computer.

"I know. Do you see the door at the back of lab?" the text bubble said.

"Yes," Mitch typed.

"Go through it and head downstairs. At the bottom of the stairs is another door. Open it and go inside. You'll find me in there."

Groaning as he got to his feet, he walked to the door and sighed before turning the handle. A darkened stairwell sat at the end of a long-neglected hall.

"Well, the only thing he can do now is kill me. I guess there are fates worse than death," he said out loud as he made his way down the stairs. The heavy door appeared locked, but when Mitch tried the latch, it swung open without much resistance.

A large room lay beyond the door, stacked with old bleachers and wrestling mats. Mitch picked his way along a shelf, stacked with textbooks lost in the past. Dust sprang up as he stepped over the debris scattered across the floor. A series of emergency exit lights lined the walls. Their orange glow allowed Mitch to find a central column between the shelves. Beyond the cluttered stack of aging materials, Mitch spotted an opening. After picking his way past some old gym equipment, he came to a wide clearing; water dripped from a thick pipe hung from the ceiling onto a cracked concrete floor. A window at the end of the room allowed for some daylight to spill in.

Drak stood in the center of the room, his long arms drooping at his side. He appeared relaxed and calm. Pausing next to a dusty bookshelf, Mitch eyed the strange young man with suspicion.

"Good to see you again, Mitch. Things are different now, yes?" Drak said while flashing that same knowing smile.

"I don't know you, and I don't know what you are up to, but I do not want to be a part of this anymore," Mitch said.

"You are a part of it now, like it or not. Things are not what they seem. More important things are happening all around us," Drak said.

"You keep saying all this vague crap. But I need you need to tell me what you are up to. You know what? Don't tell me. I don't want to know. I'm not involved in what you are doing. I think you are going to get into a lot of trouble, and maybe that's what you want. I just want things to go back to the way they were, before all of this craziness."

"No going back now. I need to show you something. You saw the news yesterday? The MindHIve guy announced a big new thing - inReal. This is big news for people here," Drak said. "Come, I'll show you something."

Reaching to the ground, Drak pulled up a drainage grate in the floor beneath his feet.

"Follow me," he said as he hopped down.

"You want me to follow you into the sewer?" Mitch said while screwing up his face.

"It's not a sewer. You'll see. You will not be disappointed," Drak said, and he flashed his all too familiar grin.

"Oh fine, but if this gets gross, I'm turning back," Mitch said before lowering himself into the drainage system. Landing on his feet, he found himself in a tunnel large enough to walk through without crouching.

"Come this way," Drak said as he pushed deeper into the tunnel. After a few dozen steps the passage ended, and a formidable metal door embedded into a concrete wall stood in their way. Reaching out with his hand, Drak made a strange gesture, and the door opened, bringing forth a rush of cold air.

"We're going in here?" Mitch said, peering into the blackness. "Where does this go to? I didn't even know this was here."

"You know Kingsford is an old mining town? Well, this is an old mining cave, and it goes deep underground," Drak said before stepping through the doorway.

"All right, but I've got a bad feeling about this," Mitch said as he followed Drak into the blackness. Pulling his phone out of his pocket, he activated the light.

The tunnel went on for a few hundred feet at a downward slope. Mitch felt a change in the air, and it felt like the roof was rising. Shining his flashlight overhead, he saw they had entered an open cavern. All this time he had lived in Kingsford, he had no idea this place existed. Everybody in town knew about the old mining caves, but they were abandoned long ago.

Drak stopped in front of him and turned around. Reaching into his pocket, he pulled out a small square and held it in his hand before Mitch.

"Seems like nothing, yes?" he said before placing the cube back in his pocket. "Now watch this."

Crossing his arms over his chest, a blue glow covered his body.

"What is that?" Mitch asked as he jumped back.

"This is the same technology MindHIve introduced yesterday," Drak said.

"Where did you get it? They haven't released any devices yet. Did you steal it? Is that what they want?" Mitch demanded.

"I did not steal it from MindHIve. They did not invent this. Like I said, things are not what they seem," Drak said while crossing his arms.

"Where did you get it then? It must've come from somewhere. Where are you from anyway? I thought you were like a refugee or something," Mitch asked.

Drak reached into his pocket and took out the cube and placed it on the floor.

"I need to explain some things, but you need to listen. Open your mind. See clearly," Drak said as he raised his arms above his head. A blue sphere appeared above the phone, illuminating the cave. Reaching out, Drak touched the orb and made a few gestures with his fingers before flicking his wrist to the left, causing the globe to spin.

Flickering through the opaque surface, an image appeared in the sphere. Mitch spotted dozens of humanoid figures huddled in a dusty wind as he stared at the orb in awe. The people toiled over a dry surface, swinging long spike tools in a slow repetitive rhythm. Hovering in the air above, larger figures imbued with an orange glow oversaw the workers struggling under the hot sun. As one of the diggers stumbled and fell, one of the massive guards flew to the slumped body. Making a gesture with its hands, two orbs of light blasted into the fallen form, disintegrating them.

"These are my people. The ones digging. We are slaves now to the Masters," Drak said. His face was tense.

"What? Where is this happening? What Masters?" Mitch asked.

"As I said before, I am not from here. I am from another place. That place is not here. It is difficult to understand," Drak said.

"So what, you're a space alien?" Mitch said.

"I said open your mind," Drak said, looking at Mitch in earnest. "Space is not a place. I have come here using a special technology, the Masters' technology. They are bad people, but they know how to use technology to move between places."

"You mean like a different dimension or something?" Mitch asked.

"Yes and no," Drak said, struggling to find the right words. "Time is all the same. Everything is here. Everything is now. Everything is connected."

"Like wormholes? I've heard about those things. They don't know if they exist. I don't believe you. Where did you get this stuff? You probably bought it on the dark web."

"You're not listening. This is no joke. Let me show you. It is easier with pictures, I think," Drak said while reaching out to the orb again. He made a few gestures, and an image of the Earth appeared.

"That's earth," Mitch said.

"Right, but here is not here," Drak said before he spun the orb again. The planet is not what it seems. "None of this is real. Well, it's all real, but not what we think it is," Drak said,

"Like a simulation," Mitch said, cutting Drak off. "I've heard that too, but It sounds crazy. Are you trying to say this whole thing is a computer game?"

"You are not listening, and this is not a joke. We don't know what it is. We just know we are in it. My home is like this planet, but in another space. The Masters know how to connect these spaces and what you call wormholes exists everywhere," Drak said while spinning the orb again. A new image of the earth appeared in the sphere.

"This space is connected to all other spaces. The Masters know how to control wormholes, and they can move between worlds easily," Drak said while his voice grew distant.

"My home is like this place." Drak said. He flicked his wrist again, and a purple and yellow planet appeared in the orb. "This is my home, we call it: 'Chalthantar.'"

Reaching into the sphere, he zoomed into the planet's surface, revealing the skyline of an enormous city. People, similar to Drak in appearance, walked through wide parks in a beautiful and ornate city while strange vehicles moved through the air in all directions. There were older people and young children, and what seemed like markets and shops.

"Although this may seem foreign to you, my people are not much different from earthlings. We have families and friends, but we also have problems," Drak said, flicking his wrist again and a new image appeared.

Angry men in armor marched in lockstep as giant ships flew overhead.

"As our civilization progressed, wars broke out among my people. Our planet plunged into chaos for many years."

Spinning the orb again, Drak summoned a new image. A gigantic crowd gathered around a large glowing orb similar to the one in the room as massive hooded figure emerged from an opening.

"One day the Masters come from out of nowhere and say they want to help. My people get crazy. They think the Gods have come to help make our world a better place. The Masters say they can end our wars. My people surrendered and let the Masters take control."

As the image shifted, an immense gathering of people bowed before several hulking forms while thousands of soldiers, imbued with an orange aura, hovered in the air over the crowd.

While the scene changed, Mitch glanced away from the orb and noticed the tension in Drak's face before turning his attention back to the sphere.

The people wore glowing collars around their necks as they marched along in columns while soldiers kept watch from the air.

"The Masters tricked my people. Made them slaves. Now we work for the Masters. They have powerful weapons and amazing technology. My people cannot stop them."

Images of the hooded figures shooting light from their hand and levitating into the air flashed before Mitch's eyes.

"I lost my mother, my father, and my family. We are separated. Now I don't know where they are," Drak said as he spun the orb again.

"The Masters sent me to a mine. I worked all day digging for a special energy the Masters need for their technology," Drak said as he wiped tears from his eyes. "Some of my people fight back. We stole the Masters' technology and made it our own. We tried to resist, but the Masters are strong. They make life more difficult for our people. But we learned how the technology works, and we learned how the world works - our world. This technology uses special energy, negative energy, or dark energy. It's like gravity, but opposite."

"I read that too. They say most of the universe is missing or something. I think it was like 85% percent if I remember right. I saw a video about it on MindHIve," Mitch said.

"It's not missing. It's all around us. We just can't see it. The Masters technology uses this energy to power their devices. But, it is actually the user that powers the device, not the other way around. The Device channels positive energy and creates a push against the dark energy allowing the user to manipulate reality," Drak finished speaking and looked at Mitch.

"I don't know what to think. I can't believe I'm sitting here talking to a visitor from another dimension. I must be going schizo right now. You're not real, are you? You're some figment of my imagination. I've obviously gone insane because of all the stress, and now I'm in the middle of a psychotic breakdown. It's only a matter of time before somebody figures it out, and I wind up in a vegetative state in a mental hospital," Mitch said out loud.

"Crazy is a good place to start. Everything crazy. But the story is not finished. You need to know why I have come here and how I did it," Drak said before he changed the image again.

"We know how the Masters jump through worlds, but we don't have access. They use big machines, but the technology needs a lot of energy. The gateway in our world is heavily guarded. We cannot destroy it or control it, but we have learned about many things. We have spies all over, and we learn new information. Other places and other people like us exist, all slaves."

Drak continued to flick his wrist, summoning images of technology and equipment Mitch struggled to comprehend.

"The Masters are constantly in search of new energy sources. Like everything else, dark energy is strong in some places and weak in others. We learned that the Masters have plans for a new place. Your planet, Earth, has a high concentration of dark matter. We learned they were building a new portal. It is not protected like the one on Chalthantar. If one of us could sneak through, maybe they can destroy the gateway and bring down the Masters' network. Maybe their people can fight back if they have the technology before the Masters come. It's a long shot, but it's worth it. I volunteer for the mission. We make a big plan and find out how to access the gateway. When the time is right, I sneak through. But the Masters learn of our plan and attack. My comrades fought back and hold the gateway open. I was able to sneak through. It's a dangerous journey, but the device protected me. The gateway is not finished on this side, and I arrived in a cave similar to this one. After getting my bearings, I explored my surroundings. I found a large community nearby. Using my device to manipulate the system, I created an earthling identity. The best place to hide is in plain sight, so I became a student and went to school. Here I have learned many things. Your language and culture are still strange to me, but I understand enough to get by. My people send me info, and I am learning who is working for the Masters in this place. I started sending out information into your network. Trying to warn people that the Masters will come here and make your people slaves like mine." Drak stopped speaking for a moment and looked at Mitch.

"I just don't believe it. If this is all true, then why me? Why did you need me? Why did you drag me into all of this?" Mitch asked.

"Opportunity. You were in the right place at the right time."

"More like the wrong place at the wrong time. The story of my life."

"No, you are so selfish. This is not about you. This is about everything. I choose you because you are the closest best thing to help my mission. I need to let the tech loose in the system so people here can find it, but I can't let the system know it is disseminating the information. Your video is only a joke, but many people watch it. The algorithm embedded the code into the video file to spread the technology around the network. If somebody finds the code, they can use the algorithm to fight back against the Masters if I fail my mission. The tech will spreading wide while the Masters try to control the system. This is one way to fight back. The Masters are not in control here yet. We will try to fight back here before they become too powerful. But after releasing tech into the system, the Masters must know I'm here now. They are searching for me. That's why they are coming here, to Kingsford. This is good. They think they can trap me, but it's a part of the plan. I need to get into MindHIve's system. There I can destroy the gateway before it is finished. But this will not stop the Masters for long. They need energy, and this place has plenty. Even If I destroy the gateway, they will come again. If your people don't fight back, the Masters will take this place too. Soon, the Masters will control everything and we will all be slaves. They are coming, and I must stop them. Will you help me or not?"

"You want me to go and fight with you? I knew you were some kind of terrorist. I've got other problems to deal with than your imaginary war. These are some really nice toys you've got, but I'm not going to go off and battle your wormhole masters."

"This is not a joke. I'll show you how serious this is," Drak said while making two fists over his head. He lowered his arms, and the orb disappeared. Picking up the cube, he placed it back in his pocket. Once again, he crossed his arms, and he was immersed in the same blue glow. Placing his hands at his side, he levitated into the air.

Mitch fell backward and stumbled over a large rock. He got back to his feet and stood before Drak, aghast. Swinging his arms, Drak moved from side to side before Mitch. Simple gestures allowed him to maneuver easily about the cavern. He made two fists, and a pair of orbs encased his hands. Flicking his wrist, he shot the ball at a rock and it burst into flames before crumbling into a pile of ash.

"Ok, enough, I get it. You're not joking. Just don't shoot me with that thing," Mitch shouted out. "How did I get involved in all this? This is a nightmare."

"No, the nightmare is coming and the battle will begin soon. There is no looking back now," Drak said while lowering himself to the ground.

"What time is it? I've got to get to class. If I'm late, Mr. O'Hare will extend my suspension," Mitch said while searching for a way out.

"We will be in touch, Mitch Mythic," Drak said. "I told you, things are different now."

"Yeah, I got that," Mitch called back as he made his way to the tunnel.

14

Moon SoHee did not want to go to America. She hated public events, and there was nothing more public than MindHIve's annual tech convention. The invitation arrived via email earlier that day, and when the CEO of MindHIve mentioned her name during the news briefing, she fell into a state of shock. The Korean media plastered her face across every imaginable surface after catching wind of her invitation, as a horde of reporters blew up her inbox. She sat alone in her room in her family's apartment in Seoul, leaving her Mother to deal with the media. The light spilled in through the large window above her bed, casting light on the aquariums SoHee set up around her room.

She heard her mother's muted voice talking on the phone in the living room. SoHee's mother had nothing but her daughter's best interests in mind, but Sohee's best interests were a matter of debate between the two of them. It was her mother's life goal to get SoHee into an Ivy League University in America. Anything less than Harvard would be considered a complete failure. SoHee, on the other hand, only wanted to work on her projects. Her mother and father held high standards for their daughter, and much to their surprise, her achievements far exceeded their lofty expectations.

From a young age, SoHee attended academies and cram schools that specialized in getting students into top universities. Thrust into the competitive world of Korean education, SoHee competed alongside her peers for to secure a place at one of the top schools in the city.

Even among such a competitive field, SoHee stood out immediately. Studying came easy to her, and she picked up on ideas quickly. Her mother had her tested at several places, and the results were somewhat startling. SoHee certainly fell into the gifted category, and being categorized as such only encouraged her mother more. She set about finding the best academies in the city and enrolling her daughter in every single one of them.

All the attention SoHee received made her immensely shy, and she hated being thrust into the spotlight. A great deal of people made a fuss about her from early on, and she often felt isolated and alone. When pushed to speak in front of people, she froze up and burst into tears. She hated losing control, and she became angry with herself for showing her emotions. Soon, she learned to bottle her feelings, and she developed a thick shell of wit and sarcasm to deflect any attempts to gauge her emotional state.

Although she resisted specialists eager to analyze her, she couldn't ignore her immense curiosity for the world. At the elite kindergarten she attended, the administrators developed an extensive Earth Science program, filling the school with all kinds of strange and wonderful creatures. She fell in love with the tadpoles right away. Watching them grow thrilled her in ways she never thought possible. As cute as they were, the tadpoles were cruel and vicious to each other. They cannibalized the dead, and they ate each other's growing limbs right before SoHee's eyes. It was disgusting yet fascinating. Her secret obsession became things that were small and strange, much like herself.

The first time she looked through a microscope, she was awestruck. Her teacher brought in water from a nearby swamp, and all the students received samples. She couldn't believe what she saw as she peered through the magnified lens. A microscopic universe right before her eyes. Fascinated by her discovery, she plunged into the dense field of microbiology with eager optimism.

SoHee ate up any information on micro-organisms she could get her hands on. If she heard about a new development, she would actively try to reproduce it. Her room at home became a miniature laboratory. Vials, jars, and tanks lined the walls. Each container filled with different specimens and samples from one of her many expeditions to a local swamp or estuary.

Her mother had no choice but to indulge her daughter. She provided SoHee with everything she needed to excel in her field. Her father, absentee as he was, had no problem footing the bill. An executive at DaeHwa, one of Korea's massive corporations, he hardly saw his daughter, but, when it came to her education, he did not spare any expense. Being the daughter of a DH executive certainly had its perks. She enrolled in the company's junior scientist program at an early age. In the beginning, she received limited access to the company's facilities, but as her experiments grew in size and scope, she soon took up an entire section of the laboratory.

At the age of 12, she published her first paper on bacterial adaptation in a journal called Korean Science Today. The paper reported how certain bacteria had adapted to live in local water systems around Seoul. It was a good paper filled with well-researched information, but the fact that a young girl wrote it grabbed media attention. As a result, SoHee found herself featured in all kinds of TV programs and newspapers. Several international journals published her article, launching her career as a young scientist.

Upper management at DH caught wind of SoHee's developments. They quickly seized the opportunity to steal some media headlines and dump a chunk of their profits into education-based tax credits. The junior science program at DH expanded at a rapid rate and SoHee was allowed to spend long hours in the laboratory, building bacteria habitats and carrying out experiments. Her mother fretted about SoHee ignoring her other studies, but her success in the laboratory trumped her mother's education plans.

The cram schools she attended could not fulfill her needs. Craving new information, the rote learning systems of the schools only stymied her appetite for knowledge. She devoured international science journals and research papers. Over time, she was taught herself how to use new technology, and the scientists at DH labs took notice.

During this time, she actively posted her achievements to her MindHIve science blog. She found it easier to express herself and her ideas through these mediums than to say them out loud to other people. Within a short time, she built up a substantial following. Although most of the comments on her post were positive, she found a particular pleasure in confronting her detractors. She possessed a knack for facing trolls, and she used her immense knowledge of the scientific world to take apart anyone that challenged her or her theories.

As her abilities and understanding progressed, so did her social status. Known in Korea as 'Miss Science,' she turned the moniker into her online identity. But her growing popularity placed pressure on her to produce more scientific material.

When she discovered the work of the renowned scientist, Herbert Boyer, and his work on recombinant DNA technology, her entire worldview shattered. The very notion that microbial DNA could be genetically modified changed the game in more ways than she could comprehend. As her research into cellular modification techniques intensified, she came across CRISPR genome editing techniques, and she implemented this practice into her work without hesitation.

Due to her work with sewage samples, SoHee could not ignore the impact humanity had on the planet. Her career began based on changes she discovered to bacteria in the local water systems surrounding Seoul. She gathered samples throughout the city, and then traveled upstream to collect more samples. The results of the test she ran on the different samples shocked her, but she found the resiliency of the bacteria far more impressive. Adapting to their environment in astonishing ways, they were intelligent, after all.

As she studied more about recombinant DNA, she realized it may be possible to develop a microbe capable of altering the environment rather than merely adapting to it. Just imagine if a bacterium could be developed that could eat the contaminants in the water supply, she had thought to herself. It was heady and challenging work, but she managed to create a gene splicing system in the DH laboratory. She started working on it on her own, but after a few posts to her MindHIve account went viral, the executive of the science department at DH caught wind of her activities. Without consulting SoHee, they decided it would be best for the company if they pitched in. No scientist wants to be on the wrong side of history, and no adult wants to be on the wrong side of a kid with a huge Internet following.

After a few months of testing, SoHee and the scientists at DH laboratories successfully modified several species of microbial bacteria. SoHee submitted her findings and work to the Journal of Scientific Discoveries. After her work was published, the media hailed her as the "Whiz Kid from Korea."

She found it difficult to keep her head above water as her scientific credibility and online status ballooned. Although it was tough to keep things straight, SoHee continued to pour her efforts into the projects she developed. Horrified about the state of the environment, she applied all she learned into producing work capable of changing the course of human history.

When scientists discovered bacteria that ate plastic at a Japanese garbage dump in 2016, SoHee realized what she needed to do. The enzyme present in the bacteria in Japan held the key to the future. After several months and a lot of setbacks, she successfully synthesized a protein with similar capacities as the ones found in Japan. With the right tools at her disposal, she ran dozens of experiments in her state-of-the-art lab at DH headquarters. After several attempts, she managed to produce bacteria capable of devouring any waste particle put in its path, with only one problem: the bacteria assumed properties of the material it consumed. It was an incredible phenomenon. Thinking of different ways to apply her discovery, she experimented with an array of waste particles, and she even went so far as to throw random objects into petri dishes filled with her modified bacteria. When the bacteria consumed a small computer chip in a week, SoHee knew her discovery possessed the potential to change the game.

Although it was possible for the bacteria to consume electronic components, it would take millions of years for the process to have any impact on the environment. The major obstacle to any further development in her research had to do with the relative size of the microbes and the immense amount of trash occupying the earth. Even though she felt she hadn't made any substantial breakthrough, she published the findings in several journals.

Her paper: entitled 'Microbes of the future' found an international audience almost immediately, and her post about the microbes devouring the microchip received millions of likes on MindHIve. Headlines around the world read: 'Girl in Korea creates miracle bacteria,' and 'Whiz kid solves world trash problem,' and on and on. She couldn't deny she discovered something, but there were too many variables at play to say for certain what the outcome of her discovery would bring, and she was terrified that her discovery would not provide the miracle solution people hoped for.

This fear and apprehension wrestled in her gut as she listened to her mother speaking on the phone in the next room with SoHee's newly hired agent. As much as her mother enjoyed the spotlight, they were overwhelmed by the attention and they needed to hire outside help.

"I just spoke with your agent, and we have a full slate of interviews scheduled for tomorrow. We're also setting up everything now for our trip to America. Isn't it all so exciting?" her mother asked while she walked into the living room. SoHee didn't say anything.

"Sohee, what's the matter?"

"I don't want to go."

"Don't be ridiculous. Just think about how good this will look on your university application."

Mitch book one grammarly

15

When Mitch returned to the computer lab in the afternoon, he walked into an empty room. He sat down in his chair and let the solitude wash over him, relieved to be out of the spotlight.

After the announcement and his trip underground with Drak, the feverish excitement of the day accelerated the passage of time to a dizzying rate. He reached history class a couple of minutes late, but Mr. Horowitz decided only to give Mitch a look rather than report him to Mr. O'Hare.

Everybody wanted to talk about what had happened to him and what he could expect at the tech convention. The students and teachers were beyond themselves after hearing the MindHIve chose Kingsford to host their convention. He tried to smile while everybody poured attention upon him, but he knew a more sinister motive influenced MindHIve's decision. Whether or not Drak told the truth of his origins, the massive corporation had certainly caught wind of the strange young man's whereabouts, and Mitch, through no fault of his own, found himself caught in his companions inescapable web of deceit and conspiracy.

Although the circumstances elevated his status on a global scale, locally, his problems remained unresolved. Passing Sage in the hall, his former friend glared at him but kept silent as he walked by. He wanted Mitch to be humiliated at the meeting that evening. If he acted the part of the aggressor again, he would be exposed. Mitch, for his part, had no desire to draw any more attention to the situation. He planned to apologize to the team and get the whole thing over with. There were far more important things for Mitch to worry about than making an insincere apology.

"Working hard or hardly working, Mitch?" Mr. O'hare chuckled as he popped his head in the door.

"Working hard, sir," Mitch said, turning to face the Vice-Principal.

"You hang in there, Mr. Mythic. Things are looking up for you. Once you change your attitude, that changes everything," Mr. O'Hare continued. "Drak isn't here? That's strange. If you see him, let him know I need him to look at the computer in my office. Some Chinese website keeps popping up on my desktop, and I can't get rid of it."

"Will do, sir," Mitch said as Mr. O'Hare left the room.

Where did Drak go, he wondered to himself. Getting up from his chair, he walked to the back of the lab and peered out into the hallway. He went down the forlorn-looking stairwell and tried the door, but it wouldn't budge. Shrugging, he returned to the computer lab and glanced at the clock: 3:30. He had another 90 minutes to kill before Mr. O'Hare released him.

Returning to his chair, he picked up his phone and read a text message from his mom.

"Be at the arena at 7:00 pm sharp. We won't be home. We're making some arrangements for the meeting. Congratulations! We're so proud of you.".

"This is going to be a strange meeting," he said aloud. Without a doubt, his mother was at the arena arranging chairs and tables in the large meeting room that sat beyond the bleachers of the arena before she ordered pizza and made coffee.

Standing up, he raised his arms over his head and stretched toward the ceiling while the fans of the old computers whirred around him. Outside, the soccer team practiced on the field. The sounds of feet kicking balls and the coach blowing into his whistle echoed up from the playing field.

He couldn't believe how simple his life had been before the events of the last few days. Even worse, and he had no idea how to make his life go back to normal. The whole town was making a huge fuss out of the tech convention, and if he refused to go, he would be letting everybody down. But after witnessing the power Drak possessed and hearing the story he told, Mitch knew a dangerous time fast approached with implications that went far beyond Kingsford.

If MindHIve knew about Drak, then Mitch would be on their list as well. They were, most likely, profiling him as he sat alone in the computer room. He needed to convince Drak to call the whole thing off and get out of town. But with Drak gone, all eyes would fall onto

Mitch. He sighed and sat down in the chair.

Mr. O'Hare popped his head in the door again. "Hey, Mitch, it's been a pretty crazy day. You can take off early. I know you've got that meeting tonight."

"Thank you, sir," Mitch said while he reached for his backpack.

Walking at a brisk pace, he wanted to get home without being noticed, but his newfound fame proved difficult to escape. People honked their horns as they drove by and recognized him.

Prior to the current state of affairs, Mitch had enjoyed semi-celebrity status because of his role on the hockey team. But in the few hours since the MindHIve announcement, he had morphed into a full-blown celebrity. He waved as politely as he could, but he couldn't help but shake his head. It was hard enough being the laughingstock of town, but now they had made him a hero for it. He couldn't imagine what would happen if they found out the truth.

He arrived home with enough time to have a shower and get changed. At team meetings players were required to wear a tie and Mitch always kept one pre-tied hanging in the closet. He wasn't very good at tying them, so it was easier to keep one at the ready rather than battle with it every time he needed to wear it. He didn't have much time to get to the arena. Grabbing his bike out of the garage, he pedaled out into the evening light.

As he rode through his neighborhood, the giddiness of the community flared up at every turn. Restaurants and shops placed signs in their windows, welcoming the massive company to Kingsford as people flooded the streets to celebrate amongst their friends.

Mitch arrived at the Arena before 7 pm. He recognized most of the vehicles in the parking lot. Near the front of the lot sat his mother's minivan and his father's pickup truck. Both vehicles were emblazoned with the "Mythic Sports" logo. Locking his bike outside, he made his way into the arena.

He always loved the smell of the rink, fresh ice, and old sweat. It reminded him of the joy hockey brought him. Some of the greatest moments in his life occurred inside those walls, but it also the happened to be the beginning of his current predicament.

The double doors to the meeting room sat wide open. His father stood at the podium while addressing his audience. Glancing at Mitch as he slid into a seat near the back, he greeted everyone that had come out.

"Good to see everyone could come down on such short notice.

Considering everything that has happened in the last 24 hours, I think it's important we get together as a team and see where we stand."

Mitch spotted the back of his mother's head. She sat in the front row with Toby, his little brother. Turning back, she spotted Mitch and gestured for him to come up with her. As he got out of his seat to join her, his father continued with his speech.

"We all know what has happened in the last little while, and I think it's time we put the past behind us and start thinking about the future. There is a young man here that has been through a lot, and he said he would like to come up here and say a few words. Mitch, do you want to come up here now?"

Mitch hesitated for a second before climbing got out of his seat. The entire room hushed as he walked to the podium. Mitch hadn't prepared anything to say. He planned to go up and say sorry, and he hoped it would be enough.

His father patted him on the shoulder as he stepped aside. He stood before the crowd of people he knew so well as the faces of his teammates and their families looked back at him. Sage sat near the back with a snarl on his face.

"I know I let everybody here down. I made a big mistake, and I let my emotions get the better of me. I just want to say to everybody that I'm sorry for what happened, and it won't happen again," he said as he gripped the edge of the lectern.

"Sage, I'm sorry I hit you. It was wrong for me to do what I did. Please forgive me," He said through clenched teeth. "In my heart, I want what's best for the team. Playing hockey with you guys is amazing. I love representing my town, and I want people to know I am a team player. So, once again, I'm sorry."

After a few moments of uncomfortable silence, everybody stood and cheered while his mother raced out of her chair and gave him a big hug.

"I knew you could do it, Mitch," she said through teary eyes. From the back of the room, a loud voice cut through the clamor.

"Let's see you put that fighting spirit of yours to work for next season, Mitch. But we all want some of those new gadgets from MindHIve. Why don't you get us all a team set while you're at the tech party?" he bellowed, and everybody laughed.

"I'll see what I can do," Mitch said as he sat down next to his mother. Mike Mythic got back on the podium and started to speak.

"We're all proud of you, Mitch. It takes a lot of guts to come out and own your mistakes. That's the mark of a leader," He paused, and everybody clapped.

"It seems like things are going to be really interesting for you in the next while. It's amazing what you've gone and done with your situation. You managed to take a terrible situation and turn it into something positive. Now, I don't know a lot about MindHIve and all this internet stuff, but I know it's a great opportunity for you, and it looks like it's going to be a great opportunity for our town,"

He paused, and everybody clapped again. Mike Mythic loved speaking in front of people. It reminded him of his playing days doing press conferences.

"We'd like to take this opportunity to further congratulate you, Mitch. I hope you don't mind, but we had a cake made up at the Kingsford supermarket in your honor."

Mike grabbed a large cake sitting on a table nearby and held it up for everybody to see.

'Congratulations, Mitch,' sat stenciled across the top of a large rectangular cake. A very creative baker managed to etch the exact image of Mitch catapulting over the net onto the cake above the #epiccrotchshot hash tag.

Everybody in the room laughed out loud. Mitch laughed along with them. He wanted to strangle his father, but he had no choice but to keep his.

"Now, who wants some cake?" His father said, and everybody laughed again.

16

After the #epiccrotchshot cake vanished down the throats of the Kingsford Crusher's players and alumni, plenty of people wanted to speak with Mitch and congratulate him on his invite to the tech convention.

Mitch's uneasy feelings hung about the back of his mind as he tried to smile his way through conversations with parents and team supporters. The local media caught wind of the meeting, and a small contingency of reporters gathered outside hoping to catch Mitch for an interview.

"Were you surprised MindHIve selected you to attend the convention?" one reporter asked Mitch as he exited the meeting room.

"Of course I was surprised," he said. "Who wouldn't be?"

"How does it feel to be the subject of a viral video?" another reporter asked.

"It's a little overwhelming," Mitch said, trying his best to seem amicable in spite of the situation.

"Why do you think MindHIve picked Kingsford over any other town?" a different reporter chimed in.

"Well, that's a pretty good question," Mitch said. An image of Drak floating in the storage room flashed through his mind. "It's like that CEO guy said, I guess. We're a small town with a big heart."

"Why don't you leave this kid alone? He's had a long day," Mike Mythic said, cutting in while grinning for the camera. Putting his arm around Mitch, he posed like he just won an award.

"Mr. Mythic, do you think it's a blessing or a burden that MindHIve will take over this town for an entire week next month?" a reporter asked.

"Well, I support any opportunity to promote Kingsford. If one of the biggest companies in the world wants to come to our town, then I would definitely say we've been blessed. I'm certain our community will not be the same when this is all said and done, but I'm excited about the convention, and I'm proud of my son for being invited to attend. Now if you'll excuse us, we're all a little tired after an eventful day," Mike Mythic said, leading his son away from the reporters. "Grab your bike and throw it in the back of the truck. We can't have Kingsford's biggest celebrity riding around on a bicycle,"

Mitch rolled his eyes and went to fetch his bike. They rode home together in silence.

"You know, we're really proud of you," Mitch's father said, trying to break the quiet. "That was a brave thing you did today. Owning up to your mistakes is the mark of a strong leader."

Mitch exhaled deeply as his father spoke.

"You seem like something's bothering you. You should be beaming right now. You've just been handed an amazing opportunity," his father continued.

"I'm sorry, dad. I'm just really tired," Mitch said while leaning his head against the passenger side window.

"I guess that's understandable," Mike Mythic said while pulling his truck into the driveway of the Mythic's home. "Let's get inside and get some rest. Tomorrow's another big day."

When he got inside, his mother stood waiting for him in the kitchen.

"I'm so proud of you," she said, as she threw her arms around him. "It was really brave what you did tonight. The team will be stronger now because of all this. Are you hungry? I could make you a sandwich?"

"It's ok, Mom," Mitch said. "I'm exhausted, and I think I just need to go to bed."

"That seems like the right thing to do. We all need a good night sleep. Toby passed out in the car on the way home. He's already in bed. Get some sleep, Mitch. We love you so much, and we are so proud of you," she said while hugging him again.

"Thanks, Mom. I love you too," Mitch said before heading downstairs to his bedroom.

As soon as he got in his room he undressed, shut off the lights, and crawled under his blanket. Although he felt overwhelmed by his circumstances, he managed to fall asleep in a matter of moments.

Drifting through a dream world, he found himself naked in front of a crowd of people watching him in amusement. At the back of the room, someone knocked on the door. The sound grew louder as Mitch made his way through the crowd. Approaching the door, he struggled to find a handle or a knob. As hard as he tried, he couldn't find a way to open it. He called out, but whoever stood behind the door refused to answer.

Snapping out of sleep, he wiped away the saliva dripping out of his mouth with his hand. Glancing at his dresser in the dark, the clock read 1:07. A quiet knocking rattled the window near his bed. Terrified, he leaned over and peered into the dark beyond the glass.

"Mitch, get up. I need to show you something," Drak whispered.

"What are you doing here? It's the middle of the night," Mitch seethed through clenched teeth.

"It is important. Come with me.".

"Dude, I just need some sleep. Can't this wait until tomorrow?"

"It can't wait. Time is short. We need to hurry. This is a dangerous time."

"This is insane. I'm not going out there with you."

"You come now and I'll show you. If you want me to go away after, I will go. I promise."

"You'll stop bothering me anymore if I come with you now?"

"Yes, come now and I will go away after, if you want."

"I'll come with you now, as long as you promise to leave me alone."

"Fine, I promise. Just come now, after, you decide."

"Hold on. I've got to put on some clothes."

Mitch got out bed while shaking his head. What have I gotten myself into, he thought to himself as he slid on a pair of pants and a hoodie.

Unlatching his window, he slithered out into the backyard. His mother's garden gnomes peered at him through the darkness, but Drak had vanished.

"This way," a voice whispered in the dark. Mitch made his way towards Drak's voice, careful not to trip the motion detector lights his father installed to keep away any night prowlers.

"We're not going far," Drak said while hopping over the fence that lined the Mythic's backyard. Mitch followed suit, and they made their way to the path that led to the greenbelt nearby. Within the confines of the forest, they slowed their pace.

"What the hell are we doing out here in the middle of the night? This better be good," Mitch said.

"We'll go in here," Drak said as he approached a massive storm drain tucked into the side of the ravine.

"Into the sewer again?" Mitch said with a look of disgust on his face.

"I told you already, there are many caves around here. The whole place is connected underground," Drak said.

"You want to go crawl around in the old mining caves in the middle of the night? I don't know, man."

"Don't worry, I have a plan."

"Yeah, you've always got a plan."

"Trust me. You will not be disappointed," Drak said before he popped open the steel grate blocking the entrance to the drain.

"Ughh man, what am I doing here?" Mitch said as he walked into the sewer. "And what is that smell?"

Entering the culvert, Drak produced a light from his pocket to guide the way, and Mitch pulled out his phone, activating its flashlight. Tall enough for them to walk upright and wide enough for them to walk side by side, the culvert smelled of rot and decay.

After a few minutes, Drak stopped before a large metal door similar to the one under the school.

"In here," he said as he cranked the door open. Its rusty hinges creaked while it swung open, revealing a rocky tunnel descending into the darkness.

"We're going in here? All of these tunnels are barricaded for a reason. They are super dangerous. Kids got hurt or vanished without a trace in these things," Mitch said as he peered into the blackness of the tunnel.

"It fine. I've been here before, safe, for now," Drak said with a grin.

"Ugh, what am I doing?" Mitch said while followed Drak into the tunnel.

The air grew colder as they walked, and Mitch felt a breeze on his face. After several minutes of stumbling over rocks, Drak stopped and looked up.

"We're here."

"What's here?" Mitch asked as he peered into the dark.

In a flash, the space around him illuminated, and he found himself standing in a cavern much larger than the one beneath the school. Drak stood to his right, holding a bright orb in his hand to light up their surroundings.

"Give me your phone," Drak said.

"What do you need my phone for? The last time I went along with something like this, you blew up my MindHIve account and dragged me into this mess. I'm not sure if I should just hand over my phone to you."

"Don't worry. This is good. You will like it. I promise. You've come this far. You are ready to level up."

"Level up? What are you talking about?"

"Give me your phone, and I will show you."

"Well, it's already this messed up. I'm probably a wanted criminal, anyway. Fine, take it."

Grabbing the phone, Drak reached into his pocket and drew out the black cube he showed Mitch earlier.

"These two things are very similar. They use the same technology. The Masters gave their earth people information many years ago, and they used it to make phones and many things — it's all part of the plan. The same thing happened in my home. But, it is not so hard to make changes if you know what to do," Drak said while placing the two devices side by side on the ground.

"What are you going to do to my phone?" Mitch asked.

"It's an upgrade," Drak said while he extended both of his hands out over the devices.

He opened his hands and raised them over his head. The orb appeared again, but on a much smaller scale. Reaching into the sphere, he made a gesture with his fingers and a long tentacle-like beam extended out of the orb and picked up Mitch's phone.

"Hey, what's going on?" Mitch half shouted.

"Like I said, upgrade. We are giving your old phone new powers. You will need this when we fight the Masters and their servants."

"I'm not fighting any Masters."

"Then you'll be a slave."

As Mitch's phone floated within the center of the orb, more blue tentacles wrapped around it, infusing the device with light.

"Almost finished," Drak said.

Mitch stared at the orb in disbelief. A brief flash lit up the cavern as the light dispersed, leaving his phone rotating in the center of the orb. Drak reached in and grabbed it before handing it to Mitch.

"Your upgrade is complete, Mitch Mythic," he said and smiled.

"What happened? What did you change?" Mitch asked.

"Everything. But nothing at the same time. Like I said, your phone has the same tech from the Masters. I added new abilities, but it is all based on the same idea. Everything we see and touch is not what we think it is. The same with power and energy. Your phone uses energy differently than before. It works with the energy field around you. Now you can do as I do. Here, see," Drak said as he stepped back from Mitch.

Placing the cube back into the pocket of his jacket, he crossed his arms over his chest and a blue glow appeared around him.

"You do the same. It's no problem," Drak said while gesturing for Mitch to follow suit. "Just like me."

Drak crossed his arms over his chest again, and the glow disappeared.

"Copy me, Mitch," he said.

"Oh, this is nuts," Mitch said after exhaling. "Fine, let's see what this is all about."

Mitch crossed his arms over his chest, copying Drak. He stepped back in shock as the blue aura spread across his body.

"What the hell? What is this?" Mitch said, trying not to panic.

"The device makes energy all around us work together. Your body is not just what you see but an entire field of vibrations. Matter and energy are the same thing. This technology allows you to use matter like energy and energy like matter," Drak said while he waved his hand in front of his face summoning a blue sphere. "Now, if you think it, you do it, like this. This energy is created when we push against dark matter. Thoughts are energy, too. If I think it, my mind pushes against dark matter, creating what I think. I can do many things with it. It's a weapon. It's a shield. Learn to control it and you will become a powerful warrior, but there is great danger here. Like everything, it does good, but it also does bad. We must be careful."

Mitch watched the ball of energy pass back and forth between Drak's hands.

"You must learn to use it, if you are to help me fight the Masters," Drak said. "A big fight is coming. We need to prepare."

"How am I supposed to fight some alien Masters?" Mitch said. "What am I even doing here? This is crazy."

"Yes, it's very crazy," Drak said. "Come. follow me,"

Pushing down with his arms, he elevated off of the ground.

"What are you doing?" Mitch asked while he looked up in awe.

"Don't be scared," Drak said. "It's safe. You can use the device to make a light like this."

Putting his arms out straight, he bent them at the elbow and waved his hands across his body in one motion, causing the light to intensify.

"You do the same, just like me," he said and grinned again. Mitch copied Drak's actions, and he found himself immersed in light.

"Ok, now follow me," Drak said before he crouched down and leaped into the air, stopping about ten feet above Mitch. "Do it just like I did. Make two fists and imagine yourself rising off the ground."

Shaking his head, he made two fists by his side, mirroring Drak, and he felt himself pop off of the ground. In shock, he stumbled backward and fell to the stone floor. As he got back up, Drak lowered himself down.

"It'll take some getting used to, huh?" Drak said before flashing a grin. "Bend your knees before you start. You need balance just like anything. Try it one more time. This time, be ready."

"What am I doing? I can't believe this is happening," Mitch said.

"Believe it. This is real. This is no joke?" Drak snapped at him. "The only thing that matters is what you believe in. If you believe it, it is possible. Bend your knees, time to go."

Following Drak's instructions, Mitch bent his knees with his hands at his side before making a fist and he felt himself rising into the air.

"Hey, ok, I think I can do this," he said as he tested his balance.

"Start small. Make some simple movements. See how it feels, like this." Drak said while he moved his legs back and forth. Copying Drak, he found himself gliding across the cavern.

"Hey, I think I'm getting the hang of this," he said as he came to a stop in front of Drak.

"Maybe, now we need to go up," Drak said. "Don't worry, it's the same as down here, just high up," he said, and he grinned again. "Here, crouch down like this and push. Up we go."

"This is nuts," Mitch said as he crouched down. Pushing off, he launched into the air. His legs came out from behind him, and he faced Drak upside down.

"I told you. You need balance and control," Drak said while he moved over to Mitch. He grabbed Mitch's leg and righted him. "You must think it and then do it. See what you do in your mind, and everything will follow. You are in control. You must believe it. Everything is in your mind. Copy my motion and do as I do."

He turned his side and crouched into a diving position. Leaping forward, he moved through the air easily.

"Like this, Mitch. It's no problem," Drak said from a distance.

Crouching down, Mitch pushed off against the air, and he felt himself speed up.

"Now think stop and make yourself stop," Drak yelled.

Mitch imagined himself stopping on his hockey skates. Turning sideways, he kicked against the air and came to an abrupt stop.

"See, you can do it. Just think it. If only you could see the look on your face now. This is the first time I've seen you happy," Drak said.

As a smile crept across his face, Mitch jumped up and he felt himself rocket upward. But panic seized him when he spotted the stalactites hanging from the ceiling of the cavern. He pushed his hands out, and he came to a stop again.

"Ok, you ready?" Drak said as he joined Mitch at the roof of the cavern. "Follow me. Don't worry. I'll go slow at first."

Shoving off across the cavern, Drak glided through the dark with ease. Mitch sucked in a breath of air and followed after him.

By pushing with his hands and feet, Drak changed his course at will. As Mitch copied his movements, he found he could maneuver with agility and speed.

"This place is where I come into this world," Drak said as he came to a stop at the edge of the massive cavern. "Everything was dark in the cave when I arrived, and I couldn't see anything. At first, I thought I made a mistake. No people, no nothing, just blackness and rock. I stayed here for some time. Got used to the air and gravity. When I felt ok, I started to look around. Find a way out. Slowly, I moved further. Careful not to be seen. I Found a town and more people. I made up a name for myself, a new identity, but I never forget this place here."

"Wait a minute. Your real name isn't Drakon Trendago?" Mitch asked.

"Well, my real name is a little hard to pronounce, so it's better if I made up a new one," Drak said. He let loose a short series of grunts and clicks that made Mitch jump back in Horror.

"What was that?" Mitch asked in shock.

"That's my real name. Told you it was difficult for people to pronounce," Drak said as he grinned again.

"You got that right," Mitch said before he laughed out loud. "How did you get in here? Is there a gateway or something?"

"No gateway here, it's just a cavern," Drak said before he sat down on a ledge. "The Wormhole spat me out here, but I can't open it. Need a big machine to open the gateway."

"If you can't open the gate, then you can't go back."

"Yes, that's true. Unless I find the gateway, for me this was always a one-way mission."

"Why did you volunteer for it? Are you suicidal? What about your family?"

"My family is dead, Mitch. I searched for them for a long time. I tried not to give up hope, but they are gone. The Masters killed them."

"What? How do you know that's true?"

"I just know. What I do now, I do for all my people. The Masters can't control everything. I will fight back — this is my revenge. If we destroy the network, they have no power. The Masters are no different from any other people. They lie and cheat, and people believe them — that's how they have power. Take away the technology, and they are weak, like everybody else."

"How are you going to destroy the network?"

"The Master's network is all connected. If we destroy one gateway, then we can destroy all gateways. A Chain reaction."

"Where is the gateway?"

"The Gateway is not anywhere. It is everywhere, but to use it you need powerful energy and special technology that only the Masters have. We are still learning how it works. If you push against dark matter strong enough with positive energy, a portal opens on the other side. Enough energy and the gateway opens. Not enough, the gateway closes. Too much energy and the gateway explodes."

"So you want to blow up the gateway? What happens when you blow it up? Is it like a nuke or something?"

"Bigger than that. If too much of the wrong energy goes through the gateway, it causes an explosion."

"How do you plan on setting off a negative energy explosion?"

"I must get into the system here and find when and where the Masters' plan to activate the gateway. If I find this, I can set off a reaction using my device."

"How will you do that?"

"I must enter the gateway and set off a reaction."

"You're going to blow up the gateway from the inside. How will you get out?"

"I won't."

"So, this is a suicide mission, and you've dragged me into it. What am I doing here? I can't believe I was almost ok with this. Oh my God, what time is it? I've got to get home," Mitch said as he dropped to the bottom of the cavern and walked toward the tunnel leading to surface. Following after him, Drak caught up to him at the mouth of the tunnel.

"I'm sorry that you are involved now, but this bigger than you, bigger than anyone. If you saw what happened to my people, then you would feel the same way," Drak said while keeping pace with Mitch as they made their way along the tunnel.

"I'm not sure how it works where you're from, but you can't just go dumping this kind of thing on people," Mitch said when they reached the door.

"I know it is a lot to think about, but time is short. Things will start happening faster now. Soon, you will see I'm not a liar. You will see the danger we are all in," Drak said as he swung open the metal door leading to the sewage drain. Mitch made out a faint light at the opening of the tunnel as the pre-dawn light crept over the horizon.

"I know you're not lying. I just don't know what I can do about any of this," Mitch said when they stepped out of the storm drain.

"You can try, and that's all that matters. Your time will come, and it may be sooner than you think," Drak said while the first rays of sunshine filtered through the pine trees.

17

"How do you respond to the allegations being made that your company is operating outside of the law?" Senator Brigsby asked as flashes popped and the TV cameras recorded away.

"Well, Senator, that's an incredibly difficult question to answer due to the circumstances we are discussing," Robert said. "We sit upon the precipice of a bold new frontier in technological development. It is impossible for me to say what is legal and what isn't legal if the laws are yet to be written. But to answer your question directly, it has always been company policy at MindHIve to put our users first. Because of this policy our technology has become a staple of modern life in the United States, and the American people repeatedly choose our products over any other, and they have, in no way, been forced to do so. If our company is operating outside of the law, then the people of this country are all criminals," Robert said.

"Mr. Chapman, I do believe you have failed to understand the scope of my question," Senator Bigsby said. "Our sources revealed proof that your company has obtained access to surveillance equipment off-limits to the private sector. If this is true, then you are in direct violation of the terms of the FTC's service compliance charter. How do you respond to these allegations?"

"The very fact that we are being accused of accessing and misusing technology and data that our company develops and operates on behalf of the government is absurd, to say the least. MindHIve has never in any way compromised the security of this country, and it is for this reason, the government chose our company to develop the technology that now monitors and protects the security of the American people. If my company is operating outside of the law, then it is the duty of this government to change that law. It is companies like MindHive and the innovations and developments we produce that have allowed this country to thrive. Government chokeholds like this only serve to hinder our economy," Robert boomed into the mic.

Days earlier, he agreed to appear at the hearing at the behest of the president and several senators. They believed it would be for the best if he sat in front of the committee to let the press and the people believe MindHIve followed the law and that the company's interests would be of benefit to the people. He personally donated millions to Senator Bigsby's re-election campaign the year before, so Robert knew there wouldn't be any surprises. All the politicians he had access to were involved in his clandestine operation in some form or another, and they knew the risks if they should cross him. He continued to answer the questions asked by each the senators as vaguely as possible. Before the hearing began, he went over every question with his lawyers and he knew nothing he said would incriminate him or his company.

This hearing had been called to investigate MindHIve's use of security satellites ahead of the tech convention. It was all theater. MindHIve had already been using the system for weeks now. But Robert didn't want some nosy reporter making a freedom of information request and discover what he was up to. Soon it wouldn't matter, but for now, it was best to play it safe. He continued to smile and answer questions.

After the hearing adjourned, a scrum of reporters surrounded him on the steps of the Senate and forcing Robert to answer more questions.

"Mr. Chapman, when will the inReal devices be released?" one reporter asked.

"I appeared before the Senate today to address issues regarding our latest developments. We are here to ensure the American people that MindHIve holds their best interests in mind. The government is doing its job, and we are doing ours. As to your question, the security issues at the forefront of this hearing address how MindHIve will implement our inReal devices into real-world scenarios. We will be making our first live testing of the beta network at our annual tech convention, which will be held for the first time in a remote location. We've had a busy day, and I have a plane to catch. Thank you all for being the voice of the people," Robert said as his security detail cleared a path for him through the crowd to a waiting limousine. As Allan stepped into the vehicle, Robert waved him off.

"You follow in the other car. There are things I need to discuss with Mr. Tobero."

Allan made a face before he went to the next car in the procession. As the door shut amidst the crowd, reporters shouted at Robert for a final soundbite.

"Good afternoon, Gerald. I hear you have some news for me," Robert said, settling into his seat after the car cleared a throng of protestors.

"That's correct, sir. We detected the signature in the area where we believed it to be active. We continue to monitor it around the clock, and we are certain it can be detained at any time," Gerald said from a screen on the opposite end of the limo.

"For now, it's best if we stand back and observe," Robert said. "Once we have secured the area, we will be able to contain the situation. What I just did today should give us total control of everything within the jurisdiction. Until that time comes, I don't want any local law enforcement catching wind of what we are doing. This operation requires absolute secrecy. If all goes well, we'll be able to kill two birds with one stone."

"Agreed, sir. We don't believe the subject represents a flight risk. They appear to be following a set pattern of movement and shouldn't be difficult to track down," Gerald said.

"Doesn't it seem too easy, though?" Robert thought out loud. "Once again, it's strange how easily we located the fugitive."

"Although it's possible the culprit is unaware of our monitoring capabilities, it does appear a little too easy. As we discussed earlier, we are aware of the possibilities of a trap, and we have simulated several scenarios, all of which indicate our forces will be able to detain the fugitive," Gerald responded.

"We need him alive. I need to know what he knows before I hand him over to the proper authorities. Is everything ready for this evening's exercises?"

"Yes, sir. The team has been preparing all day. Are you sure it is the best way to proceed? This type of combat exercise, training, or not, is quite dangerous. I want to ensure you aren't taking any unnecessary risks."

"I am well aware of the risks. I'm the one who made this stuff, and I'm the one who tested it out. Who else but I should continue with these developments? Hand to hand combat is the next likely step. Just think of the practical applications for this type of technology. It could be used for crowd control during protests or in prisons. The possibilities really are endless, and you are aware I am one of the world's greatest innovators, aren't you? I fully intend to be the one taking this technology to the limit."

"I understand, sir. You truly are ahead of your time. Your plane is waiting on the tarmac. All security protocols have been followed to the letter. You should be back safely at MindHIve headquarters in a few hours."

"Excellent Gerald, keep up the good work," Robert said before ending the call.

The limousine pulled up to the awaiting plane as a soft rain pelted the runway. Allan opened the door of the limo and held an umbrella out to cover Robert's head in the downpour. The media mob followed the MindHIve procession to the airport, and Robert waved to the reporters before he rushed onto the plane.

MindHIve Air, as the plane was known, taxied to the runway and took off in the air in a matter of moments. It set down on MindHIve's private runway a few hours later and rolled into the hangar. Robert stepped off of his private jet as several members of his staff rushed out to congratulate him while he strode across the concrete floor to an awaiting car.

"Thank you, people — all in a day's work. Somebody's got to make sure the government doesn't get their hands on this place, right?" he said.

"You are getting really positive responses from the media. It looks like the Senate will approve the new legislation and hand it over to the president by week's end," an executive said.

"Of course they will. If not, heads will roll," Roberts said and chuckled to himself. "None of those straw men will stand in my way. But that is the least of my worries. Is everything ready in building there? I'm excited to get underway. My body feels stiff after sitting around all day answering boring questions."

"The security forces and the engineers are standing by awaiting your arrival as instructed, Sir," Allan said from just behind Robert and a little to his right.

"Very good, let's head over. I feel like I need some action," Robert said while cracking his knuckles.

Building three now served as the official headquarters of MindHIve's inReal force. Gerald hand picked the most elite squad of mercenary soldiers available and recruited them for Robert's special project. A lucrative contract and access to advanced technology made it an easy sell. The team consisted of several dozen of the finest soldiers money could buy.

Two burly men from Robert's security detail opened a set of doors as he walked into the cavernous office space. Several members of the inReal force hovered in the air at the center of the room, engaged in a combat training scenario that required them to bring their shields together to form a protective front. They moved about together much like Roman Legionnaires. On either side of the action, the remaining soldiers practiced motion or took shots at holographic enemies.

"Working hard, or hardly working?" Robert shouted as his mercenaries dropped what they were doing and gathered themselves at attention. "At ease, soldiers. I'm not some slave-driving general. Well, maybe I am, but don't tell anyone? Now, who's ready to bust some heads? I just sat through three hours of Senate hearings. I'm ready to snap someone in half."

As he shouted at his soldiers, he crossed his arms and engaged his device. Rising into the air, he stalked forward predator-like and hovered in the middle of the room.

"I hear you have all been preparing for today's exercise," Robert shouted out. "Who among you is ready to take me on?"

"I am, sir," said a brave looking young man with a beard.

"Well, come up. It's Davis, right?" Robert asked as the soldier stepped forward.

"That's correct, sir. Lieutenant Jordan Davis Navy Seal retired."

"You look a little young to be retired. How is that possible?"

"It had something to do with a lucrative private sector contract a friend urged me to take."

"I heard the boss is a real jerk. I bet you'd like to kick his ass."

"I'll take on anyone I'm instructed to, sir. I follow my orders."

"Well then, Lieutenant Davis, your jerk boss orders you to come at him with all you got. Engage your weapon system and attack."

"Yes, sir," Davis said as he crossed his arms over his chest.

"Come get some, Davis," Robert said while he elevated into the air. Davis charged at him, and Robert blasted him with several orbs while he came forward. The ex-navy seal drew up his arms and created a shield around him, deflecting Robert's orbs to the side. Changing directions, Davis raised both of his fists and struck at Robert's side. Robert blocked the onslaught and backed up.

"You bad boy," he said as he glared at his opponent.

Davis charged again, but Robert made a shield to block the blow. As Davis swung out, Robert pushed to the side at the last moment. Davis spun around, only to see Robert charging at him with a glowing fist. Throwing up his shield, he caught Robert's arm in the nick of time. Robert tried to counter, but the Marine saw his other hand coming. Their arms locked for a moment, but the younger Davis managed to shove Robert back. As Robert gathered his balance, the soldier charged at him through the air. Inches from impact, Robert slipped to the side, avoiding the onslaught.

They battled back and forth for several minutes while the other members of the security force watched in awe. Davis seemed to gain the upper hand as Robert sucked back breath, and stumbled several times. Poised for the kill, the Marine came in ready to take down his boss.

Cowering as the soldier struck out, Robert dropped below at the last moment, causing Davis to miss and lose his balance. He pushed up level with Davis and hit the Marine hard from behind. A red light went off in the room, followed by a loud horn, indicating a confirmed kill.

Lowering himself to the ground, Robert disengaged his device. Davis followed behind him, and Robert wrapped up the soldier in a big hug after he dropped to the floor.

"What an incredible battle, people. Give it up for Lieutenant Davis," Robert shouted as the other mercenaries cheered and clapped.

"What did we just witness people?" Robert asked. "This is something I learned a long time ago as a young executive. You can never be sure of your victory, no matter how certain it is. Always be ready and never underestimate your opponent. The battlefield and the boardroom are not that much different. Both require skill and tactics, and the army with greater discipline is all but guaranteed a victory."

Robert paused for a moment and looked around at his forces."Now, who's next?"

"Ready sir," all the soldiers shouted out.

"Ok, you there," Robert said, pointing at a battle-hardened soldier. "Step forward. What's your name?"

"McDavid. Sergeant Grant McDavid U.S. Army retired, at your service, sir," McDavid said.

"Another retired guy. How old are you?" Robert asked.

"I'm 34, sir," McDavid replied.

"No kidding, I'm 52, and I'm not even close to retiring. What's going on in this world?" Robert scoffed. "Now, people, who wants to take on Sergeant McDavid?"

"I do, sir," said a young woman from the back.

"Excuse me, what do we have here?" Robert said.

"Agent Babcock, sir. Natalie Babcock."

"What outfit were you with?"

"Intelligence, sir."

"And what intelligence is that?"

"Central Intelligence, sir."

"Oh, did you hear that everybody? Central Intelligence. The CIA. We've got brawn versus brains live for you in Building Three of MindHIve headquarters. Get your popcorn ready everybody because this is going to be a show. McDavid, Babcock, engage your devices. Let's get this party started."

The two mercenaries walked out to the center of the room and engaged their devices. Rising into the air, the two combatants squared off against each other as a clamor of cheers and whistles filled the empty office space.

"McDavid, are you ready?" Robert shouted.

"Yes, sir."

"Babcock, are you ready?"

"Absolutely, sir."

"Ok, let's get going. Soldiers engage."

Charging forward, McDavid came at his opponent with a lunging strike, but Babcock deflected the blow with her shield. The big soldier continued to strike away, but he couldn't break the defenses of the much smaller woman. Counter-attacking, Babcock's caught the bigger man off guard, and he stumbled back in shock. Lashing out in anger, he stumbled forward after his blow missed the nimble intelligence officer. As she danced around the enraged soldier, Babcock settled into a groove, counter striking as McDavid swung at her in a wild rage. After dodging another desperate swipe, she stepped to the side and struck the hulking sergeant in the back of the head. The red light lit up the room, and the fight was over. Both soldiers descended to the ground amidst a throng of cheers.

"That was beyond impressive. Babcock, you are a fearless warrior. McDavid, well-fought," Robert shouted. "All right, who's next?"

18

The afternoon light glittered across the pond. SoHee crouched beside the water and peered into the murky depths, hoping to catch a glimpse of anything hiding in the water. Behind her loomed the headquarters of DH Incorporated. From early on, she made it a daily habit to stop at this pond on her way to the laboratory after school. As an elementary school student, she wore rain boots every day, no matter what, in case she saw some water that needed exploring. After kids started to tease her, she would pack her boots into a plastic bag and carry them in her backpack. Even as a high school student, she kept her boots with her. People would often stare at the girl wading in the water as they walked along the bridge above the pond.

That afternoon, SoHee didn't put on her boots. She only stared into the water. If she went home, her mother would make her prepare for her trip or study English, which showed how much her mother knew. SoHee had a knack for languages she picked up English early She read every English Science book she could get her hands on and she always posted and commented on MindHIve in English, not to mention the hundreds of video testimonials and mini-documentaries showcasing, all of which she produced and edited herself.

On the other hand, if she went to the lab, a throng of reporter waited to pounce on her when she arrived. "Anything biting down there?" a voice said from above. SoHee looked up and saw her father standing on the bridge, smiling.

"What are you doing here, Dad?" Sohee said, and she smiled for the first time in a long time. Her father walked off the bridge and down to the set of concrete stairs that led to the pond. His hair had grayed as he aged, and a soft pot belly hung over his belt.

"l knew I'd find you here. You were always drawn to the water, right from the start."

"Who let you out of your office?" SoHee said as her father approached.

"I can come and go as I please. I'm the boss, right?"

"You are a slave, and you know it."

She loved her father. Her father held her hand the first time she waded into a pond. If her mother had been there, there was no way she would have let SoHee play in the mud, but her father encouraged her to go dig around and get dirty.

He caught tadpoles for her and turned over rocks with her. SoHee remembered squealing with delight as the insects under the rocks scurried away.

Every night when she was little, she tried to wait up for him to come home, so she could show him the things she had found that day, but she always fell asleep before he came back.

"Don't be like me," he said to her one day. "All I do is work for someone else and make other people rich. Always follow your heart and do what you know is right. Be your own person."

Her father was the only person whom she could confide in. She felt awkward talking about her feelings with her mother or anybody else she knew, but her father had a way of understanding how she felt, and it was easy to open up to him.

"It looks like big things are on the horizon for you, my daughter," he said as he gave her a hug by the pond. She felt the tears welling up in her eyes again at the mention of the future.

"I don't want to go, Dad," SoHee said as she fought back her tears.

"Don't be scared, SoHee. I always knew you could change the world, and it looks like you are going to now. You can't hide out in your laboratory if you want things to happen. You've got to get out there."

"I am scared, though. What happens if it doesn't work? What happens if I fail? So many people are watching. There is so much pressure."

"That's because you are doing great things. Did you think it would be easy to change the world? It's scary and difficult because you are creating a new path. If it were easy, everybody would be doing it. There has always been something special about you. You never were like the other kids, and that's what is amazing about you. You're following your heart, and it has led you to new and incredible discoveries. Now it looks like the world is starting to pay attention."

"But I haven't really done anything all that special. I used other people's ideas and changed some things. It's not magic or anything."

"Isn't that what they say about science? Something about standing on the shoulders of giants to reach the stars?"

"Yeah, I've heard that one before."

"Well, there's nothing I can teach you then, is there? What could I teach the smartest girl in the world? I'm proud of you, my daughter. It's funny how life works, isn't it? It never really turns out how you think it would. Do you think I thought I would be a fat old man locked in an office tower? But I get to be your father, and that's the greatest thing in the world to me. Come on, let's go get some dukboki in the park. It was always your favorite. The mosquitos in this ditch are going to eat you alive."

She parted ways with her father after they snuck in through a side entrance of DH headquarters to avoid the reporters.

"Thanks for making me feel better, Dad," she said as he made his way to the elevator.

"Anything for my daughter, you know that," he said as he got on the elevator and waved goodbye.

She turned and nodded to the security guard standing near the doorway of the lab. The security system scanned her ID, and the door opened after verifying her identity.

The entrance to the bio lab and at the end of the hall, and SoHee arrived to find some researchers gathered around her bacteria colony.

"SoHee, come quick. You've got to see this," one scientist said as he beckoned her over.

"Look, it's growing at an incredible rate," another researcher said. The bacteria colony that ate the computer chip earlier grew at an astonishing rate over the night. The green mass of bacteria had been tiny when she left the night before, no bigger than a bottle cap, but now it spilled out of the dish it occupied and was spreading across the base of the aquarium. Still quite small, but its growth rate exceeded anything SoHee expected.

"This is amazing," SoHee said. "I wonder what caused this spike in growth. Do you think the chip accelerated its reproductive capacities?"

"Perhaps, but we'll need to run more tests to be sure," one of the researchers said.

"Of course, but first I'm going to post about this," SoHee said. "This is fantastic. Now I'll be able to bring a sample when I go to the

MindHIve convention."

"Congratulations, by the way," said the one researcher.

"Yes, congratulations, you earned it," added another.

"Thank you. I owe all of my success to the people here. It's time our hard work got the recognition it deserves. I'm going to America, and I'm going to show everybody we have made something that will make a difference," she said as she pulled out her phone and snapped a picture.

19

Kingsford transformed at a rapid rate during the weeks leading up to the tech convention. MindHIve brought the full force of its corporate powers to town, and what they did was nothing short of miraculous. Kingsford lacked the proper facilities to host an event of that magnitude, but MindHIve just happened to hold a patent on bio-dome structures designed to colonize Mars. They brought this very same technology to Kingsford and erected several large domes at the fairground. Arranged in a wide circle, the domes connected to each other through a series of tunnels. In the center of the ring sat the largest of the domes. It towered into the air, a white bulbous mass looming over the dusty fairgrounds at the edge of town.

Along with the massive bio-dome, convention participants and a whole army of support staff flooded the city in the weeks leading up to the convention. Kingsford had never looked so busy. The restaurants were jammed, and every hotel was booked solid. Mythic Sports sold all their summer camping gear in a week, as people who were unable to get a room decided they could rough it in one of Kingsford's many campgrounds.

An ecstatic mood hovered over Kingsford high. The excitement surrounding the convention consumed every student at the school. There were rumors of celebrity guests in attendance, and everyone hoped they would have a chance to get their hands on the inReal tech the world was buzzing about.

Mitch Mythic was not excited. Along with all the media attention he had been receiving both online and in real life, the secret he carried in his pocket was proving to be a heavy burden to bear.

Throughout the chaos, he managed to keep up a cheerful demeanor in spite of the stress and anxiety eating away at him from the inside. He had gone from being a loathsome creature at Kingsford High to being touted once again as a hero in a matter of minutes. Forgiving him for what had taken place prior to the MindHIve announcements, his teammates had welcomed him back into the fold, all except for Sage.

His hostility towards Mitch amplified after Mitch received the invitation to the convention, and his jealousy was evident in everything he did. After the fight, Sage and Candace McAllister started dating. The two of them, drawn together in a mutual dislike of Mitch Mythic. As he walked by the new couple in the hallway at school, they both shot matching dirty looks in his direction.

Sage and Candace were the least of his worries. His current situation had, so far, proven inescapable, with every available option offering an equal amount of risk. If he went to the police, he would automatically be detained for questioning, but if he did nothing, he was certain something horrible would happen.

After his in-school suspension finished, he was free to come and go as he pleased during his free time, but he no longer felt comfortable around everyone. There was too much attention and too much pressure. Returning to the computer lab during lunch break a few days after the suspension was over, he found Drak sitting near the front with his feet up on a desk eating a bowl of instant noodles sold from one of the vending machines around the school.

"This is good. What do you call it?" Drak asked as Mitch walked in.

"It's ramen. You don't have those where you come from?" Mitch replied.

"Nothing like this," Drak said while slurping up some noodles before tossing the cup into the trash. "Come. I'll show you something special."

"If you've taken a hostage, I'm going to be really upset."

"I'll only take a hostage if the need arises," Drak said as they ascended into the storage room that led to the cavern beneath the school.

"Where do you live, anyway?" Mitch asked as they walked past stacks of old textbooks.

"Here and there. I don't need one place," Drak said as he edged along a narrow shelf.

"Are you living down in that cave?"

"Ha, maybe. You don't worry about me, Mitch Mythic. Things are happening fast now," Drak said before he stepped over the drain and hoisted it up.

"What's the hurry?" Mitch said after he dropped into the tunnel.

"There are many things I need to show you. You need to know how to spread the tech before it is too late. The time will come when more are needed. We must be ready now," Drak said while he swung open the door to the cavern. Engaging his device on the move, he activated the light beam he used earlier, flooding the tunnel with light.

"Hand me the phone, and I'll show you what I mean," Drak said as he came to a halt in the middle of the cavern.

"So now I'm going to be the one going around spreading this stuff. I'm going to wind up in prison. I just know it," Mitch said, catching his breath.

"You are going to be in more than prison. The whole planet will belong to the Masters soon if you do nothing. They are coming, like it or not," Drak said while taking out another phone from his pocket.

"Where do you get all these phones from?" Mitch asked in wonder.

"I Have my ways," Drak said again. "Take your phone out and place on the floor."

"Uh, fine," Mitch said, placing his phone on the ground.

"Now, do as I say, Mitch Mythic. It is not hard," Drak said. "Put your hands over the device like this,"

Extending his hands straight out in front of him, Drak made two fists and raised his arms. While he copied Drak, his face lit up as the sphere appeared in front of him.

"Now reach into the sphere like this," Drak said while he pushed his hand out horizontally, palm down. Mitch followed the motion and inserted his hand into the sphere.

"Turn it over palm up and make a fist like this." Drak said before a panel appeared in the globe.

"It looks so familiar," Mitch said in amazement. "Like in a video game."

"What you see is what you want to see. The device uses your energy and your eyes see what they know. The technology molds itself to you, and you put out what you put in." Drak said, handing Mitch the other phone. "Now place the phone inside," he said.

Taking the phone, he placed it in the sphere. Just as before, the phone hovered in the opaque ball of light and rotated slowly while it hung in the air. A panel appeared above the phone, and several functions flashed within rectangular boxes.

"There, at the end. Press that button. This is the transfer button," Drak said. At the far right end of the panel, Mitch found a button with two arrows. The button responded to his touch, and he leaped back in shock as the function activated. Pulsing with light, the same strange tentacles appeared within the sphere and wrapped themselves around the phone before a flash lit up the cavern. After the burst subsided, the phone sat stationary at the center of the sphere.

"It's finished now. Easy, yes?" Drak asked Mitch.

"It seems simple enough. But who am I supposed to give this to? I'm not going to go around handing this stuff out to kids. I'll get arrested for sure."

"When the time is right, you will know what to do."

"This is pretty impressive, but how am I supposed to know you're not the bad guy here? You could be some lone wolf schizo that wants to blow up the world."

"Ha, good question. You always have many questions. That is good. If I am a liar, then this is a pretty good lie. A Lot of work to make a lie like this," Drak said as he raised himself off the ground "I'll show you how to use the weapon system now. This very dangerous, but you must know."

"I can't believe I'm going along with this," Mitch said while he crossed his arms over his chest.

"You need to stop thinking like that, Mitch. If you continue this way, you are going to be caught unaware and then it will be too late to fight back," Drak said as he hovered nearby.

"Well, give me a break. It's not every day somebody comes along and drops a bomb on me like this," Mitch said, lifting off the ground. "Well, it is hard to deny that this stuff is beyond impressive."

"You are only scratching the surface," Drak said. "Watch what I do and copy."

Making two fists, Drak's his hands were enveloped in a blue glow.

"Do as I do, Mitch," Drak demanded.

"Sorry, I'm just a little blown away is all," Mitch said as he raised his arms.

"You must think it, and it will happen," Drak said while looking at Mitch. "Imagine your hands are weapons and believe it is so."

Mitch looked at his hands, and then he thought of Death World. His character had just unlocked the snake armor and with the armor came the snake sword. Imagining the sword in his mind, a long blue blade extended from his hand. He recoiled in shock and the blade disappeared as quickly as it appeared.

"You must stay focused. If you lose your concentration, you will lose control of the tech. It is you in control of the device. Without the user, the tech is nothing. Use your power to control the device," Drak said as he watched Mitch. "Try to imagine fire shooting out of your fists."

"All right, focus. I got it," Mitch said, turning his thoughts to DeathWorld again. His character could also cast spells from his hand, and he imagined himself shooting out the energy as he had in the video game. A pulse of light shot out from his hand, and it knocked over several stones nearby.

"Defenses are the same. Imagine a shield, and it will appear," Drak said as he walked in front of Mitch and placed his forearm in front of him. "Fire at me. It's no problem,"

"Are you sure?" Mitch said.

"Yes, do it. It's fine. The worst thing that will happen is you kill me, right?" Drak said before a grin flashed across his face.

"Man, don't talk like that. I don't want to be a murderer, too," Mitch said. Taking a big breath, he imagined himself casting the spell again, and a ball of light shot out of his hands and connected with Drak's shield.

"Again," Drak said with a smile.

"I think I can arrange something," Mitch said as he felt a surge of energy run up his spine. Pulses moved down his arm, and a burst of orbs shot forth from his hand. Slamming into Drak's shield, impact pushed him backward, and he stumbled to his knees.

"Ok, maybe you are getting the hang of this. Now, it's your turn," Drak said, and he grinned again. "Ready your shield."

"I'm not sure if I'm ready for this," Mitch gulped and held his arm up to protect himself. He thought of his DeathWorld character battling against the massive foes he faced in the game. The character always carried a shield to defend itself against any attack. Mitch imagined himself doing the same, and a bright blue shield appeared around his arm. As Drak fired upon him, he cowered behind his shield and closed his eyes. Feeling the thud of the blast, he opened his eyes to discover he was still in one piece.

"You are smiling again, Mitch," Drak said while he aimed at Mitch. Raising his shield, he deflected every shot with ease before laughing out loud.

"The system is very strong, but you will still take damage," Drak said, bring up his control panel. "This is the status panel. You can see the shield percentage, and it shows much energy is left. The device will recharge using your energy field, but it will need. If you take too much damage, or use too much energy the device will fail. You must be careful not to take too many hits, go too fast, or too far."

"What happens if your device fails?" Mitch asked.

"Well, you fall out of the sky and crack your head on a rock, or your opponent takes your head off," Drak said with a grin. "The device has safety features. It stores a small amount of energy if shields fail or if energy is lost. If either happens, the backup shield will engage, but all system functions will be lost until the device has enough energy restored. But enough of this boring talk. Let's have some fun."

Stepping back, Drak's manifested a blade in his hand. "You did it once before. Try to do it again."

"Make a sword?" Is that how you want to play?" Mitch said, thinking of his character again. A long blade extended out from his hand, and he pointed it at Drak.

"I want to see what you've got, Mitch Mythic," Drak snarled as an orb shot out of his fist.

"I'm just getting going," Mitch said, blocking the attack with his shield.

"You think you can defeat me?" Drak grinned.

"Well, I can definitely try," Mitch said while raising his sword.

"You're going to have to do more than try," Drak said before he struck at Mitch with his sword.

"Is that all you've got," Mitch said as he deflected the illuminated blade and swung out with his sword. Connecting with Drak's shield, the force of the blow staggered him, but he caught his balance and looked at Mitch in surprise.

"Not bad, Mitch," he said as he moved forward with his shield up. "Let's turn up the heat a little, shall we?"

Mitch raised his shield again as Drak struck out before he struck Drak in the shoulder.

"Ha, is that how you want to play?" Drak said.

"Bring it," Mitch said through gritted teeth.

20

MindHIve's massive transport helicopter made a slow pass over the fairground. Looking out the window, Robert observed the circle of domes spread out below him. Maybe someday they would be used to settle Mars, but in the time being, Kingsford would have to do.

As the helicopter descended toward the landing zone, Robert stood and the inspected his strike force. They were all elite soldiers on their own, but when equipped with weaponized inReal tech, they were living gods. Outfitted with a protective jumpsuit and helmets emblazoned with the MindHIve logo, the soldiers sat at the ready as the helicopter landed. The suits were made from a stretchable metallic alloy MindHIve developed for space travel. Although it wasn't Mars, the suits were fully appropriate for the strike team to make their glorious introduction to the world.

A large crowd of reporters and onlookers stood a few hundred feet away awaiting the arrival, and Robert planned on making a grand entrance.

"Alpha team, prepare to disembark. Beta team get ready cause you are going next," he commanded. All the members of Alpha team stood and moved to the rear doors of the helicopter.

"Engage your tech and prepare to exit as planned," Natalie Babcock shouted. Robert made her a squad leader after her exceptional performance during hand to hand combat.

"Open the doors," Robert ordered the pilot. The pilot pressed a button on the dash of the helicopter, and the large bay doors swung open.

"Alpha team go, go, go," Babcock shouted as each member of alpha raised themselves off of the deck and shot out of the helicopter.

"Beta team get in position," Lieutenant Davis ordered. Robert appointed Davis as the other squad leader after the retired navy seal proved himself to be a soldier of outstanding caliber.

"let's move," Davis shouted, and Beta team rocketed out of the rear doors and into the bright morning light.

Robert crossed his arms over his chest and engaged his device. Exiting the helicopter, he made one giant swoop around the landing zone before coming to a resting position between the two teams of soldiers hovering in mid-air about 30 feet from the crowd of reporters.

Robert stepped down to the ground and disengaged his tech. Removing his helmet, and the crowd gasped as they realized who he was.

"Ladies and Gentlemen, I know you must have a thousand questions. I would love to answer them all right now, but you are going to have to wait until the convention starts. Behind you is the MindHIve inReal security team. Along with all the other surprises we have in store for the world, the inReal tech can also provide protection and mobility. This team of elite security advisors will be on hand at all times to ensure the safety of every convention participant and the town of Kingsford as well. We're not expecting any trouble, but this is an excellent opportunity for the inReal tech to be used in a real-world situation. I told you before inReal will change the world, and as you can see, it already has. Thank you very much for coming out and get ready to be amazed over the next few days," Robert said while he engaged his device again and raised himself above the crowd. Saluting everyone, he moved back to join the strike force.

At Robert's command, the team moved forward above the crowd and circled over the complex. Robert instructed his team to come down next to the large center dome between the interlinking tunnels where a group of MindHIve employees stood waiting for their arrival.

The strike force descended into the compound while the cameras continued to roll. Robert spotted Gerald Tobero's bald head glistening in the sunlight as he dropped to the ground. Allan stood beside him, holding his clipboard. Behind them, several MindHIve executives and the inReal engineering team looked on. As Robert stepped back down to earth and disengaged his device, his security advisor stepped forward to greet him.

"Welcome to Kingsford, sir. I hope you enjoyed making the grand entrance you planned for," Gerald said while he shook Robert's hand.

"Of course I enjoyed it, Gerald. Why do you always have to be such a killjoy? It was a spectacle for the world, and I'm certain it was jaw-dropping in every way," Robert said as he took off his helmet. "Bring me up to speed on our security situation, but keep it brief. I've got a lot of fish to fry today."

"No unusual activity to report. We should be able to contain and apprehend the culprit on your order," Gerald said while he and Robert strode toward an entrance leading to the central dome.

"That's good to hear. I'd like to have our little problem contained before the convention kicks off, but I also don't want to rush anything. When do you think we should make our move?"

"I think it would be best to wait for our subject to show himself before we spring the trap. He, I'm assuming it's a man, will most likely attempt some type of reconnaissance. To do so, they will have to engage their device in some way. Even if they don't, our satellites should be able to pick up any traces of energy should they enter the perimeter surrounding the trap. When we detect anything, we will deploy the strike force to obtain the subject, on your order, of course."

Passing through a large doorway, they entered into the cavernous main dome of the complex while a horde of workers prepared for the opening ceremony.

"Once again, that is why I pay you so well. How did your wife like the beach house, by the way?" Robert said, removing his gloves.

"She was delighted, sir. She said I should keep doing my best to make you happy," Gerald said.

"She sounds like a good woman, Gerald. I look forward to meeting her," Robert replied. "How is the drilling going? Were we able to get deep enough to access the energy field?"

"Yes, sir. While we still have a little way to go, we should be deep enough within the allotted time frame. The generator has been installed, and it is currently powering up. We will still need to drill deeper in order to draw enough power for the procedure, but the readings indicate there is more than enough energy present."

"Gerald, I don't know if I could do any of this without you. You truly are worth every penny. Keep me posted of any developments, even if they seem insignificant. Now, if you'll forgive me, I have other matters that require my attention."

"Of course, Sir," Gerald said as Robert stepped up onto the massive stage in the center of the dome. Rowed seating surrounded the stage on every side.

"Allan, has my speech been prepared?" Robert asked, striding across the stage. "I hope those spineless writers made the changes I requested."

"I believe everything has been updated. It should be ready for the opening ceremony tomorrow," Allan said.

"It better be ready, or I'll have the entire writing department executed. I cannot stress the importance of tomorrow's opening ceremony," Robert said as he stepped off the stage. "Have my quarters been prepared? I need to change out of this space suit. I want to do a full inspection of the facilities myself."

"Yes, sir. Everything has been prepared as you requested," Allan said while he followed after Robert just slightly behind and a little to his right. "There have been a lot of technical difficulties in setting everything up. We still don't have enough bedding for the participants, and there are some problems with the lavatories. Apparently, the toilets were designed with Martian gravity in mind, and we've had a few problems with waste disposal."

"Are you telling me the most important tech convention in MindHIve's history is about to be smeared with human feces?" Robert said, stalking down the long white tunnel linking the main dome to the outer ring.

"We managed to get an engineer from NASA flown in, and they are working on the problem. It looks like it should be fine before things get underway."

"Aside from the poop, what other pains in the butt do I have to contend with?" Robert snapped as they entered a dome buzzing with activity. Workers assembled equipment while others answered phones and typed into computers. The wall was lined with sleeping coffins for MindHIve's employees. Each arched window emitted a soft blue glow, creating a hive like environment.

"Participant intake has been a bit of a problem. We're still setting up the security protocols, and there appears to be a problem with the local infrastructure. Although our facilities will accommodate the participants and the support staff, the town just wasn't meant to handle this much outside traffic," Allan said while stepping around a pair of technicians installing computer equipment.

"So, not my problem then. I'm sure the good folks of Kingsford will thank us for all the business we're bringing in. If they don't like money, then these aren't the kind of people I want to deal with. Where are my rooms already? I hope no one is expecting me to sleep in one of these coffins."

"Right this way, sir," Allan said, leading him past a row of workstations. "We've prepared the Captain's Cabins for your arrival."

"Well, that sounds more like it," Robert said while Allan guided him through a set of double doors guarded by two towering security officers. The captain's quarters were spacious yet spartan. There was a desk with a phone, and several hutches were built into the walls.

"You'll find all the necessary amenities within this space, sir. In the next room there is a bed built into the wall, and everything can be accessed via MindHIve's untouch technology."

"I'll have it rigged with inReal in no time. Now Allan, if you don't mind I'd like to get out of this sweatbox without you gawking at me," Robert said before he turned away.

"Of course, sir, I'll be outside when you need me."

After a few minutes, Robert emerged from his quarters in a tailored suit.

"That was fast, sir," Allan said as he jumped up and stuffed his phone into his pocket.

"I hope I'm not interrupting your gaming schedule, Allan. What level is your DeathWorld character at now?" Roberts said with a knowing grin.

"I'm only at 57, but I started a new character. I'm trying a mage build this time," Allan responded.

"I don't give a damn what level you are. I've got an inspection to do. I'm heading down to engineering. It's off-limits to unauthorized personnel, so I won't be needing you. And Allan, nobody ever respects a mage build. Go for ranger or maybe orc. That might suit you better. Tell Gerald I'm on the way and clear my schedule for the afternoon. I've got work to do."

A doorway stood to the left of the main entrance of the MindHIve employee dome. Two security guards leaned against the wall next to the door, but they jumped to attention as Robert approached.

"At ease, boys. I hope you guys are ready for practice tonight because I've got a few surprises scheduled," Robert said before the door slid open.

"Sounds good, sir," one officer said while he stepped aside for Robert to pass.

"Looking forward to it," the other guard said.

"Don't stiffen up guarding this door. Stay loose, and I'll be seeing you soon," Robert said as the door slid shut behind him. Walking down a short hall, he came to a closed door and scanned his pass on the security panel. The doors opened to reveal a steel elevator cage. He stepped in and pressed a button on a control panel to the right of the door, and the cage descended into the depths. Through the steel cage, he spotted solid rock walls and the marks where the drill bored through the granite. After a few moments, the elevator stopped, and the steel cage opened.

"Welcome to the basement, sir. Did you have a pleasant trip?" Gerald said after Robert stepped off of the elevator.

"Very funny. It's freezing down here," Robert said while he and his security adviser made their way down a dimly lit tunnel.

A light up ahead signaled they were approaching some type of opening, and Robert had to cover his eyes as they neared.

"I suggest you put these on," Gerald said, handing Robert a pair of dark industrial goggles before they reached the opening. "It's a little bright up ahead."

"I can see that," Robert said, slipping on the goggles.

The tunnel led to an observation deck that stood on the edge of a vast cavern. In the center of the cavern, a thick pillar of blue and white light flowed up into the rock above.

"The engineering department followed the specs provided with incredible attention to detail. We were able to bore through the surface crust with relative ease, using the technology developed by MindHIve's space exploration department, and the energy converter apparatus was inserted with only a few hiccups. Power is flowing directly to the main dome, and the engineering department is running tests on the generator as we speak to detect any stability issues," Gerald said as he stood beside Robert.

"Excellent work, Gerald. We'll be putting that generator to the test in the next few days, the first being the opening ceremony tomorrow," Robert said while he watched several engineers use their inReal devices to maneuver some large scaffolding into place near the column of light. "Then we'll see what this stuff can really do."

21

SoHee was absolutely exhausted. The jet lag, coupled with the grueling travel, had left her in a hopeless state. On top of all that, her mother, who had accompanied her for the journey, was driving her up the wall. She couldn't speak English, so SoHee had to communicate everything for her. Complaining about everything from the bathrooms to the smell of the air, she was also horribly picky about any of the food they encountered. Why did she even come, SoHee thought to herself, but she knew she couldn't keep her mother away from something as important as the MindHIve convention.

They needed to make several connections to get to Longdale, the closest city to Kingsford with an airport. After arriving, they still needed to take a 2-hour bus ride to get to the event. As tired as she felt, she stared out of the window in awe as the bus wound its way past towering mountain peaks lit up by the afternoon sun. The bus rounded a bend and SoHee saw a valley spread out before her. At the base of the valley, a river wound through stands of green trees dotted by buildings and farmland.

A large sign on the Highway said: "Welcome to Kingsford, the Home of the Crushers." She wondered who these Crushers were and what they crushed.

Kingsford was fully buzzing with excitement and activity the day before the convention. Stepping off the bus, SoHee looked around in disbelief. There were crowds of people on the sidewalks, and cars jammed the streets. She felt like she was back in Seoul at rush hour, if not for all the western faces she saw.

Every single hotel and motel had their no vacancy signs lit up. Luckily, SoHee's mother booked her room weeks in advance through her agent.

The Evergreen Motel was only a short distance from the fairground, but it wasn't the five-star accommodation her mother expected. The motel had, no doubt, seen better days. Cracked stucco and peeling paint greeted them as they walked into the parking lot, and the outdoor pool looked like it hadn't been filled in years. The office was located on the first floor of the two-story building. SoHee could barely keep her eyes open while they walked up to the reception desk. Laying her head down on the counter, she rang the bell. From a back room, a heavyset middle-aged woman appeared holding a fly swatter.

"We're all booked up. No rooms available," the lady said as she sat herself down in a chair at the desk.

"We have a reservation. Here is the booking information," SoHee said, handing over the paper with her mother's information.

"Yes, here you are. Song Doo-Ahk, that's a heck of a name. Where are you two from?" The receptionist asked.

"We're from Korea," SoHee replied.

"Well, Konichiwa to you then," the lady said with a smile.

"Actually, that is Japanese. In Korea we say 'Annyeonghaseyo'," SoHee said.

"Anyong-howyadoing and welcome to Kingsford. Follow me. I'll show you to your room. There's only one bed. How are you two going to fit in there?"

"Only my mother will be staying here. I'll be attending the convention, and they have provided lodgings," SoHee said while trying to keep it together.

"Oh, I see. You must be pretty smart, getting invited to this big hullabaloo. You speak English pretty good too," The lady said as they walked along a concrete sidewalk past several numbered doors.

"This is the room here," the lady said. "And here is the key. If you need anything else, just holler at me. I'll be in the office and Anyongeeyo to you both again."

The room wasn't as run down as the outside of the hotel. A well-made bed sat beneath a framed painting of a mountainous landscape, and shag carpet lined the floor. Her mother placed her bags on the ground and sat on the bed. The digital clock on the nightstand said 7:07 pm. According to the itinerary, SoHee had to be checked in by 8, or she would have to go through intake tomorrow morning. She needed to hurry if she wanted to make it on time, and she did not want to spend another night with her mother.

"Mom, I've got to get going if I want to make it on time. Text me if you need anything," she said.

"Just go. I'm going to sleep. This whole ordeal has been so exhausting," She said as she laid her head on the bed. "This room smells like dog piss."

"Ok Mom, I'm going. Just text me, ok?" SoHee said while she gathered her bags and closed the door.

Stepped outside into the evening air, she let out a deep exhale. Although she felt tired beyond belief, it was a relief to be rid of her mother. The June weather in Kingsford was sunny and arid, a refreshing change from the stifling humidity of Seoul.

According to the map on her phone, the motel stood in close proximity to the fairgrounds. As she looked up, she spotted several white domes rising above the treetops not too far away. Taking a deep breath of the fresh summer air, she walked towards the bulbous white buildings in the distance.

Along with her belongings, she carried the only thing in the world that truly mattered to her. The bacteria sample sat strapped to the top of her suitcase in a special containment unit, bearing a yellow biohazard mark. 'Cleared inspection' was stamped in red across the top. It had been a giant hassle getting the bacteria sample through customs. Fortunately, DH had an army of corporate lawyers capable of handling the massive load of paperwork in Korea to ready the sample and MindHIve took care of American customs. But when they arrived at the international airport in Los Angeles, they were hustled into quarantine, while the customs officials made dozens of phone calls before approving the documents.

As she turned the corner and entered the massive fairgrounds, she was astounded by the size of the gigantic complex. The domes seemed like alien structures from another planet. Before them stood a massive gate emblazoned with the MindHIve logo, looming above a crowd of people clamoring before the entrance.

Television cameras and reporters stood beside vans that boasted network logos unfamiliar to her. There were thousands of people milling about the front gate, some of whom wore blue collared shirts with the MindHIve logo stenciled across the front and back.

"I need to get inside. Where do I go?" she asked a young woman dressed in blue.

"Nobody's getting in there unless you've got a pass," the woman said.

"I have a pass," SoHee said, producing the participant pass she received in the mail.

"Well, then you should come with me," the woman said after she looked over SoHee's pass. "This place is an absolute nuthouse right now. I've never seen anything like it. Let's get you inside, Miss Moon SoHee,"

Following her escort through the crowd of people, SoHee encountered all walks of life outside of the gates. Some held up up signs of protest, and others seemed to be from religious cults. There were prayer circles and drummers everywhere.

Along with the wild cavalcade of people, a heavy security presence stood watch over the festivities, and a wall of armed guards in black uniforms positioned themselves before the gates. Several feet of no-man's-land stood between the guards and the swell of people.

"I've got a participant coming through," the young woman said as she approached one of the guards.

"Let's see your pass," he said to SoHee through a scowl.

As SoHee reached for her credentials, a young man wearing ski goggles and a black bandana over his face ran froward and threw an egg into the face of one of the guards.

"inReal is a Nazi scam," he screamed before several guards rushed out to corral the boy. One guard deployed a taser, and the boy went down, screaming and foaming at the mouth a few feet from Sohee.

"Well, it looks like you're clear. Take these documents to the reception area," the guard said while a medical team came in to take the tasered boy away. "And don't do anything stupid while you're here, or you'll wind up like him,"

Watching the boy go past her on a stretcher, she could see the foam bubbling on his lips.

"Let's go before a riot breaks out," the girl in the blue shirt said. SoHee didn't need to be asked twice. Following the girl through a metal gate and into a long corridor walled with chain-link fences, the screaming and shouting echoed behind her, but she didn't dare to look back.

After SoHee and the young woman cleared a maze of corners, they came to a large open area filled with kiosks. Above each booth was a MindHIve logo. The girl led SoHee to a stall where a young man wearing the same blue shirt greeted her with an appropriate amount of cheer.

"We have a participant here who is ready to be admitted into the facilities. She has the proper paperwork," the young woman said.

"Excellent," the young man replied. "May I see your pass and your ID, please?"

SoHee handed over her passport and her ID to the young man, who looked at her picture and read her name.

"Wow, are you Miss Science? I've been following you for years. It's amazing what you've done," the young man said.

"Thank you," she managed to say, blushing as the boy handed her back her ID and pass.

"Please head through those gates there," the boy said, indicating another set of chain-link gates. "On the other side, you will receive your greeting package and gift basket, and then a MindHIve host will show you to your quarters. Welcome to the MindHIve tech convention, Miss Science. Before you go, can we take a picture?" he asked as he pulled out his phone. Before SoHee could respond, he snapped a photo of the two of them together, and SoHee tried her best to make a happy face.

Whisked through the gate, another young woman wearing a blue shirt handed her a package of papers and a gift basket wrapped in cellophane.

"Follow me," she said as she pressed the button on a large metallic gate. As the doors slid open, they revealed a massive dome bustling with activity. There were colossal company banners displayed above elaborate booths and people hustled about, setting up strange and intricate equipment.

"The participant quarters are in the next dome," the new young woman said as she strode forward. "Stick close, or I'll lose you in this mess."

SoHee did her best to keep up, but she had to dodge all types of people and obstacles moving around her. They reached a metal archway that led to a long white hallway. People were coming and going in both directions, and SoHee had to continue weaving between people. Just like Hongik station at rush hour, she thought to herself as she tried to keep up with her guide.

The next dome was a completely different world from the one she first entered. There were all types of strange looking furniture set on a patchwork of terraced work stations. Mood walls with shifting pictures wove between the terraces. Beyond the strange-looking work stations, stacks of dark blue sleeping capsules reached up to the top of the dome. Each column was equipped with a series of platforms that gave access to the capsules. Elevators and winding staircases connected to each floor while soft blue light emanated from the portal windows of the coffins.

"So you are in W-927," the young woman said. "That's this way towards the back."

Following along behind the woman, she stared up in awe at the stacks of capsules. There were thousands of them. SoHee saw a large glowing "W" above an elevator, and she knew she had finally arrived. She was asked to show her credentials to another young man in a blue shirt who scanned her pass with a transparent device. It flashed green, and SoHee stepped into a simple metallic elevator.

The young woman accompanied her into the tight quarters and pressed "9" on a panel beside them. After the elevator whisked them up to the ninth floor, they both spilled out onto a narrow walkway. Each capsule that lined the catwalk displayed a glowing number, and SoHee scanned the units until they arrived at 927.

"Here we are," the young lady said. "Scan your pass here, and the door should open."

SoHee took out her pass and pressed it onto a translucent pad to the left of the door. There was an audible bing, and the door popped open to reveal a narrow bed and a small storage area.

"This is where I leave you. You'll find all the information you need is in the orientation package you received at reception. There is a lot of information to go over, but I'm sure you must be exhausted. Orientation will begin tomorrow morning, but you'll need to go over your orientation package beforehand. The bathroom and showers are located at the end of the walkway. I'd love to show you more, but I've really got to get going. I just got an alert saying there is a malfunction at the front gate," the young woman said as she jogged to the exit at the end of the walkway.

"Thanks," SoHee half murmured before her guide jumped on the elevator. SoHee turned and looked at her capsule. She had seen worse. Slipping inside, she shut the door behind her. There was a panel that showed different light settings, and she pressed the button indicating darkness. Dropping onto the bed, she fell asleep in her clothes.

22

Mitch tossed and turned, but try as he might, he couldn't get to sleep. The pressure had mounted in the days and weeks leading up to the convention. On the eve of the big event, a ball of anxiety churned in his guts.

Tossing his blanket off of his body, he rolled onto his back. The air in his room was stiflingly hot, so he got out of bed and opened his window. He crawled back in bed, and he closed his eyes.

Feeling the cool night air seeping into his room, he stared up at the ceiling while an endless stream of anxious thoughts ran amok in his brain.

Of all the things bothering him, he was most concerned about Drak. The elusive character hadn't been seen in a few days, and Mitch was reluctant to admit that he might actually miss him. He still had no idea what Drak planned to do, or how he planned to do it.

All of this talk about wormholes and Masters seemed so farfetched at first, but now he couldn't tell fact from fiction. As he lay there trying to make sense of it all, he heard a familiar tapping at his window. Rolling over, he looked up to see Drak's outline in the darkness.

"Come quickly, Mitch. I Must tell you something. There's not much time," Drak whispered.

"Dude, you've got to stop sneaking around like this. Couldn't you just send a text or something? Oh yeah, they're watching everything you do, right?"

"You know I'm serious, Mitch. This is a dangerous time."

"Yeah, yeah, I know, dangerous times. Masters are coming, blah blah blah. I'm coming. Just let me put my pants on."

"Find me by the stream. I'll wait there."

"Ok, just give me a sec."

Slipping on a hoodie, he tucked his phone into his pocket and clambered out of his bedroom window. After checking to see if it was clear, he scampered across the road and onto the path. Drak crouched by the creek, and he rose to his feet as Mitch approaching.

"Let me see your phone," Drak said, extending his hand.

"What are you going to arm it with nukes now?"

"Not quite, but close," Drak said while locking eyes with Mitch. "When I am gone, this will be the last free device in the world. It must not fall into the wrong hands. I will show you how to destroy it if somehow you get caught."

"What do you mean caught? What are you going to do now? Is this where your end game starts, and you blow everything up?"

"I may not come back. I may fail. You must be ready to act. If they find you, they cannot find the device. You are in more danger than you think."

"Oh, you don't have to convince me now. I already know I'm through the looking glass. But who, exactly, is going to come for me? And where are you going?"

"You saw on TV today. Those men flying around with the MindHIve CEO. They are not here for security. They have another reason. If they find you, it will be very bad," Drak said after Mitch handed over his phone.

"Well, what do I do if they start closing in?"

"We cannot activate the device now, or they will see us, but I can tell you how it is done easily. The device may be destroyed using the self-destruct function. It is in the panel beside the transfer button. If this button is pressed, the device will destroyed itself after a few minutes. It will make a big explosion, similar to the portal energy but not the same," Drak said as he held Mitch's phone. "If I fail, and I might fail, then you are the last chance. It's not too late, but this is a bad time for this place. I know you make jokes and this is hard to believe, but believe it or suffer the fate of my people. You are not slaves yet. You must fight back now or lose everything."

They stood in silence for a moment. A soft breeze blew through the night air, and the forest was filled with the sound of the babbling creek and nocturnal insects.

"What will you do now?" Mitch asked.

"I must find access. It's risky, but I don't have a choice. Time is running out," Drak said.

"You don't have to go," Mitch said.

"That's true, I could stay and do nothing, stay safe. But we are not safe now. None of us are safe. My people will stay slaves, and your people will become slaves. I cannot live like that. I am never a slave. I will fight forever until my people are free," Drak said while he looked up at the night sky.

"Will you go tonight?"

"I'll leave you now. Don't follow. It's too dangerous. If I succeed, it will be like I was never here. If I fail, then you will be the last hope. The people here don't know what is coming, but you have the power to change it all, Mitch," Drak said as he reached out and touched Mitch on the shoulder. "I know you don't believe me. You still think I'm crazy. I know this is all craziness. Before the Masters came to my home, I was just like you. A simple life, no problem. Then everything changed. Now I am here doing this. I know it's crazy, but I must fight on."

"Well, thanks for everything, Drak. This is just my luck."

"Luck has nothing to do with it. You are in control of your destiny. My path lies on a different course. If the Masters can be stopped, I must try. After I go, you are the only one left."

"And you'll just leave me here to take all the blame. If you go, it's going to be me cleaning up the mess. They'll probably pin the whole thing on me."

"Don't worry. They won't blame you. I have a plan."

"Yeah, you always have a plan. Just run off and do your mysterious plan. You know what? Go. It's better if you go. Even after all the stunts you pulled and madness that you dragged me into, I have to admit I thought we were friends. How can you just leave a friend like this?"

"I am going now to protect you, don't you see? I know you're angry, but you will see that this is the right thing to do. If this is last time we meet, I am happy to be friends with you," Drak said as he reached out and hugged Mitch.

"Don't hug me. If you're going to go, just go. Get out of here," Mitch said, pushing Drak away.

"You have the power now, Mitch. Just believe in yourself. The world needs you. Now, I must go."

"Thanks for everything. I look forward to seeing you on the news," Mitch shouted after him.

Drak didn't look back while he made his way up the trail and into the darkness. Turning away in the opposite direction, Mitch's head reeled as he walked back to his house. Reaching the end of the path, he stopped dead in his tracks before he turned in the opposite direction. He had to know what Drak was up to.

Certain Drak would be headed to the MindHIve complex, Mitch hustled up the trail, hoping to catch him before he reached the site. The Kingsford Hockey-plex was situated on the same grounds, and it wasn't too far away from his house. He also knew a few short cuts Drak probably didn't know about. Picking his pace up to a jog, he felt his phone bounce in his pocket as he ran.

The grounds were skirted by a dense forest sloping up the mountains. Through the trees, a path snaked up the hill to a lookout that offered a good view of the grounds. Fighting through fatigue, Mitch pushed up the trail in the hopes of spotting Drak before he tried to enter the complex.

The wooden deck of the lookout had been built years ago. Rotten in a few places, it was still structurally sound. At this time of night, the lookout was vacant, but with such a heavy security presence nearby, he stayed underneath the deck in order to avoid detection. Before him stood the massive domes towering into the night sky. Glowing softly under the bright moonlight, the whole place seemed to emit an otherworldly aura.

Several columns of container trucks sat parked in a fenced off enclosure at the back of the complex, which connected to a much more intricate barricade of corrugated metal that made up the perimeter of the complex. Mitch spotted several pairs of security guards holding posts at regular intervals along the wall while other guards walked the fence line.

Mitch had no idea how Drak could get past those security guards undetected, let alone get over that fence unless he were to use his device. MindHIve had probably set up all kinds of security measures within the complex and satellites were, no doubt, monitoring all activity from above. Even if Drak was suicidal, the chances of successfully pulling off his plan seemed beyond unlikely.

He couldn't understand why Drak was doing what he was doing. Sneaking into the complex was stupid and reckless. The guy had been nothing but careful up until then. Why was he charging in there like that when there was no way he could pull it off, Mitch thought to himself as he kept a careful watch for his friend.

After a few tense moments, Mitch caught a glimpse of a figure crouched in the tree line. If he could only get down to him, he could tell him to stop. They could go back and find another way.

Attempting to rise, he watched Drak engage his device as he crept forward. Stalking beside a set of cars in the parking lot, a soft blue glow covered his body.

As he watched from the hilltop, Mitch knew it was too late to do anything. Drak repeatedly warned him not to come. If Mitch were to be captured by MindHIve security, he would have more than his reputation to worry about. Not knowing what to do, he stood frozen with fear while he watched Drak edge closer to the complex.

Ducking under a truck, Drak seemed to be scanning for any patrols. In a blur of light, he launched into the air and disappeared over the fence. For several moments Mitch remained still. He felt his heart beating in his chest as the tall grass beneath the rotten deck rustled in the night breeze.

23

Coming down behind a storage unit, Drak disengaged his device to avoid detection. After diving into the shadows, he scanned the area and spotted the security cameras and motion detectors over a door leading into the complex.

If the security system caught wind of his presence, his element of surprise would vanish along with his chances of accessing the generator.

His target was located inside the engineering station underneath the main dome. He knew this because he had obtained the MindHive Tech Conventions layout by having his algorithm harvest a wide swathe of deep web data. It took some time, but he had finally hit the jackpot after he narrowed the metadata filter to focus on MindHIve structural developments. The layout for a future MindHIve martian colony had been leaked some time ago, and it contained the floor plan for an exact replica of the structure sitting in the Kingsford exhibition grounds. It wasn't too hard to identify the location of the generator. He had no doubt it was the central power supply for the complex.

According to the layout, a vent large enough for him to sneak through sat on the wall opposite the door. He needed to sneak past the cameras and get to the vent or the door undetected. The conversation with Mitch still rang in his ears as he contemplated his approach.

It seemed the cameras had a blind spot between two of the columns. If he could move slowly enough, he wouldn't trigger the motion detectors and draw any attention to the area. While he edged his way along the storage unit towards the grate, he heard the access door slide open. Glancing around the corner, he saw a man in a chef's uniform walking through the door, pushing a large cart.

Although it was still the middle of the night, there were a lot of people to feed in the complex and the kitchen staff would be preparing for a busy morning. Drak watched as the chef raised his badge and opened a door.

Taking a deep breath, he followed behind the chef before the door could close. The rattling of the cart covered the sound of Drak's movements, and he managed to sneak in without the chef noticing. In a flash, he grabbed the chef from behind and choked him to the ground. The unconscious torso was difficult to maneuver in the tight space of the storage room, but he managed to drag him to a spot where he wouldn't be detected, at least for the time being. After he removed the man's clothes, he took some twine from his backpack and tied him up. Making sure the ID card was still attached, he emerged from the unit pushing the cart. He walked to the door and pressed the badge as he had seen the chef do moments before. The door slid open, and Drak stepped inside the massive complex.

Even late at night there was still plenty of activity throughout the complex. People were coming and going in different directions, and nobody noticed a humble cook walking by pushing a cart.

Trying his best to appear casual, he made his way down the long circular corridor which formed the circumference of the complex. He saw a sign on the ceiling indicating access to the inner quadrant.

As he made his way down the hall, he spotted two security guards standing at a set of doors. They watched as people walked by, but they didn't seem to be scanning passes.

Walking toward the door, he hoped they wouldn't glance at his ID. There was absolutely no resemblance between himself and the cook. If anyone looked, his cover would be blown. Luckily, there was enough activity to cover any suspicions, and Drak whistled while he walked so as not to seem out of place. The guards didn't pay much attention to him while he walked through the doors and entered the tunnel.

As he made his way toward the main dome, he followed behind a couple of people carrying boxes filled with merchandise of some kind. There were more people scurrying through the tunnel, but the guards at the doorway leading to the main chamber seemed a little less relaxed than the guards he encountered earlier. Giving them a nod as he walked by, the guards scowled but didn't say anything.

"Hold on a minute," shouted one of the guards.

"What's that?" Drak said while looking back.

"Where are you going with that cart? The mess hall is the other way," the other guard asked.

"Ah, I'm just taking these snacks to the main chamber. Some engineers are pulling an all-nighter in there. Big day tomorrow, you know," he said, trying to keep a straight face.

"What kind of snacks?" the other guard asked.

"Oh, you know, kind of snacks that go well with coffee," Drak said. "There are plenty here. You guys look like you could use something to pick you up. It's pretty late."

"I don't want any pastries. Do I look like I eat carbs?" the skinnier of the guards said.

"I like carbs. Show me what you got," said the other guard.

The skinny guard looked away while his companion grabbed two filling stuffed pastries before waving Drak on his way.

Letting loose a huge sigh of relief as he turned on his heel, he wheeled the cart down the hall.

He had been lucky, but there wasn't any time to sit around and appreciate his good fortune. It was only a matter of time before the cook was reported missing.

According to the floor plan, the way to the generator was through the electrical service entrance. Moving down the wide hall circling the dome, his eyes scanned for electrical symbols while armed guards walked in pairs along the hallway.

If the guards saw him wandering the halls multiple times, they would get suspicious, and it was only a matter of time until somebody glanced at his badge. Spotting a door marked with a lightning bolt, he engaged his device and slid his hand over the doorknob. A slight surge leaped from his hand, and the door jolted open. Stepping into the narrow passage, he got himself out of the baggy and cumbersome chef's uniform and grabbed his backpack from under the cart.

A steep metallic stairwell dropped down several feet into a world of soft buzzing light and dark shadows. Slipping down the stairs, he made his way along a metal catwalk that sat above an intricate network of wires and glowing devices. Alongside the catwalk, an endless wall of servers stretched into the darkness. MindHIve had brought along an entire server farm to keep the network stable for the convention. Further ahead, he spotted an odd purple glow coming from what appeared to be the end of the walkway. While he neared, the light grew stronger, and he gasped as he came to the end of the catwalk.

Before him stood the massive power generator. This huge device had been developed using the Masters' knowledge. Drak could see traces of their handiwork all over the glowing apparatus. Housed within a large mesh cube, the generator pulsed within the frame. The MindHIve engineers had been able to find a way to retrofit a coupling device to the generator. Drak could see where they had attached their crude instrument to the unit. Engaging his device, he opened up his access panel and prepared to sync with the generator.

Just as he established a connection, a lurch beneath his feet caught his attention. Looking up, he saw the ceiling part as the floor rose toward the opening.

Passing through the gap, he found himself in a large auditorium. The entire room was dark except for the purple glow from the generator.

A flash of light blinded him for a moment before dozens of figures appeared from the darkness and formed a perimeter around him. They wore metallic outfits, and orange auras encased their bodies. None of them moved.

"How do you like my little trap?" a voice asked from behind.

Turning around, he saw a tall man with a graying beard sitting casually in a chair on a podium. The man wore the same uniform as the hovering figures, but he let his helmet sit on his knee.

"You'll never win," Drak said through gritted teeth.

"It looks like I already have," Robert Chapman said after he got to his feet. "I burned through a lot of resources trying to find you. But all I had to do was roll open my door, and you just came running in."

"You think you know what you're doing, but you will be a slave just like the rest of them."

"Really now. Is that what became of your people? It's amusing that lower life forms always think they have some right to freedom. It's the same here as it is anywhere, I guess. I know all about what became of your world, and I know all about you. You were nothing but trouble from the start and look at you now. I guess nobody can break their old habits," Robert stopped for a moment and stared Drak in the eyes.

"You think you can set your people free, but the thing is people don't want freedom. They want what we give them and what we offer is security and safety. In turn, they provide us with a valuable resource: their indentured service. That is how it has always been, and that is how it always will be. All living things bow before the powerful because we set the natural order. If everybody were free, it would be chaos."

"You only think you have power," Drak said as Robert approached him.

"We'll see about that, but in the meantime, what am I supposed to do with you? Should I kill you or keep you around for entertainment? Now, I'm sure you're going to say: 'you'll never take me alive or something like that'. The truth is I don't really care how I take you. I just hope you put up a bit of a fight. We've been itching for this for a while," Robert said as he stopped a few feet away from Drak.

"You have no idea what you are doing," Drak said, backing away.

"You look like a scrawny kid. I'm not sure why they made such a fuss about you," Robert said while he looked out at his strike force. "What do you think fellas? Can we handle this punk? There's like fifty of us and one of him. I got a question, though, who wants the first piece?"

"I do, sir," several voices shouted out.

"Babcock, come on down here," Robert said, glaring at Drak.

"Look at this little snot," Robert said to Babcock. "You think you can handle him?"

"With pleasure, sir," she said.

As the woman bore down on him, Drak crouched down into a ball. Before she could strike, Drak leaped out of his ball, and a massive wave of energy erupted from his body. The pulse sent every single member of the strike force flying backward. Propelling himself upward, Drak raised his fists above his head and charged towards the ceiling of the dome. In an explosion of fire and light, he burst through the roof of the dome and disappeared out into the night.

"What are you waiting for? After him," Robert shouted as he gathered himself up.

Rising into the air, the soldiers shot toward the hole Drak had blown through in hot pursuit of their target.

After racing past the rooftops of Kingsford's suburbs, Drak headed straight for the mountains away from the city with the MindHIve security force hot on his tail. With no cloud cover overhead, dropped down into the forest in order to shield himself from the attacking guards. As he shot between the trees, the strike force volleyed shots at him, but the thick trunks of the evergreens provided Drak with excellent protection.

Approaching the mountains, the grade rose at a sharp incline, causing several soldiers to strike trees or rocks as they attempted to obtain their quarry. After he cleared the tree line, a steep gorge with rocky cliffs reared up before him. Below Drak, soldiers shot out of the trees and opened fire. Rising through the canyon, Drak blasted the steep walls, causing massive rocks to fall from the edges, forcing the guards to fall back.

Cresting the summit, he hovered at the top of the gorge and fired at the cliffs again, letting loose more rocks before he rocketed over the ledge and descended into the next valley. As he dropped into the valley, he was blindsided by Robert Chapman barreling in from his left flank.

"Leaving so soon? And we were just getting acquainted," Robert shouted while they careened down the boulder-strewn hillside.

"I know all I need to know about you," Drak said after they came to a rest at the base of the narrow valley.

"All opinions aside, I'll have to admit that was an impressive display, young man," Robert said, leveling his outstretched arms at Drak. "You just took on a whole squadron of some of the best soldiers on this planet. You are a force to be reckoned with, but, unfortunately for you, this is not the kind of force I need disrupting my convention."

"I'm not trying to impress you," Drak said, shielding himself from Robert's attack before he fired back.

"You're pretty brave," Robert said while steering aside the counter-attack "You're alone here, but you don't seem fazed one bit. Your plan failed, and now there is no hope for you. The only way you can possibly return to your home is as a prisoner."

"We will all be slaves soon thanks to you," Drak said before he raised his hand and created a long staff and struck out at his opponent.

"Impressive stuff, but two can play at that game," Robert said while a long whip extended out from his hand. Lashing out at Drak, the whip wrapped around the young man's arm.

Drak pulled back, but his hand was caught. Slashing the whip with his staff, he broke free only to catch a blow from Robert's opposite hand. Descending into the valley, the remaining soldiers rocketed towards Robert and Drak as they fought in the field.

Striking at Drak with his whip again, Robert's lash wrapped around his opponent's gangly arm again. As the MindHive soldiers closed in, they all extended whips from their hands and struck out at Drak. He tried to fend off their strikes, but as more soldiers arrived, they were able to latch onto him from all angles. Bound at every limb, and he struggled against his bonds. He tried to use his energy burst again, but his device lacked the necessary power. A soldier lashed out from behind him and caught him at the knees. The whip tightened around Drak's legs, and the soldier yanked his feet out from underneath him. He could feel his heart beating against the damp ground as the sun crested the horizon.

24

The main dome of the MindHIve complex bristled with excitement. It was Thursday, June 21st, the first day of the MindHIve convention. Sitting alongside thousands of excited conventions participants, Mitch was a nervous wreck as he waited for the festivities to start.

Overhead, workers patched a hole in the ceiling that had somehow opened up during the night.

He had sat beneath the deck on the hillside the night before wondering what fate possibly awaited Drak inside the complex, but he never in a million years thought he would see his friend come shooting out of the dome with all of MindHIve's security forces chasing after him. Sitting on the hilltop with his mouth agape, he watched Drak's figure disappear into the darkness, pursued by a squadron of soldiers volleying fire in his direction.

Arriving at the convention grounds that morning, he had been whisked through a series of lineups and kiosk desks. Several MindHIve employees loaded him up with all types of merchandise, including a new Hi5 phone and a textbook worth of orientation information. He arrived inside the massive auditorium overwhelmed, under slept, and anxiously waiting for the other shoe to drop.

As the dome filled up with participants, a sea of bodies jammed the entrance ways.

"Hey, it's #epiccrotchshot boy. Can we get a selfie?" a man asked as a group of people rushed to their seats.

As the selfie was snapped, more people took notice and Mitch had to submit to a round of photos before a pair of security guards came along and suggested everybody take their seats.

While he slid back into his seat, the lights in the auditorium dimmed, sending the audience into a fervor. An array of lights swirled throughout the arena, and the opening notes of the MindHIve theme filled the room.

The lights focused on the stage at the center of the dome, and the audience gasped as a crack in the flooring opened. A bright light burst out of the seam, and the audience cheered its approval as the opening enlarged.

The MindHIve strike team poured out of the top of the dome from an unseen entrance point. Joining each other in formation, the soldiers circled above the crowd before coming to a complete stop surrounding the stage.

The crowd gasped in astonishment as a giant purple cube emerged from the opening beneath the stage. As the music reached a crescendo, the stage lights flashed before an explosion of pyrotechnics brought the music to a halt.

"Ladies and gentlemen, are you ready to be a part of the future?" A voice asked over the loudspeaker. The crowd responded with wild cheers, and thunderous applause as Robert Chapman descended from the ceiling.

"Welcome to the MindHIve tech convention," he boomed to the audience while the music started again. As the crowd roared, Robert landed on the stage.

After he shook a few hands, he stepped back and stood still for a few breathless moments. Leveling his arms in front of him, he made two fists before raising his hands in the air. Rising out of the cube behind him, a massive purple orb manifested in the center of the dome. Its glow lit up the faces of everybody in the room.

Mitch stared at the orb in shock while everyone around him howled with delight. After several moments of applause, Robert raised his hands and gestured for everybody to be quiet, and a hush fell over the room.

"Once again welcome to our MindHIve convention. As you can see, there are a lot of things to talk about. I'm sure you are all wondering what this thing behind me is and what the heck it does. We'll get to that shortly. But we need to talk about all of you first. You are all here because you've done something extraordinary, and it is our hope you can use our inReal technology to further your development." Robert said as he stalked beneath the massive glowing orb.

"Now, how exactly are we going to get all of you onto the inReal system? Well, I'm excited to tell you we have come up with an incredible solution," Robert said while the crowd applauded. "All of you here today were issued a fancy new Hi5 phone as you entered the convention. I'd like all of you to take out those phones now."

There was a moment of shuffling as the audience rifled through their gift baskets in search of their phones.

"Every one of these devices is inReal ready, and we are going to activate each one right now using a brand new technology I'm sure will blow your minds. I'd like all of you to hold out your phones just like this," Robert said, reaching into his pocket and holding up a phone for all to see.

As the music started again, Robert swiped to his right with his hand above his head, causing the sphere to rotate.

"Ok, everybody, keep holding your phones up. Do not be afraid. Everything is perfectly under control," Robert said as he swiped faster. Soon, the orb was spinning at a phenomenal rate. As it turned, glowing strands appeared within the globe. Wrapping and coiling around each other, they formed an enormous purple ball of light inside the opaque sphere as shrieks of joy emitted from the crowd.

"What you are seeing now, for the first time, ladies and gentlemen, is inReal at its purest form," Robert said as he stopped accelerating the orb and turned to face the crowd. "This massive ball of energy is created within the core of the inReal generator. From this generator, we can activate the inReal capabilities of every device in this auditorium. People prepare to be amazed, and please don't panic. I'll repeat it again. Everything is perfectly under control."

From the ball of light, thousands of purple tentacles extended out into the audience. Making contact with the phones people clutched in their hands, the strands of light wrapped around the devices and elevated them into the air before the person holding it. After a quick flash of light, the tentacle retreated, leaving the phone hovering in mid-air.

"As your devices are activated, I will warn you not to attempt to use inReal at the moment. We will be unlocking the device's capabilities in seminars throughout the day. Your devices are inReal ready, and we will be going through the process of syncing your phone with the network during the orientation process which will be taking place after our opening ceremony," Robert said while he looked out at all the ecstatic faces in the crowd.

Surrounded by a crowd of ravenous spectators, Mitch watched in awe as the gigantic dome was filled with an intricate network of glowing strands of light. A tentacle reached out and took the phone he held in his hand, much like he had seen Drak do in the cave. He shook his head in disbelief as the strand retreated, leaving his device hovering in the air before him.

Despite the mass of people in the audience, the orb managed to make short work of the crowd. Before long, the tentacles all slipped back into the sphere, and the purple ball of light sat motionless in the spinning orb. Robert raised his hands over his head and crossed his arms, forcing the globe to halt.

Within the orb, a large projection of Robert's head came into focus. Three more identical projections appeared on the other sides of the sphere, allowing Robert's face to loom over everybody in the audience.

"I know you are all beyond excited to get out of here and start learning how to use your inReal devices, but I've got something very important to tell all of you before we begin our orientation sessions," Robert said, looking on the audience with sincerity. "The security and safety of every single participant in this event is of the utmost importance to myself and to the MindHIve team. We have taken every single precaution necessary to ensure your safety, but we still can't account for everything."

His face disappeared, replaced by a large holographic projection of Robert's full body.

"I'm going to tell all of you here today something nobody in the world knows about as of yet. Last night, in this very dome, there was an incident. Some people, it would seem, do not want this event to go as planned. One person, in particular, had a plan to break into this very facility and sabotage our equipment. This terrorist wanted to kill all of us and destroy the work so many people have poured their lifetimes into creating."

Robert's figure disappeared as the projection cut to a grainy video feed of the stage.

"This is actual footage of last night's incident," Robert said while the floor split apart just as it had a few minutes before.

As the cube rose through the opening, Mitch spotted Drak standing before the cube. His device was engaged, and he seemed to be trying to activate the generator.

"This brazen individual broke into this very facility and tried to destroy the main power generator. It was an act of terrorism, and it will not be tolerated," Robert said. In the projection, Drak could be seen looking around while the strike force members pulled out of the darkness and circled in on him.

"This terrorist thinks he has the right to force his opinions and viewpoints on the world, and he felt the best way to get his point across was to murder all of you. Now don't panic. The MindHIve security system detected this individual as he entered the complex, and he stupidly walked into our trap," Robert said as the camera showed Drak crouch down.

The projection cut to an image of Drak in restraints while a group of guards led him down a hallway. Zooming in, the camera showed Drak's face up close. He stared into the camera with a blank expression.

Mitch felt his heart racing in his chest as the image of Drak flooded his mind. What did they know, he wondered. Looking around to see if any security guards were closing in on him, he tried to stay composed.

"Ladies and Gentlemen, I'll have you know the MindHIve security team easily apprehended this individual, and he is currently in custody. The culprit has admitted everything, and he acted as a lone wolf. Believe me, nobody will be compromising the security of my guests or this event. I'd like you all to give a warm round of applause for the MindHIve security force and the men and women that make this bunch the greatest security team the world has ever known," Robert boomed out at the crowd. People rose to their feet and cheered with wild enthusiasm while the security team circled the dome again, waving and bowing.

"As for this guy, well, don't worry. We're about to hand him over to the proper authorities, and they will make sure he is taken care of," Robert said as the crowd booed and hissed at the image of Drak. "Once again people, we take the security of this event very seriously. Any threat or hint of violence will be investigated to the full extent of our abilities, and I assure you we have the finest assets in the world to assist in keeping you safe. I wanted to tell all of you this before you heard it somewhere else. You are safe in our hands, everybody. That brings us to the conclusion of our opening ceremony. Thank you for coming. This is going to be an amazing week. We are so pleased to have the greatest minds in the world under one roof, and I can't wait to see how all of you are able to apply the inReal tech to your work,"

The audience filled the dome with rapturous applause as Robert bowed several times in appreciation.

"As you leave the auditorium, you will need to scan your pass. Upon scanning your ID, you will have activated a small inReal chip within the card. The pass will display the information you need to know so that you can find your orientation group. Just follow the corresponding color, and you will find your destination," Robert said after an image of the event pass appeared in the orb. A hand scanned the pass, and the card emitted a soft, pink glow.

"The pulsing light indicates which dome you are to report to. As you exit the auditorium, you will see multicolored lines of light displayed on the ceiling of the connecting corridors. Follow your corresponding color until you reach your assigned dome. Scan your pass again, and you will be guided to your incubator."

The orb showed a group of people gathering within the dome under a glowing MindHive sign.

"If you have any trouble at all, please do not be afraid to ask any of our wonderful staff. They can be easily identified by their bright blue MindHIve shirts," Robert said while the display showed a group of smiling staff members waving out at everyone. "Let's have everybody slowly exit the auditorium. Just to keep some semblance of order, we are going to ask that each section exit in turn. When the lights flash in your respected section, please make your way to the nearest exit and scan your pass. Now, let's start the process."

The lights in a section across from Mitch pulsed in rhythm. Rising from their seats, the audience members made their way down the steep staircase. As Mitch's section lit up, he shook his head and grabbed his overloaded backpack.

25

The hallway surrounding the dome was jammed with people. Above them, a rainbow of flashing arrows guided the way to the outer circle. After Mitch scanned his badge at the station, his ID pulsed green. In the ceiling of the tunnel, he saw a corresponding green line with arrows indicating the direction he was to follow.

As he walked among the crowd, he couldn't shake the image of Drak standing before the soldiers out of his head. He watched Drak shoot out of the dome with his own eyes and the hole in the roof proved beyond a shadow of a doubt there was more to the story than what the CEO of MindHIve stated a few minutes before.

Mitch felt the weight of the phone in his pocket. If Drak had been telling the truth the entire time, then that phone was the last thing standing in the way of the mass enslavement of the human race. It was either that, or Drak was the insane person that Mitch had thought he was all along. There was only one problem with the latter theory: Drak was perhaps the smartest and most incredible person Mitch had ever met. If he was nuts, he certainly hadn't acted like it.

Mitch had no idea what was going to happen next, but he knew he wasn't out of the woods yet. He hadn't been captured or detained, but he was deep within the belly of the beast, and there was no way out as far as he could see. If he bolted now, they would be onto him. Even if Drak had protected him by turning himself in, whoever was watching must have some suspicions about him. He pulled his hoodie over his head, knowing full well it wouldn't hide him from the complex's ubiquitous security system.

Like it or not, he had to go forward no matter what fate awaited him. He sighed again and looked up. The green arrows were still flashing over his head. Readjusting his backpack, he followed along with the bubbling and exuberant flow of humanity surrounding him.

Before long, the green arrows indicated Mitch should turn to the left, and he found himself entering a different corridor. The ceiling of the new hallway was completely green, and a stream of arrows flowed toward a door at the end of the hall. A small crowd of people clamored at the entranceway to scan their passes before entering another enormous dome.

Waiting his turn amidst the crowd, he stepped to the next available scanner. An audible bing filled his ears before a purple 'W' appeared on his pass. Mitch entered into the dome, and he gawked at the sheer size of the open space.

A strange array of ergonomic computer work stations, beanbag chairs, and otherworldly lights and displays extended across several overlapping levels. Overhead, stood a forest of intimate and immersive lighting. Rising over the terraced work stations stood stacks of strange blue capsules.

Glancing at his feet, Mitch spotted several trails of light. A purple path lead to the right, and he followed it past a bank of walls that displayed images fading in and out of each other. There were pictures of surreal landscapes and black and white portraits interjected with inspiring quotes of all kinds. MindHIve was pulling out all the stops to get the creative juices flowing.

Kiosks along the walkway displayed different letters of the alphabet above them. As Mitch followed the purple line, he saw groups of people gathering before the stalls, scanning their badges. Finding a W overhead, he stepped up to the kiosk and scanned his badge again. The bell pinged softly, and he was greeted by a cheerful young lady wearing a blue MindHIve T-shirt.

"Welcome to The MindHIve tech convention. My name is Cindy, and I will be your liaison and inReal guide," she said as she peered at his badge. "Mitch Mythic, well isn't that a cute name? Hey, aren't you that crotch shot guy?"

"The one and only," Mitch said while trying to force a smile.

"Well, we're glad to have you with us, Mitch Mythic. This is incubator W, and it will be your home base for the next week. Please head on in and make yourself at home. If you are hungry, there is a snack and beverage section to the left. Go make yourself a coffee or a kale shake and grab a comfy chair. It looks like everybody is almost here. We'll start the orientation session in a few minutes. It's going to be an inReal day," Cindy said with a toothy grin.

Incubator W was filled with the same ergonomic office furniture Mitch spotted on the way in and there were even more bean bag chairs. Hammocks hung between the metallic tree lights, and while mood walls provided ambient light. Mitch saw several people spread out on some strange-looking chairs that resembled human torsos.

Another group of people stood at the coffee and snack stand, pouring an array of liquids into the tumblers that came with their MindHIve orientation packages. Mitch didn't drink coffee, but he needed something to keep him awake. Spotting a fridge past the coffee bar stocked with energy drinks, he grabbed a can of MassBlast. The label said it had six different kinds of taurine, and it was guaranteed to take you to the next level. Mitch popped the can open and took a sip and winced as he swallowed. It tasted horrible, like cough syrup mixed with gasoline, but he needed the energy. The second sip wasn't so bad, so he had another. A table with several baskets of baked goods sat to the left of the coffee stand. Striding across the space, he grabbed a couple of muffins and donuts.

He put the muffins and donuts on a plate and sat down at a nearby table. Grabbing a blueberry muffin, he bit into it and sighed to himself. The flavor was incredible. He finished off the muffin in no time, and he started to devour the donut. After a moment he looked up, and he realized he wasn't alone at the table.

Across from him sat a petite Asian girl wearing a pair of large glasses. She watched him in disgust as he stuffed the donut into his mouth.

"These are pretty good. You should get some," he said, trying to make light of the situation.

"I'm not hungry," she said, dropping her head down. She wore a strange pink sweater that said 'Fresh: dare to come back,' across the front. Judging from her fashion and her manner, she hailed from some other country, but there was something familiar about her. Mitch noticed a strange container beside her. About the size of a shoe box and rather nondescript, it had several odd markings on it in a language he didn't recognize.

"What's in the box?" he asked, trying to recover from his embarrassment.

"It's nothing," the girl said before she grabbed the container and placed it in her lap.

"Sorry, I didn't mean to bother you," Mitch said as he took another bite of his donut.

"You're not bothering me. I'm just a little overwhelmed is all," the girl said.

"I think I know how that feels. I'm having quite the day myself."

"I'm just nervous. This is my first time in another country, and I don't speak English very well. Everything is so strange here."

"Well, it sounds like you speak English just fine to me, and don't worry this is strange for me too and everybody else here. Do I know you from somewhere? I feel like I've seen you before."

"Uh, I have been in the news a bit. I also have a science blog."

"What's its name? I might have heard of it."

"Miss Science."

"No way, I've totally heard of you. You're that girl from Korea. You made that stuff. You were all over MindHIve a few months ago. That's amazing. It's nice to meet you. My name is Mitch. Don't worry. I'm famous too."

"I'm SoHee," the girl said, and she almost cracked a smile. "What makes you famous?"

"I'm a famous food blogger," Mitch said with a grin.

"I bet you are," SoHee said while lightening up.

"Okay people, let's all gather up," Cindy shouted from the center of the room. "If you could all come together before me and grab a seat we'll begin Orientation."

26

Peering through the tinted glass, Robert spotted a fingerprint left behind by someone who had come to gawk at the prisoner. Beyond the one-way mirror sat the gangly kid he and his minions captured the night before.

"It still seems a little hard to believe." Robert said.

"Hard to believe what, sir?" Gerald Tobero responded.

"This whole ridiculous situation we find ourselves wound up in. I'm looking in on a little punk that almost devastated all of my highly trained soldiers, and I can't make heads or tails of him. Is he a threat, or is he an asset? Do we keep him or get rid of him? No one has been able to get him to talk, but there are a few folks in high up places that want this guy bad."

"Perhaps the best thing to do in this situation is to be patient," Gerald responded. "It seems to me there are more pressing issues at play given the current situation."

"That may be true, but my window is closing, and I'm afraid I can't afford to be patient. As I said, there are individuals with considerable influence anxious to get their hands on him. I may not have much time to get the information I need," Robert said as he leaned against the glass.

Drak sat at the table with his hands cuffed. His face lacked expression, and he stared into the one-way window, fully aware he was being observed.

"There are several methods to get people talking fast and I have a few favorites."

"I am well aware of your methods, Gerald. Unfortunately, I cannot unleash you on this prisoner. He has information I would consider beyond classified. I'm afraid all of this goes above your pay grade. I'll need to talk to the prisoner alone."

"I see, sir. Would you like me to turn off the coms system?"

"And the camera too. I can't afford to have any of this getting leaked. The Internet would have a field day with this kind of video. I'm surprised nothing has turned up from last night," Robert said as he glanced at his watch. "Let's do this now. I've got a lot of things planned for today."

"Of course, sir," Gerald said before he flicked a few buttons on the control panel in front of the glass. "I've disengaged all communications and disabled the video feed. The prisoner is yours."

"Thank you, Gerald. I appreciate your sensitivity in this situation, and your loyalty shall be rewarded. But if I find out you've been snooping, then I'm sure you're fully aware of the consequences. If anyone compromises this conversation, that beach house isn't the only thing you'll have to say goodbye to," Robert said before he pressed a button beside the door that opened into the holding cell.

"I understand very well, sir," Gerald said while Robert stepped into the holding cell.

As Robert walked up to the desk, a sly little grin flashed across Drak's lips. Sitting down across from his prisoner, Robert leaned back in his chair and laced his fingers behind his head before he put his feet up on the desk.

"You know that I know everything?" he said, looking Drak square in the eye. Drak's eyes flashed, and he grinned again, but he remained silent.

"I told you before, I know why you are here, and I know about your people," Robert said. He watched Drak's eyes for any signs, but the kid's face remained an unbroken slab of restraint. "Do you really think what you are doing is going to make a difference? You do realize that the Masters have more than one gateway. Blowing up one isn't going to change anything."

Drak didn't move or say anything, but his eyes remained fixed on Robert.

"That's the thing I can't understand. If your whole goal was to come here and blow everything up, then why didn't you even try? Don't worry. I'm not trying to make you talk. I know your lips are sealed and nothing can break you. I'm just wondering aloud. It's been going through my head for the last few hours."

As he spoke, Robert watched Drak's eyes in the hopes of catching any movement that might show a crack in his facade.

"You see, I deal with all types of people all the time. I can usually figure out what somebody is after in the first couple of minutes of talking with them. It's kind of my special gift. Most people just want money, and that's easy. Others want power. Some want both, but it's usually money or power. Those people I can make deals with. We can come to some kind of agreement." Robert said as he dropped his feet to the floor.

"You, on the other hand, don't seem to care about money or power. But there must be something you care about, or you wouldn't be here. Terrorists, like yourself, often feel they are justified in doing what they do because they have been able to convince themselves they are fighting true evil. They are certain their cause is the just cause, and God is on their side. So in their minds, the destructive acts they carry out must be done for the sake of their belief."

Drak didn't flinch as Robert talked.

"Your people have been under the boot of the Masters for some time now. You've grown up a slave, and all you've known is the cruel reality the Masters have forced your people to accept. Naturally, you would want to take some kind of action. A terrorist act in these types of situations, while futile, is a natural progression. Your band of rebels hasn't made any headway against your overlords, so your leaders concocted a plan to strike back. They sent you here to find a way to do maximum damage, and you were able to penetrate right to the core," Robert said as he paced the room.

"So now we come to the point I don't understand. If you are a terrorist and you came here to wreak havoc on the Masters' plans to avenge your people, why didn't you? You didn't even try to blow anything up. There can only be one possible reason you didn't try to trigger an explosion. You are fully aware that if you went through with your plan, you would have wiped out this whole place, not just the town but everything. The power packed into that generator is big enough to cause a mini supernova. A real terrorist wouldn't have given a damn about the destruction he caused, the bigger the better in that case. You didn't want to destroy anything. That means you are trying to protect something."

"Nothing here to protect," Drak said, breaking his silence.

"Ah, he speaks," Robert said with a laugh. "It's interesting you chose to break your silence now. You are protecting something, or you would've kept up that stoic routine you maintained up until now."

"My mission failed, that's all. Now I wait for my fate."

"What was this mission, anyway? Come here and blow up a generator. That doesn't seem like a very well thought out plan. That can't be why you risked everything to come here. We've been aware of your activity for some time. Although you've been careful, you've also been sloppy. It's these mistakes that make me wonder about your motivation. You have done a wonderful job of implanting your algorithm into the system, but you easily gave away your location. We were able to track you to this point, and we were able to apprehend you with little damage. Why go to so much trouble to give yourself up? That's why I know you are protecting something. You think offering yourself up as a prize will throw us off the trail. I'll hand you over, and that'll be that. I know what you've done. You didn't come here to blow up anything. You came here to create dissent. You were clever enough using that video to spread the message, but you didn't think we were onto you from the start. #Epiccrotchshot boy, he's your friend, isn't he?" Robert said, as he smiled at his adversary. Drak's eyes steeled over.

"That's it, right there. It's fairly obvious. How much does he know? Did you tell him everything?" Robert said, searching for an answer. "This is the problem with freedom fighters like you. You let your heart get in the way of your goal. You thought you could help these people by coming here and warning them. That was your plan all along, wasn't it? Well, let me tell you something. The people of this world don't need saving. They have been slaves all along, and they don't want to be free. What they do want is comfortable bondage, and that is what I offer."

"No one wants to be a slave," Drak said. "You may think you are in control, but you not. You make a deal with Masters, and they make you a slave. That will happen matter what you do."

"I agree with you there, and I'm glad you've decided to talk with me. The Masters may like to think they know what's best for everyone, but you and I both know they are blubbering old fools. You may think I am the enemy, but that is far from the case. I am a lot like you in many ways; however, I am not the kind of person that thinks they can rush in and start a revolution. That's not how the world or the universe works. There will always be rulers and those that are ruled. It's called the natural order. The Masters may have power, but they know nothing of progress. They are doddering and decrepit relics, just clinging to their ways, and they need us to keep them in power. Soon they will be cast aside, and a new order will rise, an order that can help the sentient beings of the multi-verse realize their true potential."

"You are just like them, no different. All you do is take."

"That's not true at all. Look at what I've given back to my world. I am a benevolent ruler, and the people here bow down before me in honor. This is the type of leadership that is needed, and it is precisely what the Masters cannot offer. Join me, and together we can bring about a golden dawn. We will free your people from the Masters and create a new age, an age of progress."

"You will not save anyone. You are a liar."

"Why would I lie? I'm telling you everything. I'm also willing to let you out of these chains. I can be a very good friend, you know."

"I know what you are. You are a servant of the Masters, and you do their bidding. I will never trust you."

"Suit yourself, but I think I'll go and have a little chat with your friend Mitch Mythic. I'm certain he and I will have a lot to talk about. I bet I can convince him to help me."

"He is nothing, and he knows nothing."

"We'll see about that," Robert said, and he turned to leave. "I look forward to meeting him. He seems like a great kid. I loved his video anyway, probably the funniest thing I saw all year."

27

"As you can see, I've made a fist with my arm in front of me. This motion will activate your inReal device," Cindy said as an opaque orb encased her form.

The members of incubator W looked on from their ergonomic seating devices in awe.

"After completing this motion, you'll notice a panel appears in front of me. I can now access any of the functions available through the device. Let me show you a few of these features, and then we'll all activate our systems together,"

Her audience leaned forward as Cindy opened up photo apps and social networking tools. Mitch tried to look on with the same enthusiasm as everybody else. He fidgeted with his phone inside the pouch pocket of his hoodie.

"Let's all stand up, and we will practice a few basic motions everyone will need to remember to get the most out of their devices," Cindy instructed her audience.

Rising out of their seats, the attendees bunched together in the gaps between chairs. SoHee stood holding her box between a heavyset older man and a pair of women wearing matching yellow t-shirts endorsing a brand of environmentally friendly cleaning products.

Mitch stood on the other side of one of the chairs holding SoHee prisoner. She rolled her eyes when she saw him smirking at her situation. Reaching over, he pulled the strange-looking furniture toward him, giving SoHee a chance to escape. The man in front of her didn't look back as SoHee stepped past him. He was too busy following along with Cindy's movements. SoHee had to duck under his arm as she crept past his wide body.

"Awkward," Mitch mouthed as she stepped out into the space on the other side of the chair. Trying to hide her embarrassment, she hung her head while clinging to her container.

"Yes, let's all find some space, and we can get ready to engage our devices," Cindy said from the front of the room. "After you find a comfortable place, please take out the devices you received in your orientation packages."

Holding the slick new phone in his hand, Mitch watched as SoHee contemplated where to put her container. All the surfaces on the ergonomic chairs were oddly shaped, and she appeared reluctant to place it on the ground in fear of it getting stepped on. After a few moments of deliberation, she set her container on a table near the coffee station.

"What's in the box? Is it the stuff?" Mitch asked with curiosity. SoHee didn't respond.

"Ok people, you'll notice the devices are not powered up, and that is because we haven't connected your phones to the system. To connect your device, you will need to hold down on the power button until you see the MindHIve logo flash on the screen," Cindy said as she raised up her inReal display for everybody to see.

Mitch followed along with the crowd. He was curious to see if there was a difference between what he had in his pocket and what MindHIve intended to dole out to the masses. As he held the button, he noticed a large entourage enter the dome. Camera operators and several security guards circled around a single individual while the procession moved toward a flight of stairs. Rounding a corner, they disappeared behind a mood wall before Mitch could make out who was at the center.

"So after we've powered up our inReal devices, we'll begin the process of engaging the application. Place the device anywhere on your person. I recommend your front pocket, but anywhere is fine. If you don't have any pockets, you can use the collar and hook we have provided for you in your orientation packages," Cindy said as her audience followed her instructions.

Reaching into his pocket, Mitch made sure his other phone was switched off. A few feet away, SoHee hung the device around her neck using the collar from her orientation package. She still seemed nervous, and she kept looking back at her container on the table.

"Now that we have placed inReal on our persons, let's get to the exciting part. If all of you could do as I do and raise your arm in front of you, we will activate our devices," Cindy said with enthusiasm. All the members of Incubator W did as they were told, and the space was filled with shrieks of joy as the devices went live.

Mitch watched as everybody around him was encased in opaque bubbles. He raised his arms in front of him, and he was relieved his new device kicked in, not his hacked phone. The panel was similar to what he had grown used to, but several features were noticeably absent. Looking to his left, he saw Sohee had opened her device and connected to her MindHIve account.

"Hey, you're pretty fast," he said.

"Maybe I am, but it's actually really easy to use," she said.

As they played around with the features on their devices, the entourage of people Mitch watched enter the dome earlier rounded the corner and entered incubator W. A collective gasp filled the air as the participants realized Robert Chapman walked at the center of the group.

"Now, now, everybody carry on. Don't make a big fuss because some cameras are watching you. It's amazing to see everybody familiarizing themselves with this technology," he said into the cameras and to all the people present. "As you can see, this convention is dedicated to bringing about a fully immersive experience. We want our participants to fully engage with inReal, so we can release the very best user experience to the public."

As he came around to the front of the incubator, the camera crew fell back, and his security team positioned themselves throughout the room.

"I hope everybody is having a fantastic time. It is truly wonderful to see all of you good people experiencing inReal for the first time. This has been an incredible morning, hasn't it?" Robert said to everyone. "Now, as I said earlier, we have plenty of surprises packed into this convention, and you people are lucky enough to be able to witness something that has never happened before."

The audience members looked around with excitement as Robert prepared to make his announcement.

"There is a young lady here that has traveled all the way from Korea, and she has brought with her a special guest. I'm talking of course about 'Miss Science' herself: Moon SoHee. Everybody give her a big hand," Robert said as he applauded and everyone else in the room clapped along with him. SoHee dropped her head down in embarrassment.

"We've also got another celebrity present. I'm pretty sure you've all seen his video. #Epiccrotchshot boy is here with us as well. Everybody give a big hand to Mitch Mythic, the hometown hero. Why don't both of you come up here with me?" Robert said as he beckoned for Mitch and SoHee to step forward. Mitch gulped and looked around. Realizing everybody was looking at him, he felt a knot of anxiety tightening in his gut.

"Well, you two sure look embarrassed. That's surprising. You are both internet sensations, and a live audience has you rattled," Robert said as Mitch and SoHee approached. "I'm just giving you a hard time. I've seen that video of you going over the net, I don't know how many times, Mitch. That's got to be way more embarrassing than standing up here with some old businessman."

"You may be right," Mitch said as he tried to smile.

"Now, Moon SoHee, or do I call you SoHee Moon? I'm not sure about these things," Robert asked.

"Just call me SoHee," she said.

"Well, SoHee, we sure are glad to have you with us. I understand you brought your friends with you. As I'm sure all of you are aware, Miss Science isn't just a blogger; she's an innovator of some standing. We were all awestruck by her discovery this year. It's truly staggering what she has achieved," Robert said for the cameras.

"I only used other people's ideas. It's nothing, really," SoHee said while trying not to cry.

"How humble you are. You should take credit for all that you've done. For those of you that don't know, SoHee here has gone and invented bacteria that can consume any type of material, and in doing so, the bacteria will take on the properties of the material it has consumed. As exciting as that sounds, we'd like to push this development one step further. SoHee, I need to ask you something. Would you like to see your specimen coupled with inReal? It would be astounding to see what would happen, all for the sake of science, of course. What do you think everybody?" Robert said as he started to clap and everybody else joined in.

"I, um, I don't know. We have to conduct more research before we manipulate its properties any further. It's difficult to say what mutations may develop if the enzyme is altered."

"These scientists and their cautious approach to everything. SoHee, this week is about being bold and reaching out into the future. Let's take a chance and see what happens. I have taken the liberty of preparing an inReal prototype that is ready to be inserted into your bacteria culture, with your permission, of course. What do you think everybody? Should SoHee take the plunge? No risk no reward, right?" Robert asked to everybody watching. Incubator W responded with cheers and applause. Behind Robert, two MindHIve employees wearing blue shirts wheeled in a large cart bearing a MindHIve banner. A glass box with glowing lights sat on top. Inside sat a small black cube on a metallic pedestal.

"SoHee, are you willing to take a risk? We could be sitting on the edge of a major breakthrough. Just imagine what could happen with your bacteria and inReal. We could be talking about the end of the pollution crisis as we know it. SoHee, you stand on the cusp of greatness. It's time you step forward and take a chance like all the other great scientists that came before you," Robert shouted out, and everybody cheered.

SoHee was so shaken up by the attention, she just started nodding her head.

"She says OK. Everybody, this is incredible. SoHee, where is your sample?" Robert asked.

"It's on the table over there," Sohee said.

"Would you get it for me, please?" Robert said while he beamed for the cameras. SoHee walked over to the table. She was visibly upset, but she did her best to hold it all together.

"The world needs innovation everyone, and it's innovators like SoHee that make a difference. She seems a little shy, but think about how brave she is for coming all the way to America. Now, she is going to do something no one has done before. Let's give her another applause, people." Everybody started to clap as SoHee placed her hand on her container. Returning to Robert, she clutched the case close to her chest.

"Ahh, she's carrying it like a baby. It must mean a lot to you, doesn't it SoHee?" Robert said while he tried to take the case away from her.

"It is very important to me," SoHee said. "If anybody is going to put that device into my work, it is going to be me."

"As you like, Miss Science," Robert said. "Let's take the inReal device out of the glass."

The MindHIve workers did as they were told. Removing the case, they left the black cube sitting on the pedestal. SoHee stepped to the cart and opened her container. This was not how she had imagined sharing her findings, but she was hopelessly trapped. The cameras were rolling, and a large crowd gathered to watch. As she opened the inner chamber, vapors released from inside the container. Everybody watching gasped with astonishment.

"Now SoHee, could you hold up the container so everybody can see what we've got here," Robert asked.

Several camera people rushed in as SoHee held up her specimen.

"This is it, everybody. SoHee, is there anything you'd like to say before we drop in the device?" Robert asked.

"I hope nothing bad happens," she said, and everybody laughed. SoHee didn't find it funny. Reaching over, she grabbed the cube off of the tray. The room hushed, and time seemed to slow down. Exhaling, she lowered her hand into the tray and placed the cube alongside the specimen.

The audience held their breath, waiting for something to happen, but after a moment of silence and puzzlement, SoHee approached the container and peered in.

"Nothing's happening so far," she said.

"Well, let's hope our patience will be rewarded," Robert said for all to hear. "We'll continue to monitor this experiment all week. I'm sure we're in for a treat. Everybody give a big round of applause to SoHee."

SoHee stood beside her container as the crowd cheered and tried her best not to cry.

"You're all probably wondering why I've brought Mitch Mythic up here," Robert said after the applause subsided. "We've all seen the #epiccrotchshot video countless times, but let's not forget that in that video Mitch was playing hockey. Mitch Mythic is a great athlete, and before this video went viral, he made Kingsford quite proud playing that sport. Mitch, I'm sure you're interested in redeeming yourself to everybody here and everybody out there. How would you like a chance to participate in an extraordinary event we have planned over the next couple of days?"

"Uh, that sounds, interesting, I guess," Mitch managed to say while everybody looked on.

"Well then, let me tell everybody about our next big announcement," Robert said before he reached into his pocket. "I hold here in my hand what we call 'the inReal sport.' While this may look just like all the other devices you all have been using just now, this particular device is capable of the flight and motion functions my security team has been showing off over the last few days. During this morning's presentation, I used an inReal sport to enter the dome while all of you looked on.

Mitch, I'd like you to take this device and activate it for yourself."

Handing the device to Mitch, their eyes made contact for a second, and Mitch felt a flash of panic.

"Go ahead and activate it, Mitch. You've had a bit of practice already, right?" Robert asked. Mitch looked around for a moment, trying to find an exit. He expected the security team to pounce on him at any second. "Just now I saw you using your inReal beta, as we like to call it."

"Yeah, I was kind of getting the hang of it," Mitch said, trying not to sound flustered.

"Then this should be easy for you," Robert said. "Follow my instructions, and we'll have you using the inReal sport in no time at all. What do you think everybody? Give a big hand for Mitch Mythic."

"I'm not sure I'm ready for this," Mitch, but his response fell on dead ears. As the audience cheered him on, Robert put the device in Mitch's hand and dragged him out in front of the cameras while gesturing for everyone to be quiet.

"Mitch, I'd like you to follow my lead as I activate the inReal sport. This is the first time this has ever been shown in public. As I promised earlier, there will be a lot of surprises over the next few days," Robert said to the cameras and everybody watching. "Cross your arms like this, Mitch, and you'll activate the device,"

Doing as he was told, the crowd gasped as a blue aura spread across his body.

"You'll notice there is a little difference between the inReal beta and the sport. The inReal tech uses your available energy field to manipulate the environment, and that is exactly how the inReal sport allows us to levitate. Watch as I raise myself off of the ground."

With everyone watching, Robert lowered his hands to his side and raised himself into the air.

"Mitch, do you think you could do the same?" Robert asked as he stared at Mitch.

As the audience looked on in anticipation, he bent his knees and readied himself. Making his hands into fists, he raised himself into the air. The spectators gasped and cheered as Mitch hovered before them.

"Would you look at that, everybody? Mitch Mythic is a natural. Let's hope this video goes as viral as his #epiccrotchshot video, right? Let's try out a couple of movements, Mitch. Follow along as I show you how to get yourself in motion."

Pushing himself over the crowd, Robert raised himself higher into the air.

"Follow me up here, Mitch," Robert said as he beckoned for Mitch to follow.

Raising himself to Robert's level, Mitch looked down at the onlookers and spotted SoHee eyeing him with a look of puzzlement.

"Wow, you really figured this thing out quickly," Robert said with a grin. "Let's see if you can keep up with me while I move around."

As Robert took off across the dome, Mitch pretended not to understand for a moment.

"Like this, Mitch," Robert shouted as he pushed off with his feet. Mimicking Robert's movements, he followed after him and tried his best to play dumb.

Robert made a large swoop of the dome, and Mitch pretended he was struggling to keep up. Beneath him, people in other incubators looked up and pointed in amazement as he passed by.

Coming to a stop in the middle of the dome, Robert raised his hand, and a glowing orb encased his fist. Without warning, he launched a ball of light in Mitch's direction. Mitch instinctively brought up his shield and deflected the shot. He was about to return fire, but he caught himself as he realized he was falling into a trap.

"That was incredible, Mitch. You are a natural with this stuff," he said as they lowered down into incubator W again.

"Ladies and gentlemen, what you just witnessed was a demonstration of the inReal sport and a taste of the new game we have invented called 'inReal ball.' Over the next few days, we will be playing this game in the main dome, and I'd like all of you to come and watch. I'd also like to invite Mitch Mythic to participate in these games. He will join a team of our trained security officers in an actual game of 'InReal ball.' What do you think, Mitch? Are you ready for this kind of challenge?" Robert said.

"Uh, I guess," Mitch said.

"That sounds like a yes to me," Robert said. "Everybody give it up for Mitch Mythic. The first game is tomorrow night, and I think all of you will want to attend. You're in for a treat. The game is a mix between football and hockey, so I think Mitch will feel right at home. Won't you, Mitch?"

"Uh, do I get a chance to practice?" Mitch asked.

"Practice? That's funny. Everybody, #Epiccrotchshot boy here is asking me if he can practice. You'll get plenty of practice, Mitch. But it looks like you've got it all figured out already," Robert said with a laugh, and everybody in incubator W laughed along with him.

28

The stench of rehydrated food blanketed Incubator W. The Martian meal packs MindHIve developed for future expeditions to the red planet had been repurposed as lunch for the starving masses of the convention.

Mitch Mythic looked down at the bulging silver bag that sat before him. "Meat sauce," was written in black stencil across the bag, and at the top left corner, an arrow pointing at a broken black line, indicated where here should tear open the bag. Tugging at the line, he spilled the contents of the bag into a bowl emblazoned with the MindHIve logo.

Stepping into the ergonomic chair, he hit the button labeled food on the untouch panel embedded in the right armrest.

Several feet away, SoHee stood in front of her bacteria colony and puzzled over what she should do. She hadn't opened the container since Robert Chapman forced her to place the device inside.

In order to find out if any damage had been done, she would need to find a laser-scope. Luckily, she was at a state-of-the-art science convention. Gathering up the box and her MindHIve backpack, she made her way to the exit.

Mitch saw her leaving, and he got up and followed after her. He didn't want to be in that space anymore, and the smell of the meat sauce was making him queasy.

"Where are you going?" Mitch said as he caught up to SoHee.

"What do you want? Aren't you enjoying your Martian meat product?" SoHee said.

"I thought Miss Science would be a lot nicer," Mitch said.

"I don't like that man," SoHee said.

"Yeah, I don't know. He's kind of a big deal, but he must be hiding something," Mitch said as he tried to keep pace with SoHee.

"So how is your food blogging coming along, #epiccrotchshot boy?" SoHee asked.

"Well, I know my first post won't be praising the food at this convention. Did you smell the meat sauce? More like Martian butt sauce," Mitch said as he dodged past people.

SoHee moved through the crowd milling about the mezzanine at breakneck speed. Jogging to keep up with her, Mitch had to dodge back and forth to avoid people staring at the opaque screens in front of them.

"You didn't answer my question," he asked as she zipped ahead of him.

"I need to find a Laser-scope," SoHee said over her shoulder. "Where are you going?"

"Well, I guess I'm following you. Is that all right? And what the hell is a laser-scope?"

"A laser-scope is a microscope that can examine living cells. You can follow me if you want, but don't you think you should be getting ready? You've got a big game tomorrow." SoHee said, indicating one of the massive screens located above the door.

Mitch's face was plastered across the screen, and the hashtag #epiccrotchshot was written in bold letters below the image.

"Come see #epiccrotchchot boy play in the first-ever game of inReal ball tomorrow night at 7 pm," an announcer said. The screen then cut to a video of the MindHive security team preparing for the match. They hit and kicked a large ball of light back and forth inside the main dome while they made faces at the camera and battled against each other. Stepping away from the group, Robert Chapman approached the screen.

"Get ready to witness the future, everybody. This game will be the ultimate display of the inReal tech," Robert said as he held the ball of light in his hand. He turned to his side and raised his arm. A transparent inReal extension appeared before him. Covering his arm, it looked somewhat like a paddle. Robert maneuvered it back and forth in front of him. After a bit of posturing, he pulled up a ball of light and smacked it with his paddle. It shot across the dome into a glowing cube, and the entire dome lit up with lights and explosions. Robert cheered, and he was joined by the other players who all looked into the camera and made aggressive faces.

In horror, Mitch watched the video loop again. Turning to his left, he spotted SoHee disappearing into the tunnel that led to the next dome.

"You're still following me?" she said after he caught up with her in the hallway.

"I figured you needed a bit of protection considering you are carrying precious cargo."

"Oh, I feel much safer already. Scientists and computer nerds are known to attack at random. I'm glad you are here to keep me safe."

"Well, maybe you can protect me with your goo. I'll probably need a bodyguard now that I'm major famous."

"I'll see what I can do."

"You speak English really well."

"So do you."

"Fair enough. You talk pretty tough for a scientist, though. I thought smart Asian girls were supposed to be quiet and shy."

"Oh, so sorry. Do I not fit into your stereotype? Let me see if I can adjust myself for you."

"That's not what I meant."

"If it's not what you meant, then why did you say it?"

"I don't know. I didn't mean to make you angry."

"Well, if you aren't trying to make me angry, what are you trying to do?"

Mitch was about to answer, but they neared the entrance to the next dome, and a throng of people milled about while scanning their passes. Above the entrance, Earth Sciences scrolled across a bright electronic sign.

As they entered the dome, Mitch looked around in awe at what he saw. Brightly lit exhibits lined a pathway circling the perimeter of the structure and a massive an inReal orb swirled over the room. It displayed all types of information on its outer panel and within were simulations of different ecosystems that interacted with participants using inReal. Beneath the structure, a long line of participants waited to enter the synthetic environment.

Rising overhead, laboratories lined the walls of the dome. Hexagonal windows looked into each room, allowing observers to watch researchers as they worked.

"Do you think that stuff could do anything to your goo?" Mitch asked while SoHee darted through the crowd.

"I have no idea what will happen because I don't know what this inReal stuff actually is. The goo, as you are calling it, is capable of consuming any type of material and in doing so, it assumes the properties of the material in some way or another, essentially mimicking the world around it. So it's possible it could be inundated with the characteristics of inReal, but it is also possible the inReal could cause the cells to mutate in any number of directions."

"Mutant goo, huh, that sounds pretty cool."

"If that's what you think is cool, then I suggest you reassess your worldview. Genetic mutations are no joke, and they can have a profound effect on the world even though we are hardly able to detect them with our limited senses. Just think about all the people that have been affected by cancer if you think mutations are cool."

"I guess I never thought about it that way."

"I guess you should then," SoHee said before she made her way toward the labs along the edge of the dome.

As Mitch entered the lab, he was astonished by the level of activity in the room. Clamoring around several work stations with their devices engaged, groups of people were assembling and adjusting all types of equipment and syncing them to the inReal network.

A robot jumped off of a desk right in front of Mitch and danced around on the ground. Beside the desk, a chubby looking engineer controlled the actions of the robot using inReal. The robot mirrored his motions, and they both performed a goofy dance. Other people laughed and clapped.

"What are you looking for in here?" Mitch asked, stepping past the robot.

"I told you already. I need a laser-scope. It's the only way I can get a good look at what is happening inside the cells of the bacteria without damaging the colony," SoHee said as she scanned the room.

"Why don't you just ask somebody, instead of running around?" Mitch said. The guy with the dancing robot didn't seem very busy at the moment, so Mitch approached him.

"Have you seen a laser-scope around here?" He asked.

"You know what, I haven't, but you'd think they'd have one in this place," the robot guy replied. "There is a directory on the inReal panel, and I think we can search there."

Pulling up his inReal panel, he typed 'laser-scope' into the search box. As quickly as he typed, several entries appeared, and he clicked on an image.

"Ah, here we go. It says there is a laser-scope located on level 3 section 46. Wow, it even gives directions, cool."

"Thanks, I guess I could have done it myself."

"What do you need it for?"

"She needs it for her project," Mitch while he looked around. SoHee was nowhere to be found.

Rushing out of the room, he spotted her making her way up the stairs to level 2. He caught up to her just before she hit the staircase leading to level 3.

"You sure are in a hurry. You don't even wait for me?" Mitch said as they mounted the stairs.

"I'm not particularly concerned with you at the moment."

"Well, I'm the only person that seems to be trying to help you out, so maybe try to be a little nicer."

"Why exactly are you helping me, anyway? Do you think I'm going to fall in love with you or something? Did somebody tell you Asian girls are easily impressed by Western charm?"

"Uhm, no, I was just trying to ..."

"Don't worry #epiccrotchshot boy, I'm only teasing you," SoHee said while she looked at him sideways through her large black glasses.

Mitch made a face and groaned to himself, but decided to keep his mouth shut. He had never been taken apart by a girl like that before. He walked along beside in her shock. After a few moments, she stopped and looked up.

"Forty-six," she said and motioned upward with her eyes.

"Huh?" Mitch said and looked up.

The number 46 sat above another round portal entrance. Making their way inside, SoHee spotted what she was looking for.

A long cylindrical looking apparatus sat on a table next to a monitor and several dials. As SoHee approached the device, she was cut off by a young man and woman wearing blue MindHIve shirts.

"Hold on a second. Where are you two going?" The woman asked. "This area is restricted. Only people with the right access have permission to enter here."

"How do you know if you have permission?" Mitch asked.

"You need to scan your ID before you enter any laboratory. This place isn't a free for all," the man said.

"Let me see your ID," the woman asked. SoHee handed her ID over, and the woman looked her up and down for a moment.

"Hey, you're that girl, aren't you?" she said. "Well, you check out. You've got access. Is that the stuff there?"

"Perhaps," SoHee said.

"And you're #epiccrotchshot boy?" the young man said. "You have no idea how many times I've seen that video. I just laughed and laughed"

"I'm glad you enjoyed it," Mitch said as he looked away.

"Well, go on in, but be careful. There is some really expensive stuff in there," the girl said. "What are you trying to do, anyway?"

SoHee didn't reply. She made a direct line to the laser-scope, pressing buttons on several panels without hesitation. Mitch watched in awe as she fired up the machine and punched in a series of commands on a screen. After a few moments, she stood up and approached her box. She paused for a moment and took a big breath. Mitch heard her mutter something to herself in Korean, and it sounded kind of like a prayer.

As she opened the lid, she felt a shock of electricity ripple through her body, and she stepped back in horror before a green light burst out of the box. She backed up right into Mitch, and they both froze as a green sphere emerged from the case. Rising up above the box, it hovered in midair.

"What is that thing? Is that your goo?" Mitch asked.

"I think so. It appears to be the bacteria colony interacting with inReal, but I need to get a closer look," SoHee said.

Ripples of fear shot up her spine while she raised her arms and fired up her inReal device. As she did, the green mass moved toward her. Small extensions of light reached out of the green ball. She put up her hands to defend herself, and the green ball stopped a few feet away.

With her inReal still engaged, SoHee reached out with her hand. The tentacles coalesced together and extended toward her. As the mass of energy came into contact with SoHee, light pulsated through her device. Throbbing at a steady rate, the orb sent several flashes down the mass of tentacles connected to SoHee's display.

"What is happening?" Mitch shouted to Sohee.

"I have no idea, but I'm going to see if I can analyze it using the device," SoHee said.

"Don't try to analyze it. Just believe you can speak to it," Mitch said.

"What are you talking about?" SoHee said as she typed into the panel.

"You need to trust me. I can help you control it, but just listen to me. It is how this stuff works. Just think about what you want it to do. If you don't try, then there's no telling what will happen. Just think you can stop it. Think you can control it."

"What do you mean, think? I just think what I want, and it will do it?"

"Just try it."

Closing her eyes, she muttered to herself in Korean again. The pulses slowed, and the bright glow receded. SoHee opened her eyes and looked at the sphere in front of her.

"It seems like it is capable of interaction," she said while she peered into the swirling ball.

As she moved closer, small bursts of energy fluttered across the surface. She raised her hand, and the mass copied her, extending an appendage from its body. SoHee moved her arm, and it moved with her.

"It's linked with my device. I'm able to control it and manipulate it."

"Just think it and you will be able to do it."

"How do you know all this?"

"Uh, it's kind of a guess."

Outside, people gathered at the windows, and they watched as SoHee continued to interact with the sphere. Taking several steps around the room, the green mass followed her.

"It looks like your goo is alive," Mitch said.

"It was always alive, but this is incredible. I still need to analyze the molecules. I wonder if I can do it here?" she thought aloud, and a panel appeared in front of her. In the screen, she saw a cell from her bacteria colony. Small extensions of light reached out from within the organism.

"The makeup of the colony has changed dramatically. They are still individual organisms, but they have coordinated themselves somehow. It's unbelievable," SoHee said as she typed more commands into her inReal panel. "My device is able to send signals, and each cell responds in turn to the signals forming a single response."

Several security guards pushed their way through the mass of people watching the spectacle unfold. Forcing back the crowd, they made a perimeter around the lab. More MindHIve Security guards rushed into the room wearing blue hazmat suits. After the guards came a tall black man with a bald head wearing a dark suit. He strode into the room with his hands behind his back.

"This area is under lockdown. Our security system detected a biohazard threat in this room. We will place the affected subject and the material into quarantine after we have successfully contained the outbreak," Gerald Tobero said, eyeing the orb.

"What do you mean quarantine?" Mitch shouted back.

"It's a standard procedure. You need to step aside and let us handle this," Gerald said. "Ready your devices and prepare to activate containment measures."

On Gerald's command, the guards readied themselves, and strings of light extended from their arms.

"What are they doing, Mitch?" SoHee said as she looked around.

"Don't worry. It will be alright," Mitch said.

"Begin the containment process," Gerald ordered. Pushing their hands forward, the MindHive guards closed in on SoHee. As they approached, the lines extended out and attempted to trap the green mass.

In fear, SoHee lashed out at the lines, and the bacteria followed her actions. In a flash of light, several thick tentacles shot out of the sphere and swatted at the guards, sending them reeling backward.

"Security team, seize the girl," Gerald shouted. "Use non-lethal force."

As the team closed in on SoHee, she backed away in terror. The orb followed after her, forming a defensive position, swiping out at anything that came near.

Recovering from the initial onslaught, the MindHIve guards closed in again and one was able to wrap his rope around the glowing orb. As he pulled back on the rope, a tentacle struck him from behind and he flew into a workstation. The laser-scope fell to the ground and exploded while more guards rushed forward and wrapped their ropes around the flailing green orb.

"We've got it connected. Shut it down," Gerald said into his earpiece.

In an instant, the orb was encased in a blue aura and it froze in place as the long tentacles vanished.. Looking to his right, Mitch saw SoHee frozen inside her orb, a look of horror plastered across her face.

"Let's get 'em out of here," Gerald said.

"Where are you taking her? She didn't do anything wrong," Mitch shouted as the guards elevated SoHee off the ground.

"We're taking her somewhere safe," Gerald said. "This material is dangerous. It needs to be properly stored and examined. You'd be well advised to watch your tone, Mister Mythic."

"You can't just lock her up like that. This is MindHIve's fault, anyway. It wasn't her idea," Mitch shouted.

"It doesn't matter whose idea it was. It's my job to make sure security is maintained at all times. You better step back or you can join her."

Mitch stood there seething as he watched SoHee and her goo disappear down the stairs. The overhead sprinklers showered down water on his head while several MindHIve employees rushed in with fire extinguishers to contain the blazes ignited during the chaos.

29

Robert wiped the sweat from his brow as he removed his helmet. Above him, the strike force practiced inside the orb. Allan handed Robert a towel and a water bottle as he sat down and loosened the zipper on his uniform.

"These suits are like ovens. I am sweating like a migrant refugee in this thing," Robert said. "Let's get some lightweight stuff for the game tomorrow night."

"Noted, sir," Allan said while hovering over Robert.

"And don't stand so close to me, Allan. You're suffocating me. Don't you see I need some space? I can actually hear you breathing, and you know how much that bothers me," Robert snapped out. Opening the water bottle Allan had handed him, he dumped it on his head. "And get me some more water. I'm dying over here."

As he sat there catching his breath, he realized he was sitting right next to Gerald Tobero.

"Man, how do you keep sneaking up on me like that? I pay you to keep me safe, not give me a heart attack," Robert said in dismay.

"Apologies, sir. It was not my intention to upset you," Gerald said with his usual cool demeanor. "We've contained the outbreak, and the subjects are in stasis."

"Well played, Gerald. I'm hearing some exciting things from our scientists," Robert said as he wiped the water off his face. "It seems the mutation occurred as we predicted; however, we may have a problem with the girl."

"Yes, it's unfortunate the symbiosis of the subjects occurred before we could interfere. We're working on separating the link, but there may be a few complications. Somehow the connection between the two subjects is unrelated to the girl's device."

"You seem to know an awful lot about everything, Gerald. Just remember to keep any information from leaking out. We're discovering new things about inReal every moment. That's what this whole convention is all about. I've got the right people working on it as we speak. How are things looking for tomorrow night?"

"All is ready, as you suggested, but I would advise you to scale back your involvement in the game. Not much is known about the G forces one experiences using inReal at these velocities."

"Oh, it's cute when you worry about me like that. I'll be fine. Just make sure we don't have any more incidents or outbreaks. The world will be watching this event. It needs to be the spectacle we have been hyping."

"Understood, sir."

"You're a good soldier, Gerald," Robert said while he got to his feet. "I'm glad I can trust you to keep an eye on everything. I've got pressing matters to deal with. Inform me if anything arises that I need to know."

"Of course, sir," Gerald said.

Nodding to Gerald, Robert walked out of the dome with Allan tailed behind him and a little to his right.

"I've got some uniform designs for you to choose from. We have several options available. You can make your selection now if you like. The options are on your inReal," Allan said while he kept pace with Robert.

"Excellent work, Allan," Robert said as he brought up his inReal panel. "Oh, these look good."

Panning through several displays, he stopped at a blue and black form-fitting suit.

"These ones here, we'll need two sets. One in red and one in blue."

"I understand, sir. I'll inform the design department right away."

"And get some gum or something. Your breath smells like you've been eating Martian meal packs. Those things are disgusting. I can't believe how much money I spent on that tripe."

"I'll get right on it, sir." Allan said before they entered into the MindHIve employee dome.

As he made his way to the captain's quarters, Allan stepped ahead and opened the door before Robert could bark at him.

"Well done, Allan," Robert said after he stepped through the door. Allan was about to follow him through, but Robert stopped him.

"That's far enough. I have some important business to attend to, and

I do not want to be disturbed in any way. Post those uniforms on the official MindHIve account. I want to add some more buzz to the event."

"Understood, sir," Allan said before he stepped back and closed the door.

As the door slid shut, Robert exhaled and made his way to the inner quarters and shut the door. Stripping himself out of his damp and sweaty space suit, he dropped into an egg-shaped chair and placed his hands behind his head.

So far, the day had gone rather well, as first days go, he thought to himself. The Martian meals had been disappointing, but everybody knew those were failures even before the convention, and security only reported a few incidents at the gates. Aside from the containment issues regarding the girl and her bacteria, everything else had gone swimmingly.

The little stunt with #epiccrotchshot boy had worked out in his favor as well. The kid was rattled, and Robert was excited to see how he would perform the next day.

He had been going at a breakneck pace all from the moment he woke up, but he had one more thing to do. Sighing as he got to his feet, he went to a wall opposite the door and waved his hand in front of a panel, and a door slid open to reveal a shower stall.

Entering the enclave, he pressed a button, and he was doused in a warm spray on all sides. Soap shot out of from some unseen mechanism, and he was rinsed again. Before he knew what was happening, a warm wind covered his torso.

After a few moments to dry off, the door of the shower opened, and a robotic arm handed him a towel.

"That was refreshing, I guess," he said aloud as he stepped out of the shower stall. He touched another panel to the left, and a door slid open to reveal several suits hung in pristine condition.

After dressing himself in a gray suit with a blue tie, he walked to the center of the room and placed his inReal device on the ground. Raising his hands above his head, he brought up the orange orb. He stepped back, got down on his knees, and placed his head upon the floor.

"Robert, my humble servant, it is always a pleasure to see you bowed before me," Commander Holrathu's voice said before Robert looked up. "Rise before me, my soldier. We are all proud of the work you have done for our cause. The Emperor has even spoken of you with favor."

"It is my only wish to serve him well. The fact that the Emperor mentioned this loyal subject by name fills my heart with joy," Robert said with his head held low in reverence.

"Enough with the pleasantries. Are you prepared to transfer the prisoner? We are eager to have this nuisance put to rest."

"We believe we are prepared, but we would like to run a few more diagnostic tests to ensure everything will run smoothly. The prisoner is fully contained, and we will be able to transfer him to you once we are certain our portal is 100 percent operational. I wouldn't want to upset the Emperor with any minor errors that could have been avoided."

"That is the Robert that we know and love. Preparation is key. We all know the Emperor frowns upon mistakes. If anything were to happen to compromise the transfer of this prisoner, the Emperor would be most unforgiving. He takes this matter very personally. Any infractions will be punished to the full extent of the Emperor's law."

"I understand fully, sir. We are taking all the necessary precautions to ensure the success of this undertaking."

"The Emperor will be happy to hear everything is in good hands. I shall inform him myself. We were pleased to see you were able to create the connection, and it appears the power generator you constructed can produce the correct amount of energy to open the portal. Once you have completed your system analysis, we will begin the transfer process," Commander Holrathu said while he looked down upon Robert. "You've been a busy boy, Robert. How have the Emperor's new subjects taken to their collars?"

"We are still in the preliminary testing phases, but the responses have been beyond expectation. As predicted, the people are frothing at the mouth to get their hands on the devices. I am certain that once we are able to reach full production, containing the population will not be a problem. Given the right amount of time and the proper marketing, we can be sure none shall escape the grasp of the Emperor."

"That is wonderful to hear. Slow and steady is the best approach. We shall await your signal once you have fully stabilized the generator. This operation will be the first true test of your abilities. The Emperor will be watching. Impress him this time, and you will endear yourself to his heart, but should you fail, his wrath will be severe."

"I would never dream of failing the Emperor. Nothing will be overlooked."

"Very well then, Robert, we shall leave it at that. Glory to the Emperor."

"May his reign be infinite and just," Robert responded before the signal ended.

Robert scooped his device off the ground and walked over to another panel and pressed a button before a bed lowered itself to the ground. Stripping off his suit, he jumped in and closed his eyes.

"This might be easier than I thought," he said as he drifted into a deep and relaxing sleep.

30

SoHee awoke with a splitting headache. Realizing she was soaking wet, she looked down and found her body immersed in a strange green liquid. A soft glowing aura emanated from the eerie water, lighting up her immediate surroundings. She peered into the inky blackness that enclosed her, but she was unable to glean any information from her surroundings.

"Hello," she hollered out into the darkness, but not even an echo replied to her cry.

Her body felt weak, and she ached all over. Forcing herself to stand, the green liquid dripped off of her while she got to her feet. It was only a few inches deep, and underneath it sat a mossy bottom that gave way as she shifted her weight. She stood there for a moment, shivering with cold. The only thing she wanted to do was lie down, but there was nowhere to rest.

Pulling her left foot out of the water, she took a careful step forward. It seemed like the footing was solid, so she edged ahead into the darkness. Once she was sure she could walk through the green liquid, she decided to keep moving in the direction she started.

It was difficult telling up from down in the darkness, and she had grown more and more disoriented as she walked. Pausing for a moment, she thought she saw a speck of light in the distance. After wiping off her glasses, she blinked several times and focused her eyes on the wall of black in front of her. Letting her eyes adjust, she spotted a single point of light further ahead.

After several more minutes of sloshing through the water, she could make out a large pole or a tower rising up from the water. Before she had a chance to register what she was seeing, something brushed against her leg and she shrieked in terror.

Looking down, she saw a long black tentacle curling around her ankle. A flash of panic shot up her spine, and she jumped into the air. Screaming in horror, she ran toward the tower as more curling limbs shot out of the water and grabbed at her.

A tentacle wrapped itself around her leg as another ensnared her arm, causing her to stumble forward. As she struggled against her bonds, she felt something slip around her waist and hoist her into the air. A terrible rumbling and sucking sound tore through the darkness, and a hot stench blew against her face. Unable to see, she shrieked before more slithering limbs coiled around her torso.

While the limbs dragged her back, a flash of light burst through the blackness, revealing the immensity of her attacker, a slithering mound of flesh recoiling from the light. Pulling away from the limbs, she looked up and saw a strange energy emitting from the top of the tower.

A hissing sound shot out of the blackness behind her, and she struggled to turn around. As she looked back, she saw a gaping mouth opening to consume her. A colossal tongue-like appendage swung out at her and licked her face.

Another flash of light burst forth from the tower and a tremendous boom shook the ground beneath her. A wall of light slammed into the blackness, and SoHee felt herself dropping to the ground. The hissing head retreated while a powerful wave of energy pounded into its writhing flesh.

Scrambling away from the beast, she watched the tentacles slither through the water and out of sight while her heart pounded in her chest. The smell of the creature lingered in the air and she could see marks on her skin where the tentacles had wrapped themselves around her.

Looking up as she ran, she saw the top of the tower looming over her in the dark. Its peak consumed by a sphere of light burning into the black emptiness.

Long lines of rivets ran along the metallic surface in a strange and intricate pattern. Reaching the staircase that coiled around the structure, the railing felt cold as SoHee wrapped her hand around it and pulled herself up onto the first stair.

She watched as the green liquid gushed out of her shoes as she ran up the stairs. Although she was relieved to be out of the water, the horror of being eaten alive was still fresh in her mind. Wiping tears away from her eyes, she flung her damp hair back over her head and sat down on a step.

Taking a big breath, she rose to her feet. She put one foot on the next step and took a big breath before pulling herself up the staircase. Her headache had eased, and she felt somewhat elated after having escaped death, but she still had no idea where she was or how she came to be in that place.

As she climbed, her mind returned to what had happened to her before she awoke in the darkness. The entire experience was surreal and unexplainable, yet she had felt something coming from the green mass. As strange as it seemed, the orb had responded to her movements and her feelings. It was impossible to explain what happened to her, but she knew it occurred. Determined to get to the bottom of it, SoHee pushed herself up the stairs, confident that the answers she sought sat at the top of the tower.

Rounding the final turn, she had to cover her eyes as she approached the summit. With her hand shielding her vision, she kept her eyes fixed on the stairs in front of her and her legs shook while she forced herself up the last few steps. She stepped onto the metal landing, and fell to her knees, exhausted.

A blast of energy washed over her as she sat on her knees before the light, and she felt the strength of the illumination diminish.

Lifting her head, she found herself before a tree of billowing light. As it moved, pulses of energy emitted from its core and approached SoHee in soft waves.

Immersed in a warm glow, SoHee saw images of herself and the research she had done hovering in the air. Pulses of emotion washed over her, and she remembered the triumph and joy she felt while developing the bacteria species. More images flashed past her, and she saw herself standing at the MindHive convention alongside Robert Chapman.

Looking on in awe, she watched herself place the inReal device into the colony. As the lid closed, strings of light pulsed through the cells, but her jaw dropped when the sphere of green light rose out of the box, and she saw herself frozen before it.

Pulses of energy passed between herself and the pulsing orb as the security personnel filled the room. Terrible explosions filled the room before she was led away by the security guards alongside the sphere.

The security guards took her to a cell, and she was strapped into a gurney. A second team took the colony and entombed it inside a glass and metal cube. Waves of confusion and fear passed over her, and she watched as the square encasement rippled with a sinister-looking energy field, forcing the bacteria into a constrained ball.

The visions ceased for a moment, and the tree of light grew darker. SoHee felt anger and rage wash over her while different images appeared before her eyes. She saw large crowds of people inside their inReal spheres frozen in place. As she saw Robert Chapman ordering his security guards to seize Mitch. They lashed him with ropes of light and he fell to his knees. Another boy was brought out. SoHee recognized his face from the video shown during orientation. They were placed on the ground beside each other.

More visions flooded her eyes, and SoHee saw a giant portal imbued with energy expanding before the silhouette of Robert Chapman. Large shadowy figures stood on the other side. They had blazing eyes of light, and they glowed much like the inReal devices, but their aura was a menacing red. As they stepped through the portal, SoHee saw Robert Chapman bow before them. The figures seized the other boy while praising the MindHIve CEO.

The tree of light grew darker still, and SoHee saw more of the creatures flying out of the portal. Visions of her family passed before her, and she saw her mother and father forced onto the ground in front of the DH laboratory. Everybody she knew and cared for was there, and they were all in tears as several large metallic monsters lurked over them.

The visions ceased without warning, and the tree of light sat before her, sending pulses of energy in her direction at a slow and steady rate. SoHee felt an inner strength grow inside her, and more visions flooded her eyes. The enormous metallic beings walked towards her in lockstep.

The figures towered over her before raising their arms to strike. As they brought their fists down upon her, an intense explosion burst forth from her body and the monsters were sent flying backward.

Opening her eyes, the tower vanished. She was alone in a darkened room. Trying to move, she found herself connected to several instruments measuring her body functions. SoHee closed her eyes again, and she saw the green tree glowing gently before her again. A fresh wave of emotions passed over her, and she knew what she had to do.

31

It had been nearly twenty-four hours since the incident in the lab, and every moment that followed had been torturous for Mitch Mythic. As game time approached, new ads to promote the event popped up on every available surface and screen at a dizzying rate, and Mitch was featured in nearly all of them.

"Will he be epic or will he get it in the crotch again?" scrolled across a panel display in incubator W in bold letters, followed by the hashtag "#epiccrotchnot."

Mitch shook his head as he stuffed the remnants of a Martian meal pack into the receptacle to the left of the snack counter. Feeling his pocket, he realized his old phone was missing. A flash of panic coursed through his brain as he thought he had lost it. It must still be in his bunk, he thought as his heart pounded.

The other members of the incubator were hard at work, applying inReal to some task or other. Mitch wanted nothing to do with anything related to those devices. Tormented by yesterday's events, he had suffered through a sleepless night inside his cell.

It was only a few hours before the game of 'InReal ball,' or whatever Robert Chapman had called it, and Mitch knew he had no way out of it. He was on MindHIve turf, and all eyes were on him. Escape was impossible. Should he do anything out of line, they would hunt him down like a dog, and it would be his mugshot they were showing on the news.

He tried to slink his way out of the incubator, but Cindy saw him leaving and chased after him.

"Mitch, I'm supposed to tell you that you need to report to the main dome. They are going to fit you with your uniform, and you'll get a chance to practice before the game. It's pretty exciting, isn't it?" she said.

"I guess you could say that," Mitch said, trying to remain affable.

"Well, I hope you can handle the pressure because it looks like the whole world will be watching. I couldn't imagine having to get up there with all those people watching, but I guess that is something you are used to by now," she said with a smile. "Anyway, they are expecting you at the main dome. You should head over there now."

"Uh, just give me a second. I've got to get something from my bunk," Mitch said.

Trying his best to suppress the paranoia attacking his brain, he walked out of the incubator and headed toward the sleeping cells at the back of the dome. He wondered if security had inspected his bunk as he ate lunch. They probably already discovered his rogue phone and were preparing to swoop in at any moment. He would be whisked off to the bowels of the complex where he would join Drak and SoHee in some blacked out holding pen as they awaited the arrival of the Masters.

He sighed a breath of relief as he rounded the corner and saw no armed goons awaiting him. Climbing the staircase that led to his bunk, he looked around before he scanned his pass and entered his capsule. Nothing had been disturbed, and he found his phone stashed under the mattress. He placed the phone into a side pocket on his pants and laid down on the bed. Tossing his new inReal sport onto the bedside table, he stared up at the ceiling. If he didn't report to the main dome soon, they would become suspicious and send somebody to come and find him, but he couldn't shake the nauseating suspicion sitting in his gut.

He felt a vibration in his pants and he realized his old phone was ringing. 'Mom wants to video chat,' scrolled across the screen.

Sighing again, he pressed the green button and his mother, father, and his little brother stared back at him through a pixilated screen.

"Mitch, it looks like you've had a pretty interesting time over there. We're looking forward to this game you're going to play in. What an amazing opportunity," Mike Mythic said.

"Way to go, Mitch. We're so proud of you, honey," Mindy Mythic said.

"Kick some butt, Mitch," said his little brother.

"Ha, I'll try. It's a little crazy, but I think I'll get the hang of it," Mitch replied.

"That MindHIve guy is a real jerk. He's been saying all kinds of stuff all day. Show him how we do it in Kingsford, son," his dad said.

"I'll see what I can do," Mitch said.

"I don't like that guy at all," his mom said. "You let him know you can stand up for yourself, Mitch."

"Ha, there's a lot he doesn't know about me. I think I can show him a trick or two," Mitch said.

"You probably don't have much time, but we just wanted to let you know we will be watching. We're proud of you, buddy," his father said.

"Have you heard about that girl from Korea? Nobody knows what happened to her, and her mother has been making quite the scene. It's all over the news," his mother said.

"I haven't seen any news at all. I've got no idea what happened to her, but I'm pretty sure she is in good hands," Mitch said as he glanced at the door.

"Well, you just take care of yourself and keep your stick on the ice," Mike Mythic said.

"There isn't any ice, Dad," Mitch said.

"Well, you know what I mean," Mr. Mythic said with a laugh.

"We won't keep you too long, honey. Just know we'll be watching and we love you," Mitch's mom said.

"I love you guys too. Don't expect too much from this game. It's more for show than anything, I think. I'm just going to try to have some fun," Mitch said as he attempted to play down the situation. "I've got to get going. I'm going to hang up now."

"We love you, Mitch," his family said in unison, and the call ended. Mitch groaned to himself and stood up.

"What a nightmare," he said to himself as he stuffed his phone back in his pocket. Opening the door of the cell, he stepped out onto the walkway and got on the elevator. With his hood over his head, he managed to get himself out of the dome without drawing a crowd, and there were minimal people in the connecting tube leading to the main dome, but two security guards stopped him as he came to the entrance.

"Nobody's going in there right now, buddy. Authorized personnel only," one of the guards said.

"You might have to make an exception," Mitch said as he removed his hood.

"Ohh, I see," said the other guard. "Just scan your pass over there, Mitch. Loved your video, by the way."

"Well, hopefully, I can keep you entertained tonight," he said as he scanned his pass.

The dome was even larger empty than it was when it was filled with people. Reaching to the top of the structure, the stands seemed to take on an impossible angle as they climbed up the arched walls.

In the center of the dome, the giant sphere spun at a slow rate, casting off a soft purple glow. Within the orb, Mitch spotted several members of the security team practicing maneuvers wearing red, tight-fitting, one-piece bodysuits. There was some type of armor on the shoulders, and each player had been equipped with an aerodynamic helmet sporting a semitransparent visor.

Even from a distance, the players looked huge. Mitch gulped as he watched two muscle clad brutes tussle for the ball along the edge. They were only practicing, but they displayed an animal ferociousness as they jostled with each other.

"Are you Mythic?" a voice called out.

Mitch turned around and looked to see who had called him.

"Yup, it's you," a bearded soldier said as he tossed a uniform at Mitch. "Put this on. Let's see if it fits."

The soldier threw a blue uniform in plastic wrap at Mitch. He tried to catch it, but he bobbled the package and dropped it to the ground.

"Well, you certainly catch like a hockey player," the soldier said with a laugh. "Go on. We ain't got all day."

"Right here," Mitch asked while he looked around.

"Yeah, your dressing room isn't quite ready yet. We're still shining up the chandelier. Somebody get the princess a tiara. She's late for the ball," the soldier shouted while several other security force members laughed. "Get your butt in gear, Mythic. We've got a lot to do to get ready for this game. We're blue. I'm Lieutenant Davis. You're on our team, and your video was hilarious."

"All right, just give me a second," Mitch said before he pulled off his hoodie.

"Look, everybody. He's gearing down right here. Somebody get a camera. Mitch Mythic is putting on a show." Davis said, and everybody laughed again.

As his cheeks flushed, he struggled to put on the tight-fitting suit. After a few flustered moments, he managed to get the suit over his shoulders and zipped up while the guards laughed at his expense.

"Looking good, Mythic. You might want to start hitting the gym a bit more, but there ain't no time for that now. You still got your inReal sport on you," Davis asked.

"Yeah, I've got it right here," Mitch said while he reached for his pants. His heart seized when he only found his hacked device in the side pocket.

"Come on. Our practice session is starting now. We'll get a warm up, and then this place is going to fill up with people. You're going to need some time to get your bearings, so let's go. Don't forget your ID. You'll need it to enter the orb," Davis said as he tossed Mitch a helmet and activated his device. "Put this thing on and fire up your unit. We're going in now."

Donning his helmet, he activated the phone Drak had transformed inside the cave. As he crossed his arms over his chest, he felt the blue light cover his body.

"Move it, Mythic," Davis shouted at him again. Mitch scowled and raised himself off of the ground.

There was a round hole at the base of the sphere that allowed people to enter. While Mitch approached the sphere, it scanned his ID through his uniform. A translucent barrier faded before him, and he slunk into the globe.

"You really drag your butt around, Mythic," Davis said after Mitch reached the huddle of players at the center of the dome. "Everybody knows who you are, so don't worry about introducing yourself. Nobody is expecting you to do anything, but Chapman wants you in the game when it starts. All you need to do is stay out of the way. You understand, Mitch?"

"I guess," Mitch said.

"It's a simple game: get the ball into the other teams net. There are no off-sides or anything, and body contact is fair game, just no punching or kicking. Use the paddle on your arm to smack the ball," Davis said before he produced a ball of light using his left hand. A large inReal paddle extended from his right arm, and he smacked a ball of light at Mitch. Mitch instinctively brought up his shield to deflect the ball.

"Whoa, look at this guy go. Shields up and ready," Davis said. "Bring up your paddle like this," he said before he raised his arm and made a fist. Mitch copied the motion, and he imagined a paddle appearing along his arm. An opaque extension manifested itself in front of him.

"It looks like you're ready to go. Just hang on the edges, and you'll be out of harm's way. Watch the game for a bit, and if the ball comes at you just bat it away," Davis said and smacked another ball of light at Mitch. He was ready this time, and he sent the ball back at Davis.

"Now you're getting the hang of it. Don't get cocky and stay out of the way," Davis said after he smacked the ball towards the opposite goal.

"Let's get into position. You're on the right wing, Mitch. You're a hockey player. You'll figure it out," Davis shouted while the other players spread around the sphere.

Heading to the right as he was told, Mitch watched as his team mates scrambled after the ball. As it returned to center, Davis pounded it down the right wing. Taking his cue, Mitch bounded toward the ball and batted it back in the direction it came.

"Not bad, Mythic. Chapman was right. You are a natural. Just don't blow it like you did in that video," Davis said from nearby.

"I'll try not to disappoint you," Mitch said under his breath.

As he settled back into his spot on the wing, the ball came at him again. Instead of batting it back, he decided to keep it close and see what he could do against these guys. Copying the other players, he picked up the ball with his paddle and took off toward the net at the opposite side of the sphere. As he darted forward, the other players took notice and came at him full speed.

The first player lunged at Mitch as he crossed the opaque center line, but Mitch stepped around him with ease. It seemed like the security team hadn't yet understood how inReal worked. They were slow to react, and they moved as if they were on land, not in the air.

The next player came at him and tried to tackle him, but instead of going sideways, Mitch inverted himself and pushed down. As he rocketed to the bottom of the dome, he heard the other player curse. Angling up, he spotted the goal a short distance away. He shot upwards just as a swarm of players tried to intercept him. Changing direction again, he freed the ball from his arm after he avoided another tackler and swatted it into the net.

"What are you doing hot-dogging around like that? If you pull any stunts like that in the game, I'll bench you in a heartbeat," Davis said as he got in Mitch's face.

"It seemed like a fair move. Did I do something wrong?" Mitch asked.

"I told you to stay out of the way, but you couldn't help yourself, could you? You completely ignored my orders," Davis said.

"I was just playing the game. What's wrong with that?" Mitch asked.

"Don't ever disobey me again," Davis said as he glared at Mitch. "Everybody, let's bring it in. We're done here."

32

"The kid's got some moves. This is going to be interesting. Who are you betting on, Gerald?" Robert said while he and his chief security advisor watched Mitch Mythic and the rest of the blue team exiting the orb from the security command center situated underneath the main dome.

"I'm not a betting man, sir," Gerald responded. "But if I were to wager, I'd bet on the home team."

"What's that supposed to mean?"

"That's for you to decide, sir."

"I'm not sure why I bother with you sometimes. If you weren't so goddamn useful, I'd have fired you a long time ago."

"Understood, sir. I'll continue being useful as needed."

"Very funny. How are we with the broadcast? I want to make sure we get the widest reach as possible."

"Our entire network is fully dedicated to the game at the moment; however, it appears that the media has taken notice of the plight of the Korean girl. After her mother made a scene at the front gate, the floodgates were opened, and the story has steamrolled over the past few hours."

"Stick to the script on that one. The girl is fine, and the incident was minimal."

"The South Korean embassy has started to make a stink. I'm not sure how much longer we can keep them at bay."

"It's a quarantine situation. Although she isn't in any danger, we can't risk exposing everybody else and blah, blah, blah."

"It will be difficult without a statement from the girl."

"We haven't broken the bond yet. Once we have extracted her, we'll release her to sweet mommy dearest. Until then, everything will have to wait. That stuff is my property, and it may be one of the most significant developments in bioengineering history. There's no way I'm letting her walk out of here with it. Another 24 hours won't kill her, and it'll give the press something to talk about. In the meantime, I've got bigger fish to fry."

"Understood, sir."

"Keep at it. I need a one on one with our friend down the hall before the game starts."

"Be careful with that one," Gerald said as Robert left. "He's hiding something. I'm sure of it."

"Oh, I'll be careful," Robert said with a laugh.

As he approached the door to the holding cells, he was greeted by the two guards standing sentry before the entrance.

"Good evening sir," they said before Robert swiped his pass on the panel and the door slid open.

"It is a good evening. Are you guys going to watch the game? It's going to be a good one," Robert said with a grin.

"We're on duty, sir," one guard said.

"That's right. You are on duty and don't forget that for one second. You are guarding a dangerous criminal. You must be ever vigilant," Robert snapped as he walked by.

"Yes, sir," the soldiers chimed in unison while the door slid closed.

Nodding to the guard standing in the monitoring station, he walked past several cells packed with protestors. People banged on the glass as he strode by, but he didn't bother looking over.

He arrived at the final door at the end of the hallway and scanned his pass one more time. The room was dark, save for two video monitors and a large window looking in on the barren interrogation room. Robert spotted Drak slumped across the table. Another guard stood up as Robert walked in.

"You can wait outside," Robert said as the guard attempted to salute him. "My friend and I have something that we need to discuss in private."

"Of course, sir," the guard said before he left the room. The door shut behind him with a soft whoosh.

Looking through the glass for a moment, Robert pressed his pass on the panel next to the door and stepped into the room.

"Whoa, did you piss yourself or something?" Robert asked while holding his nose. As the door slid shut behind him, he saw Drak lift his head and glance in his direction before laying back down again.

"Still doing the whole strong silent type thing, are we? Well, let me tell you something right now," Robert said as he sat down at the table opposite Drak. "You've got about 24 more hours before your plight gets a lot worse. I'm going to hand you over to our big metal friends, and I'll wash my hands of you for good. That is unless you are willing to help me."

"Do as you please. I will not help you," Drak said without lifting his head up from the table.

"As you like, but just know I can make all of this go away and then we can work together. Do you think I want to be a slave? I have been working on a plan for some time now that will bring down the Masters. You can help me, but you need to cooperate."

"I will never trust you with anything."

"Suit yourself, but I'll let you know something else," Robert said as he got up. "Your friend Mitch and I have been getting along wonderfully. I'm going to see him in a couple of minutes, and we're going to play together in a little game I made up. The whole world will be watching, and you can watch it too. This window can act as a TV screen as well. You'll get to see me toying with our pal Mitch. I'm going to go after him with everything I've got, and when I'm finished with him, they won't be calling him #epiccrotchshot boy anymore. I imagine it will be something more like: 'accomplice to a terrorist,' or 'dangerous anarchist,' or something along those lines. Either way, it's going to be a lot of fun, and I hope you enjoy watching me bring down your friend."

"You are evil, and you will pay for it."

"Oh yeah, who's going to stop me? I gave you a chance to save yourself, but there you go again, acting all virtuous. I'm the sanest actor here, Drak. I can see the reality of the situation, and I'm making the most out of it," Robert said before he stood up. "Enjoy the game. I'm going to have a blast taking apart your friend."

Stepping to the door, Robert scanned his pass while Drak glared at him.

"Don't look at me like that. Your people did the same thing, and they are much better off now than they were before the Masters came, despite what you think," Robert said as he slid the door shut.

He laughed to himself while he walked over to the control panel underneath the window. Pressing a few buttons, the one-way window turned opaque. A view of the main dome appeared on the glass. The place was absolutely packed. As lights flashed over the crowd, two announcers stepped in front of the camera.

"It's a full house tonight, and the excitement is at a fever pitch here in the main dome of the MindHIve convention in Kingsford. What will Robert Chapman serve up for us next?" one announcer asked.

"That's a great question, Bill. They have been hyping it hard for the last 24 hours. Are we about to witness the birth of a new and exciting sport, or is this going to be some kind of publicity stunt? It looks like we're about to find out. The teams appear to be entering the dome," the other announcer said.

Both the red and blue teams floated into the dome with their inReals engaged. Upon seeing the players entering, a roar lit up the crowd. The camera panned over the players, and a despondent-looking Mitch Mythic hovered amidst the blue team.

"Almost time for my grand entrance," Robert said while smiling to himself.

33

While Mitch made his way toward the blue players' bench, the overhead lights darkened and a kaleidoscope of color cascaded over the crowd. There was a moment of silence before a voice filled the dome.

"Ladies and Gentlemen, and kids of all ages. We would like to welcome you all to a historical event. Are you ready to see the future?" the voice boomed.

The audience responded with a definitive 'yes,' followed by an ear-splitting cheer.

"You are all about to witness the first ever game of inReal ball. This game may prove to be the future of sports, as we know it. Let me introduce the man who invented this sport. He is the reason we are all here at this convention, and he is perhaps one of the greatest innovators alive today. Everybody put your hands together once again for Robert Chapman," the voice said.

The audience exploded with cheer and applause, while everybody rose to their feet. After a few moments, the entire dome went dark, save for the glow of the orb at the center of the room.

A burst of flame at the top of the dome caught everybody's attention, and a streak of light rocketed down from above. The crowd leaped to their feet again as Robert Chapman stood at the helm of a flaming chariot circling over the audience.

Beaming at the crowd as he descended, he steered the glowing vehicle toward the landing zone at the side of the sphere.

After landing with a thud, Robert jumped out of the chariot and waved to the crowd again. The roar of approval was deafening, and he bowed towards the audience, clasping his hands together in appreciation. Repeating the motion several times as he circled the main generator below the orb, he finally came to a full stop and extended his hands out over his head. Crossing his hands over his chest, he activated his inReal and rose up into the air, sending the crowd into a frenzy.

"I can't tell you how happy I am right now," Robert said, his voice projecting throughout the dome. "This is an incredible moment in human history. All of you are about to witness the truly awe-inspiring power of inReal. I couldn't think of a better way to display the power of this bold new technology than through sport," Robert said, and the crowd roared in approval.

"This is a brand new game the MindHIve security team and I invented. There are a lot of people that deserve to be recognized for their contributions to the game, but we can get to that later. Is everybody ready to see something incredible?"

The crowd was, once again, brought to their feet by Robert's overture.

"Well, let's get to it then," Robert said while he beamed at the crowd. "Before we get started, let's just make a few things clear. The object of the game is to put the ball into the other team's net. You can see two glowing cubes positioned opposite each other at the edge of the sphere. These cubes are the goals. This is a concept we are all familiar with, right? So no further explanation is needed there. While any type of contact is allowed, the referee will determine what constitutes fair play. Any violations will result in a penalty, and the offender will be sent to the 'sin bin,' shame!" Robert said as he looked out at the audience and laughed at his own joke before he continued.

"There is one other thing we would like to introduce to you, and it is something of a novel idea. Your response to the action will have an impact on how the game is played. The orb, within which we shall play this game, will respond with color to your reactions. Therefore, how you cheer will be reflected back upon you by the color of the orb itself. This is very exciting stuff, and we are using top-notch technology to achieve this. So, just know your mood and reaction will have a direct impact on the game," Robert said while the crowd roared its approval.

"So, are you all ready for some inReal ball?" Robert shouted, sending the crowd into a frenzy. "All right, let's get this party started. We've divided our forces into two squads. One in blue and one in red. Let's get everybody into the dome so we can begin."

The crowd rose to their feet as the red and blue teams entered the orb.

"I'm just as excited as all of you are about this game. As you can see, I'll be playing for the red team, and we are pleased to have the hometown hero, #epiccrotchshot boy himself, Mitch Mythic playing for the blue team," Robert said. He was met with another swell of applause.

"The blue team will be captained by Lieutenant Jordan Davis, a retired Navy Seal, and a decorated veteran. And the Red team is captained by Special Agent Natalie Babcock, formerly with the CIA. Let's give them a hand, as well as all the other members of the MindHIve security force," Robert said as the crowd cheered.

"I think I've talked enough. Just remember to cheer for red," Robert said amidst the roar of the crowd. Donning his helmet, he saluted the audience several times before he went through the opening at the bottom of the sphere.

Hovered among the blue players as they prepared to start the game, Mitch watched Robert Chapman pandering to the crowd. A scowl spread across his face as he watched the tyrannical CEO enter the dome.

"Just follow my instructions, Mythic. I don't want to see any hot-dogging like I saw earlier. You got me?" Davis said while he pushed past Mitch.

"I'll try my best," Mitch said as he followed the rest of the blue team into the orb.

"Everybody, get into position. Let's stick to our game plan, and everything should go well," Davis shouted while the blue and red teams took their positions. Mitch had listened to Davis's game plan in the dressing room, and it seemed to him that Davis was planning to lose the game. Their entire strategy was to sit back and let the red team attack. They had no plans for offense or any idea about how to score.

"Stay in your positions and play your game," Davis said. "They may have the bigger guns, but if we work together, we can shut them down."

The referee coasted to the center of the orb, carrying the ball of light in his hand. Encased in a purple sphere of his own, the time clock and the score of the game could be seen on its surface.

As He blew into a device on his fingers, a shrill whistle echoed around the dome and the orb changed its hue to a soft green. Placing the ball of light at the center of the sphere, the referee pulled back and blew into his whistle again. Davis came forward from the blue side, and Babcock came forward from the red side. Around the ball lay a translucent boundary line, and both players stopped at flashing markers opposite each other. When the referee blew his whistle, both players charged at the ball. The game was on.

Mitch stayed on the edge as he was told and watched the action unfold. The blue team was sticking to Davis's game plan, and they formed a defensive line as a red player shot toward the blue goal with the ball. Two blue players immediately attacked him, and they knocked the ball of light away. Babcock swooped in and batted the ball across the dome to Robert. The blue defenders were out of position, and Robert had a clear shot at the net. Mitch watched him saunter forward from his wing position. There was no way Mitch was going to let him walk in and score just like that. Darting in behind Robert as the CEO raised his arm to strike, Mitch lifted his paddle and stole the ball.

"You want to play that way, huh?" Robert shouted before Mitch batted the ball to one of his teammates and raced away.

Streaking down the wing, Mitch watched in anger while the ball carrier whacked the ball into the red zone and retreated to a defensive position. As the ball shot over the goal, it bounced off the wall and dropped to the base of the sphere.

From his position, Mitch was the closest to the ball, and he didn't hesitate to race after it. Scooping the ball up with his paddle, he saw a wall of defenders descending upon him. He pushed to the left before kicking up to get some space between himself and the defenders and looked for someone to pass to, but the blue players had fallen back to their defensive positions.

Without the support of his teammates, there wasn't much he could do. As More red players swarmed the ball he Mitch found himself ensnared by the opposition.

"What are you going to do, Mitch?" Robert sneered. "We got you surrounded. Now, why don't you just cough it up, so we don't have to beat it out of you."

You think I'm just going to roll over?"

"That's the idea. You're out of your league here. Do you think you can beat me at my own game?"

"That's right. I'm a kid, and I've played a lot of your games," Mitch said before he hit the ball as hard as he could right at Robert. The older man raised his paddle to block the ball, deflecting it up and to the left.

Shooting after the ball as the red players scrambled to react, Mitch scooped it up and raced toward the goal. Behind him, he could hear the red players coming after him as he closed in. With only the goalkeeper to beat, Mitch smashed the ball into the cube-shaped goal. A loud horn went off in the dome, and the crowd jumped to their feet.

"Ladies and gentlemen, we have just witnessed the first goal in a game of inReal and it was scored by #epiccrotchshot boy himself - Mitch Mythic!" An announcer said over the PA.

"CrotchShot, CrotchShot," the crowd chanted while the blue players charged toward Mitch and congratulated him.

"Nice shot, but this game ain't over yet. Stay in your position. You don't want to get burned," Davis said as they returned to the blue end.

"I'll try, but that was almost too easy," Mitch said as they made their way back to the blue end.

"Well, you pissed them off now. Chapman ain't the kind of guy to let something like that pass. You better keep your head up cause they're going to be gunning for you."

"let's just hope my teammates have my back should anything go down."

"Stick with the team, and we'll have your back, but if you think you can go it alone, you've got another thing coming, Mythic," Davis said before he positioned himself at center.

Returning to the wing, Mitch laughed to himself. Maybe he didn't stand a chance against them in a fight, but he could certainly show them a few moves they hadn't figured out yet.

As the referee reset the ball, Robert decided he would take the face-off instead of his captain and he entered the slot, squaring off against Davis.

Robert Chapman was actually a pretty big guy, and he seemed to be in good shape for a CEO. He fit right in with the brutish-looking thugs that made up the MindHIve security team.

The referee blew the whistle, and Robert charged at the ball. Even from a distance, Mitch could see the anger and intensity in his eyes.

Slamming into Davis, Robert wrestled the ball away from him and slapped the ball to Babcock, who had lined up against Mitch. As the lean-looking woman caught the ball and charged forward, her teammates surged behind, ready for the attack.

The blue defenders came forward to meet the onslaught of red, and Mitch was caught up amid a chaotic clash of bodies. Grunts and hollers could be heard everywhere while the roar of the crowd engulfed the action, driving the players into a deeper frenzy.

Reaching out to try to stop Babcock as she pounded her way through the blue defense, he was blindsided by a charging Robert Chapman. As they plummeted towards the bottom of the dome, Robert grabbed Mitch by the collar and slammed him into the wall.

"Do you really think you're fooling anyone, Mythic?" Robert said before he pushed off and rocketed back to the action above.

Righting himself, Mitch winced with pain and looked up just in time to see a red player knock the ball into the blue goal. The dome lit up again, and the crowd cheered wildly, sending waves of color cascading across the sphere.

34

In the dark, SoHee couldn't see what restrained her, but she felt electrodes pressing into her head, and an IV drip attached to her arm. Several strange looking instruments whirred and hummed on either side of her as their digital displays cast soft glows in darkness.

Feeling dizzy, she laid her head back down on the pillow. When she closed her eyes, the tremendous green tree-like entity hovered before her, energy pulsing in rhythmic waves. In a burst of light, she saw the central dome filled with people. The audience sat frozen in place. Shocked faces locked in stasis. Hovering in the center of the sphere, Mitch was surrounded on all sides by the security team and a sneering Robert Chapman.

She had to get out of that room. Those people were in great danger, and she knew if she didn't stop the CEO of MindHIve from carrying out his plan, the entire planet was in peril. Focusing on the energy pulsing between herself and the mass, she asked how she could get free of the restraints. The question was answered by a flash of light. Her physical body pulsed in sync with the rhythm of her counterpart. Concentrating on the energy, a sensation of weightlessness passed over her body.

On the other side of the complex, a team of bio-engineers stood before several monitors. Beyond the equipment, in a giant containment unit, the inReal infused mass of energy that had been SoHee's bacteria colony crackled and throbbed.

"These readings are off the charts," a woman wearing a lab coat said as her peers looked on. "It is sending out signals across the spectrum and at the same time drawing energy in. If we don't contain it, this thing is going to burst out of this unit in no time flat."

"Is it possible to drain energy away from it using some type of diffusion?" another scientist asked.

"It's possible, but we don't have any mechanism to drain that energy away. In my opinion, it would be best to use inReal to create a field around the tank. We could establish an energy barrier that would keep the subject contained while we come up with a better long-term solution," an older female scientist said.

"Are you nuts? This mutation is feeding off of the surrounding energy. If we try to use inReal to contain it, we'll just be throwing fuel onto the fire," a younger woman said.

"That may be true, but we're running out of time, and that thing is growing stronger by the second. In my opinion, we don't have any choice," the older woman said. "Unless we can come up with another solution right now, we'll have to go ahead with my plan."

"And what plan would that be?" a voice said from behind them. Turning around, they saw Gerald Tobero enter the lab.

"It seems to me this is a very serious security risk. Don't you think it would be wise to run it past me before you take further action?" Gerald said as he shot a hard look at the specimen in the tank.

"Of course, sir. We weren't about to go over your head on this, that's why we called you. We were just coming up with some plan of action. This whole thing is about to slip out of control. If we don't do something now, we'll run the risk of compromising the entire operation and endanger everybody in the vicinity," the older woman said.

"Very well. This entire situation is about to go sideways anyway, and we'll need the best minds we have to get it under control. I've brought a few security guards to assist you, should they be needed," Gerald said while several armed security guards emerged from the darkness with their inReal devices engaged.

"We're glad you're here to assist us. I'm worried this thing will breach the containment unit at any time," the older woman said.

"Let's see you carry out this plan. We're here to help, but I will step in and take command should the need arise," Gerald said.

"Understood, sir. Let's begin the connection. We'll be able to create an energy field using the laboratory's power generator and this inReal device," the older woman said, holding up a phone. "Sandra, can we calibrate the generator to produce a negative energy field?"

"I've already dialed it in," the younger woman said.

"You're going to need to hurry because this thing is multiplying like crazy. I don't know if we'll be able to contain it in time," a middle-aged male scientist said.

As the pulsing rhythm of the green orb accelerated the containment unit took on an otherworldly glow. Energy infused the beams holding the cell together, and the glass portals vibrated at an alarming rate.

"I've got the field ready. We'll just need to connect the unit," Sandra shouted while she typed commands into a control panel.

"Ready your containment prods. This is about to get interesting," Gerald commanded his team, and the security guards extended the large rods of light they used to contain the mass during the first incident.

"I'm about to make the connection. I'll just have to get close enough to establish contact," the older scientist shouted as a tumultuous roar of wind engulfed the lab. Holding the device in her hand, she struggled forward against the howling wind.

"The tank is about to blow," the middle-aged man shouted. "The levels are through the roof."

The security forces closed in as the older woman reached forward with the device. For a moment, the entire room went silent, and the pulses ceased.

"I think I can reach it," the scientist shouted. As she leaned forward, a tremendous explosion burst through the lab as the containment tank disintegrated. The orb hovered motionless for a second, assessing its surroundings.

Recovering from the blast, the security team climbed back on their feet. As they pushed forward, several arms shot out the orb and grabbed the guards. It raised the assailants into the air before tossing them in every direction.

"Seal the room," Gerald yelled out, but he was sent sprawling into a pile of debris as the orb shot past him and smashed through the door, leaving a trail of vapor behind it.

"The situation has escalated in the lab. Quarantine has been breached, and we're going to have to initiate emergency protocols," Gerald said, speaking into his device as he rose to his feet.

"Understood, sir. The game is on at the moment, and the broadcast is live. Should we inform Mr. Chapman?" A voice replied.

"I'll inform him myself," Gerald said. "Initiate the protocol. We need to lock this thing down. I want all of our resources focused on tracking that thing down. Get eyes and ears on it ASAP."

"Yes, sir," the voice said. "Initiating lockdown sequence as we speak."

"Send a team to the medical center. I think I know where that thing is headed," Gerald said while he headed for the door. "Get up and follow me. We have to contain this situation at all costs."

Roused from her trance, SoHee heard the muffled sound of men shouting and equipment being moved. As she opened her eyes, the reality of her situation hit her in the face. Lashed at the wrists and the ankles to a gurney, three bands extended over her torso and legs, making it impossible to move.

Outside, the shouting intensified, and SoHee saw several flashes of light erupt under the door. The men screamed and shouted while the light under the door grew stronger. A strange whooshing sound swallowed up the voices before several heavy thumps, and crashes filled the air.

Seeping through the wall, pulses of energy washed over her body in calming waves. As the door slid open, the room was filled with an intense light. Tentacles of light reached through the doorway and loosened the straps holding her down.

After the last belt dropped to the ground, she rolled off of the bed and fell to her knees. Raising her head, she felt the presence of the glowing sphere hovering before her.

Several branches of light reached out from the orb and raised her into the air. She hovered before the ball as pulses of light moved over her, quickening until they fused into a solid beam. Imbued with light, an intense burst of energy engulfed the room. Shed dropped to the ground after the light subsided and looked at the green orb for a moment before a slight smile spread across her lips.

More voices filled the hall as back up security personnel hurried in to corral and contain whatever they had been told was on the loose in the medical center.

As the soldiers approached, SoHee reached forward, and the orb wrapped itself around her. Raising her arms in front of herself, she watched as appendages of light wrapped around her form.

"I think it's time we showed them what we've been up to while we were away," she said before she shot out of the room.

Paul Ormond

35

The first half of the game had stacked up to the hype. Locked at one goal each, neither team managed to get an edge in play after the opening flurry of goals. Robert had certainly stacked the teams in his favor, having placed the faster and flashier players on the red side, but Davis, fully aware of the imbalance, managed to get the most out of his squad by focusing on a team effort and a commitment to defense.

Mitch, for his part, held his own against his larger and older opponents. Although he wasn't a match for them strength-wise, he used his speed and agility to give himself an edge over his opponents. Having electrified the audience with his daring moves earlier in the game, the crowd roared with approval every time he touched the ball; however, after scoring the first goal, the red defenders caught onto his abilities, and they swarmed him whenever he attempted anything threatening. He had been knocked hard a few times, but he hadn't let it get to him. In spite of Robert's comments at the bottom of the orb and all the anxiety festering in his guts, he had to admit he was actually enjoying himself.

As Mitch returned to his right wing position, the crowd was on their feet and cheering. Although Davis had rebuked Mitch at the start of the game, at halftime the consensus in the blue locker room was to form their attacks with Mitch's speed in mind.

After winning the face-off to start the second half, Davis slotted the ball to the opposite wing, and Mitch took the pass as his cue. Darting towards the bottom of the dome, he was immediately followed by two red defenders who dogged him all the way to the bottom.

"Where are you running to, Mythic?" one player jeered as he gave chase.

"You better keep moving, or you're going to get epic crushed, crotchshot boy," the other player said while they stayed hot on his heels.

Slowing down as they closed in, he dodged to the left and pushed off the wall of the sphere. The defenders weren't expecting him to bounce back so quickly, and they watched in shock as he rocketed past them towards the red goal.

As the left winger drew the red defenders to him, Mitch looked up and saw Davis rushing toward the center of the dome. The winger lobbed the ball back at Davis, and the defense pivoted toward him, unaware Mitch was shooting up from the bottom of the sphere. Robert saw him at the last second and charged forward as Davis blasted the ball to Mitch. Just before Robert made contact, Mitch one-timed the ball past the sprawling goaltender and into the red net. He and Robert tumbled away from the goal as the dome exploded with color and cheers.

"I hope you've enjoyed yourself, Mythic, because things are about to get a little more intense. Remember, you're in my world, and I make the rules," Robert said after he and Mitch untangled themselves.

"You don't think I can handle it, old man? If you thought I was just going to roll over and take it, then you've got another thing coming. You want to raise the stakes then bring it on," Mitch said before he made his way back to the blue zone. Hearing Robert's voice again, he looked back, and he saw the CEO speaking to somebody using inReal voice connect.

"Breached?" Robert asked. "I thought you had this under control? Initiate lock down immediately and damn the feed. Tell them it's just technical difficulties. Lock it down now."

Mitch went back to his position and waited for the game to start, but something was off. The dome had grown quiet and the massive sphere lost its colorful notations. Looking out at the audience, he saw the crowd frozen in place, vacant expressions occupied their faces.

A flash of panic shot up his spine as every player in the dome fixated their attention on him. The inReal glow that encased them had changed from blue to a fiery orange.

"You must be wondering what's happening now, aren't you, Mitch?" Robert said from behind him. Whirling around to face his opponent, Mitch found the CEO hovering just a few feet away, enshrouded in an orange glow identical to the other soldiers.

"We've had a security breach. It appears somebody has broken out of quarantine. You wouldn't know anything about that, would you, Mitch? Of course not, you're just a kid that has no idea what's going on here. We've had your friend Drak staying with us for a few days now, but I'm sure you don't know anything about that either. Don't worry. He didn't spill the beans or anything. He's a loyal friend, and that's a rare thing in this world or any world for that matter, isn't that right?" Robert said as he stared Mitch down.

The security team closed in on his position, and the dome was sealed shut from the outside.

"Your friend SoHee hasn't put up much of a fuss, though. She's been a model patient. I look forward to keeping her onboard. She'll make a great asset to my team. Her scientific abilities are incredible, and it looks like that stuff she made will be of great benefit to humanity. As you can see, we've taken some precautionary measures and initiated a complex wide lockdown. This is for everybody's safety, of course. Anybody using a MindHIve issued device should be in stasis at this point," Robert said while he looked directly at Mitch. "The odd thing is, you were issued a MindHIve device, but here you are fully lucid and glaring back at me with your supple brown eyes. The team and I have security clearances that have kept us active, and we've all switched over to our weaponized systems, hence the orange aura. The last time I checked, you didn't have any security clearance at all. Do you mind explaining why you, of all people, managed to be spared from the lockdown?"

Frozen with fear, Mitch didn't respond.

"Don't worry. I know you are too tough to talk. Nobody can break a guy like you. I mean, you've survived being the laughingstock of the internet. After that, you can probably put up with anything. Now, I've got a hunch you've got what we like to call in the industry a 'jailbroken' phone. I'm pretty sure this jailbroken phone is pretty special to you. So special I bet you'd be willing to do almost anything for it, but it can't be as special as your freedom. I bet Drak told you all about those big bad guys coming for him. There's not much I can do for your friend, but I'd certainly be able to help you out if you are willing to cooperate. So why don't you hand over the device, and we can sort everything out? I'll have you back in your mommy's arms in no time, and this will all be over like a bad dream," Robert said.

"What if I give it to you?" Mitch said. "What happens to me?"

"We will do everything we can to protect you. Nobody knows anything. You just hand it over, and it will all go away. I promise,"

Robert said as he cautioned the other soldiers to hang back. "You're a smart kid, and what you did today was beyond impressive. You're the first star player in the brand new game of inReal ball. The feedback we've gotten from the media after the first half has been magnificent and you were the first name off of everybody's lips. Let's end this insanity, and I'll make you a star."

Mitch gulped hard and looked around. He heard a sound from behind him, and he whirled around to see a MindHIve soldier reaching for him from behind.

"Get him," Robert shouted as the guards closed in.

Balling himself up, he shoved upward, sending a shock wave of energy in every direction. The soldiers were knocked backward by the blast as Mitch rocketed to the top of the sphere.

The soldiers recovered quickly, and a wave of blue and red swarmed towards Mitch. Holding out his right arm, a broad blade extended along his limb. He knew he didn't stand a chance against those brutes, but if he was going down, he was going down fighting.

Pushing off the top of the sphere, he dropped onto the oncoming soldiers and he was met by a volley of fire. As he dodged the onslaught, he shielded himself and narrowed in on the first attacker in range. The soldier had his shield engaged, but he wasn't prepared for a close range attack. Charging forward, Mitch undercut the guard with his sword, sending him reeling to the edge of the sphere.

After cutting through the ranks of MindHIve soldiers with several large slashes, he hit the opposite wall and spun around. Regrouping with Robert, the security force closed ranks and pushed across the sphere. They extended their containment rods as they approached, and it looked like the plan was to capture him alive.

Steeling himself, he pushed forward, ready to face his fate, but a tremendous explosion tore through the dome before he got the chance.

Recovering from the blast, Mitch watched in awe as a massive green orb burst through the hole in the floor of the dome where the explosion had occurred. Rising into the air, it hovered for a moment at the same height as the soldiers. Mitch could clearly see a feminine figure at the center of the orb.

"It looks like the situation has made its way here," Robert said into his voice connect. "Send all forces to the main dome now."

After a brief pause, the green orb rotated end over end at a slow rate while several long claw like appendages extended out from its surface. In a flash, its claws cut into the enormous sphere hovering before it.

Pushing through the gap, it sent it out blasts of light knocking the soldiers backward.

"Fire on that thing. Don't back down," Robert shouted before he glanced over his shoulder and spotted Mitch clinging to the far wall. "Davis, you've got Beta. Babcock, take Alpha. Give it everything you've got. I'm going to contain our other problem."

As the MindHIve security team fired upon SoHee in all directions, she was able to defend against the onslaught using a shield system produced by the orb. Whirling the claw-like appendages around her, she struck out at the scrambling soldiers retreating from her wrath.

After pulling away from the raging limbs tearing into the dome, Davis and Babcock re-organized their teams into a collective shield.

"Gunners, get in position. We need to hit it with the big ones now. That thing is only getting stronger. Don't forget your training. We can hold this thing off if we stick together," Davis shouted as the four assigned gunners fabricated large inReal guns that they extended through the shielded wall of soldiers.

"Fire when ready. Let's see how she handles the heavy stuff," Davis ordered, and a firestorm erupted from the guns, sending SoHee reeling backward.

Across the sphere, Robert closed in on Mitch. With his shield drawn and his sword hanging at his side, he circled near the young kid who hadn't moved since the green orb cut through the sphere.

"I know you're probably scared, and that's ok, but I can still help you if you are willing to cooperate. It's not too late, Mitch," Robert said.

"It's not too late for me. That's true," Mitch said as he pushed off of the wall. "But it's too late for you. I know what you're up to, and there is no way I'm going to let you get away with it."

"Oh, #epiccrotchshot boy knows everything, does he? Look, just put the sword away before you get hurt. You're confused, and a terrorist has told you a bunch of lies. Don't make me do anything I'll regret later," Robert said while he extended his sword in front of him.

"Let's just see who the liar is," Mitch said before he shot at Robert with his blade raised. Robert backed up defensively as Mitch swung out and caught his shield.

"Is that all you got?" Robert said as he brought his sword down upon Mitch.

"I've got all kinds of tricks up my sleeve," Mitch said, dodging Robert's attack.

"You've figured it all out, haven't you, Mitch?" Robert said while they circled each other. "You're the guy that's going to defeat the evil just like all those movies you've watched and games you've played, but remember I'm the guy that pays people to make that nonsense and here's why we make them: to give people hope. Now, I'm going to tell you something that might shock you, but, there is no hope, never has been. The powerful will always triumph over the weak, and you will never defeat me."

"We'll see about that," Mitch said before he struck at Robert again.

Recovering from the initial attack from the larger guns, SoHee pushed all of her shield energy into the direction of the fortification. The shots kept coming, but she was able to take the blasts with minimal damage. Several long appendages extended from her orb as she closed in on the fortified soldiers. Lobbing giant balls of fire upon their shields, she forced her assailants back to the wall of the sphere.

"Prepare to split just as we practiced," Davis shouted while the green orb bore down upon their position. "Babcock, take Alpha company and circle around from behind. Beta company, stay with me we're going to continue to draw her fire."

"Keep it distracted. We'll try to find an opening," Babcock shouted at Davis before Alpha team broke away and maneuvered around the green orb reaching out to consume them.

"Do you really think you'll be able to escape, and everything will go back to normal, Mitch?" Robert shouted at Mitch as they continued to exchange blows. "Best-case scenario is you admit your friend and his cult brainwashed you and you'll probably get a light sentence because you're a kid. I imagine you'll be out of jail before you're 30." '

"Wait until they hear what you've done," Mitch said as he deflected Robert's strike and counterattacked with a slash at his opponents thigh.

"What exactly is it I have done, Mitch? Aside from being one of the greatest innovators of all time and elevating humanity to near impossible levels," Robert said, avoiding Mitch's sword.

"You've sold us down the river, or more like across the universe," Mitch said while he dodged to his right.

"Is that so? Who told you that? Your friend, the terrorist?" Robert said with a laugh before launching into an attack. "Did Drak tell you the Masters are going to enslave us all, and we don't stand a chance? If you haven't figured it out already, Mitch, I'll lay it out for you nice and clear. You already are a slave. You always have been a slave, and you always will be a slave. Your father was a slave and so was his father and your children will be slaves as well."

"Well, you'll be a slave too. The Masters will turn you into a lap dog if that isn't what you are already," Mitch snapped back and knocked the older man backward.

"Well, it looks like you've thought of everything, haven't you, Mitch?" Robert replied through gritted teeth. "Now that you've figured everything out, you can sing it from the mountaintop. I'm sure everybody will believe #epiccrotchshot boy's grand conspiracy theory about inter-dimensional slave masters and the evil CEO of MindHIve. The thing is, Mitch, nothing is quite what it seems. If you think I was foolish enough to enter into an agreement with a bunch of creepy aliens, then you are dumber than you look, and that's pretty dumb, all things considered."

"Say what you want, but I didn't sell out the human race," Mitch said while he slashed at Robert's side before pushing himself up to the top of the sphere to gain some space. As he shot away, he saw an incredible scene playing out on the other side of the sphere.

A heavy barrage of fire pummeled SoHee from both sides while she attempted to dismantle the shields of the security guards. She appeared to be holding her own, but Mitch could see she was outgunned and outnumbered. Glancing beneath his feet, he saw Robert charging up at him. Mitch pushed off of the wall of the sphere with his sword raised. Just as Robert was about to reach him, Mitch darted to the left, causing Robert to stumble in mid-air. Swiveling around the larger man, he brought his sword down across his opponents back, sending him spinning head over heels to the bottom of the sphere.

Mitch didn't waste any time watching Robert tumble away. As he Rocketed toward SoHee, he spotted Davis commanding a squadron of shielded soldiers. Blasting at the guards from behind, their shield collapsed under his attack and they scrambled across the dome in an attempt to recover from the ambush. In the melee, he spotted Davis attempting to escape. Pulling up his sword, he darted towards the soldier and struck him across the shoulder. Davis was knocked toward the opposite wall, and Mitch saw the look of disbelief on the soldier's face while he spun away.

SoHee was still under fire from the other squad, and Mitch rushed to join her, but as he did, he saw reinforcements flooding the entrances of the dome.

"Nice of you to pop in," Mitch shouted at SoHee.

"I figured you could use a hand. Besides, I needed somewhere to stretch out. Quarantine was getting a little stuffy," SoHee hollered over the din.

"I see you made a new friend," Mitch shouted before he sent a volley of fire at the shielded squadron.

"It's more like an old friend," SoHee said while she shot a blast of her own.

"And where would we be without our friends?" Mitch said while a surge of guards piled into the sphere, fresh and ready for the fight.

"Come to me. My shield will protect you," Sohee screeched.

"Any chance we'll get out of here?" Mitch said while he shot to her side.

"Uh, I might have a few tricks up my sleeve, but it looks like we better act fast. This place is starting to get crowded," SoHee shouted.

"You don't need to convince me," Mitch said. "If you've got a plan, now would be the time."

As the dome filled with re-enforcements, Mitch looked around and his heart sank. It was over, and there was no escape. They had fought hard, but defeat was inevitable. Maybe Robert was right. If they surrendered, the authorities would probably go easier on them, Mitch thought to himself while they were bombarded by fire. But just as the attack reached its crescendo, it stopped. The soldiers had ceased firing, and Mitch looked around in disbelief before he saw the mass of soldiers part to let Robert through.

"Well, look at this lovely little couple," Robert said after he stopped a few meters away from Mitch and SoHee. "There ain't nothing quite as cute as two kids falling in love at summer camp, isn't that right fellas? You two lovebirds sure have caused us a lot of headaches. I hope you had your fill because it looks like this is the end of the road. As far as I can tell, you've got two options: Shut it down and go quietly, or we'll light the two of you up like the 4th of July."

"There's just a couple of things I want to know before it's over," Mitch said. "What's it all for? What's the point of doing all this? Where does it get you?"

"Oh Mitch, you can't go and get all esoteric on me now. Not in front of the guys anyway," Robert sneered, and the soldiers all laughed. "There's only one thing that matters in this whole world, and that's power. Whoever has the power makes the rules. The world needs powerful people to make the rules, so everything functions well. Without guys like me, you and your people would all be living in caves and eating rats."

"So it's about you and your power trip? Well, isn't that just typical? I hope you've got what you wanted. How does it feel to be the guy that sold the world?" Mitch said before raising his voice so that everybody could hear. "I bet Robert Chapman hasn't told you guys what's actually going on. You'll find out soon enough when you're in chains too."

"Mitch, I hope you realize how silly you sound when you talk like that. This is why nobody will believe anything you say. You sound like all the other lunatics on the Internet ranting about conspiracy theories. What makes you think anybody will believe a word you say. By tomorrow morning, you'll be the most famous terrorist in the western world and your story will confirm the fact that you are completely unhinged. You'll be buried in a federal prison where you'll spend the rest of your days battling off rapists and killing cockroaches. Or you can come out now, and everything will be ok," Robert said.

The room fell silent once again. Mitch could feel the glares of the soldiers as they hovered nearby. Beyond the security forces and the sphere, Mitch could make out the faces of the people in the crowd. Frozen in place, their dead eyes stared back at Mitch.

As ripples of light reflected off the soldiers' masks, he turned around to find SoHee immersed in a great ball of light. Several more pulses sent shock waves through the dome, forcing the guards backward.

"Concentrate all your fire on that girl," Robert hollered. "She's going to blow this place up."

As the soldiers opened fire, SoHee raised her hands above her head, and the light around her grew in intensity. Screaming as she brought her hands down, the dome was rocked by an explosion of light and sound. Mitch felt his stomach drop as the light consumed everything around him.

36

Still clutching his head, Mitch found himself crouching in an empty blackness. As he peeled his hands off his head, his eyes adjusted to the dark, and he realized he stood in a rocky tunnel. In the distance, he spotted a source of light reflecting off a pool of water.

A chill washed over him, and he felt a cold breeze blowing up the tunnel from the opposite direction of the light. Flipping the visor on his helmet up, he moved toward the light.

The cave opened up further ahead, and a familiar green hue accented the glow. Mitch was not surprised to see SoHee sitting on a rock surrounded by her orb of light as he entered a large cavern.

"Is this what you meant by a trick up your sleeve?" Mitch asked when she saw him approaching.

"Maybe, but I'm not exactly sure what happened," she said after she hopped off the rock. "Where is this place?"

"I think we're in the mines underneath Kingsford, but I'm not entirely sure. There is a network of caves that have been here for centuries, but they haven't been fully explored," Mitch said as he sat down.

"I had no idea," SoHee said.

"Well, there's obviously a lot we don't know," Mitch, with a laugh. "How come none of this is surprising to me right now? This is the new normal for me, I guess - absolute insanity. A few weeks ago, I was the laughingstock of the internet, and now I'm lost in a cave with Miss Science, and we're both fugitives from the law. That is just typical."

"Do you think this is funny?"

"I don't know what it is, but I'm laughing, anyway. If you had any idea what I've been through in the last while, you'd laugh too. Actually, what am I talking about? I'm telling you about my insane life, and you're sitting here a million miles from home with your magical goo ball best friend - yes, absolute insanity."

"I saw your friend. He's in trouble,"

"Which friend? Oh, you mean Drak. Where did you see him? Was he locked up with you? He's the reason we're all in this mess. Well, it's not really his fault, but if not for him, none of us would be here. Oh, it's a long story. Of course, he's in danger, they've got him," Mitch felt himself babbling away, and he could see the look of confusion on SoHee's face as he spoke.

"There are others coming, terrible things," SoHee said. "We're all in danger."

"How do you know this? Did you talk to Drak?"

"I've seen it."

"What do you mean 'seen it'?'"

"This stuff lets me see all kinds of things, and it showed me horrible images of what may come and what has happened. I saw Robert Chapman opening a giant gateway or portal, and I saw massive metal figures entering our world. They handed your friend over to them, to the monsters, and they took him away."

"So, you've seen these Masters in your visions?" Mitch said, laughing in spite of himself.

"This is no joke. Why are you laughing?" SoHee said in dismay.

"I'm sorry. It's just that I've heard it all before. Hearing you say it means I'm not crazy, and all of this is really happening."

"It is really happening, and that's what frightens me. The things I've seen are horrible."

"You don't have to convince me. I've already been down the rabbit hole. I just have no idea what we're supposed to do about it."

"We have to stop them."

"Yeah, sure, but how? Chapman has an entire army backing him up. He's probably going around telling everybody we are terrorists too. The whole world is most likely hunting us down as we speak. If we ever get out of this cave, we'll probably spend the rest of our days rotting away in some black site."

"We can stop them. I have seen it."

"Oh, the oracle has spoken. I'm sorry I forgot about your magical powers. How do you propose we stop them? I know you've got your friend and I've got my ...," Mitch stopped talking and patted himself

until he found his phone. He pulled it out and then frowned.
"Oh great, it's dead."

"Don't lose hope," SoHee said as the orb fluttered behind her. "All is not lost. Let me see your phone for a moment."

"Yeah sure, but unless you've got charging station in there, I'm straight out of luck."

Mitch stopped talking as he watched SoHee turn around and face her glowing mass. A beam of light reached out from the orb and took his device. The sphere placed the phone into its core, and a flash of light blasted the cavern walls. As quickly as it happened the orb handed back the phone and SoHee, in turn, handed it over to Mitch.

A brief smile flashed across his face as she returned it to him, but he frowned again and sat down deep in thought. The cavern grew silent save for some water dripping into a shallow pool.

"First of all, we've got to figure out where we are. Can't your thingy do some kind of thing and whisk us out of here?" Mitch asked, breaking the silence. "What happened up there, anyway? I thought we were dead for sure, and then that thing did whatever it did, and now we're here."

"From what I've been able to understand, the orb created a temporary wormhole, and it sent us here."

"Ha, that thing can make wormholes too. Well, I guess that shouldn't be surprising."

"I still don't understand why you are laughing."

"I'm not laughing. Well, I'm laughing, but I'm not laughing because I think it is funny. I guess I'm laughing because I don't know what else I am supposed to do. Do you think it could wormhole us out of here? Actually, don't, they'll find us in a heartbeat. We need to get out of here manually and go find help. Can your thing just tell us where we are?"

"Just give me a second," SoHee said, and she closed her eyes. Pulses exchanged between her and the orb, and after a few seconds, she opened her eyes again. A holographic 3D map appeared before the sphere. "It appears you were correct. We are directly underneath the city. There's a way out at the opposite end of the cavern."

"That's crazy," Mitch said while he peered at the map of their location. "Hey, can you zoom out a bit?"

"I think so," SoHee said before she closed her eyes again. The image expanded to reveal a wide swathe of the area.

"No way. We're right beside the Pits. That's pretty funny," Mitch said.

"What are the Pits?" SoHee asked.

"It's a Kingsford thing," Mitch said with a laugh. "What else did the orb tell you?"

"It also says there is a lot of action happening deep underground, and it appears to be connected to the MindHIve complex. A massive energy field is active beneath us."

"The portal. They are going to open the gateway. Drak really is in trouble, and so are we. We need to get moving. Time is running out, and we're going to need some help if we want to stop all of this from happening. And with your thingy, I think I know how."

"Who do you think will help us? We can't go to the authorities."

"Yeah, the cops are out, but, I think I know a few guys that can lend a hand," Mitch said before he walked toward the other end of the cavern. "Come on. Let's go save the world."

37

"What exactly happened during the game to cause a blackout? Some are saying this situation is slipping out of control," a reporter shouted out.

"I would say the notion that our little convention is slipping out of control is preposterous," Robert said from behind a podium while he stood for questions before a large group of reporters and television cameras. "We've had a few hiccups, but that's to be expected when you take on something as bold as what we are doing. MindHIve is a company that takes great leaps forward, and in doing so, one must anticipate a bit of collateral damage along the way."

"But you still haven't addressed what happened during the blackout, and where are the missing attendants?" another reporter shouted out.

"That was a simple power surge brought about by an overload on the system, but we've been able to solve the problem. Like I said earlier, we're working out the kinks and over all the convention has been a tremendous success." Robert said with his trademark charm.

"Where are Mitch Mythic and SoHee Moon? Why all the secrecy surrounding their whereabouts?" A reporter shouted from the back.

"Miss Moon is safe and sound in our medical complex recovering from a bio-shock scare caused by some reckless material handling. She will be fine, and once she is out of quarantine, you'll have a chance to talk with her. I spoke with her a few hours ago, and she was in good spirits. As for Mitch Mythic, he was injured during the surge, and he is recovering as well. He had an amazing game, and we sure are excited about his future. In the meantime, I think everybody needs to stop worrying and pay attention to the all the good things happening all around us at this convention. We are not running some prison camp, nor do we have some diabolical plan to take over the world. MindHIve is committed to bringing the greatest technological innovations to the people of this planet, and our conference only adds more weight to that statement," Robert said as flashes popped all around him.

"What about the mother of the girl? She is hysterical, and she wants to see her daughter. It has turned into a diplomatic nightmare that the president is about to weigh in on," a reporter shouted.

"Of course SoHee's mother should be concerned about her daughter's well-being, and I can understand why she would be upset, but we have quarantine regulations in place to ensure the safety of everybody within the complex. It's unfortunate Miss Moon was exposed as she was, but accidents happen and luckily nobody got hurt. We are simply taking the necessary precautions to prevent any large-scale disaster and to understand the nature of the substance in question. I can assure all of you here and anybody watching at home SoHee is unhurt, and she will be released from quarantine as soon as possible," Robert said.

"What is the substance you are speaking about? Strange reports are circulating on the internet," another reporter shouted out.

"For now, that will remain classified," Robert said while maintaining his cool.

"People are reporting they experienced blackouts and loss of memory during the supposed energy surge. Can you elaborate on what happened during that time?" someone shouted from the throng of media huddled before Robert.

"The power surge created an unstable environment for the inReal program, and we implemented security measures to, once again, ensure the safety of all involved. I understand there is a great deal of speculation and hearsay whipping up controversy all over the internet, but these reports should be seen for what they are: hysterical reactions and ridiculous conspiracy theories. I'm surprised I have to answer these kinds of questions. Any reporter of substance would have thrown these notions out the window as soon as they crossed their desk. I've read all kinds of ridiculous things on my MindHIve feed. 'We're planning to enslave the planet' and all of this nonsense. It's unbelievable people would suggest such a thing. With that in mind, I think I'm done answering questions. Tomorrow is another big day, and I'm certain we will be seeing even more incredible developments as this convention continues."

Robert walked off of the stage as the cameras continued to flash, and reporters shouted more questions. He smiled and waved once more before two security guards ushered him out the door.

"Ughh, the things I've got to put up with," Robert said after the door closed behind him.

"You handled it beautifully, sir. I'm always impressed with how you stuff it to the media," Allan said as he followed Robert down a long hallway, making sure to stay just a little behind and to the right.

"There's no reason to go brown-nosing right now, Allan. Just keep your head down and know your place. You'll get recognition when you deserve it. In the meantime, get me a new towel. This thing is soaked," Robert said before he tossed a wet towel at Allan.

"Will you be retiring for the evening, sir?" Allan asked as he handed the towel off to a young man wearing a blue MindHIve shirt.

"Indeed, I will Allan, but I've got a couple of calls to make before I do. It's a never-ending battle when you're at the top. Play your cards right, and maybe one day you'll find yourself up to your elbows in idiots like I am," Robert said with a laugh.

"Understood, sir. Is there anything else I can do for you?" Allan asked.

"You can get out of my face with that cat food breath. I thought I told you to get some gum or something," Robert snapped while he approached a closed door. A security panel scanned his face, and the door slid open. "That will be enough for tonight, Allan. Thank you very much."

As the door whisked shut, he walked down a short hallway and stepped into the captain's quarters, his temporary home away from home. Throwing his device onto the table, he made a sweeping gesture to activate his inReal. As the panel came to life, an orange banner flashed indicating he had an incoming call. He pressed the button and frowned as the video came up.

"Hello Daddy," two children chimed as the video call connected.

"Everybody wave to Daddy," a woman's voice said before Robert's wife peered into the camera alongside the children. "We love you and we miss you."

"Hey guys," Robert said with a grin. "Who wants to see Daddy?"

"We do," a boy and a girl said.

"When are you coming home, Daddy?" the older boy asked.

"I'll be home soon. Daddy has more work to do, son," Robert said.

"How are you doing, honey? You've been all over the news. People are saying crazy things," his wife asked.

"I thought I told you not to believe what you see on TV. Isn't that right, sport?" Robert said, while looking at his son. "Do you think your daddy is a big bad meanie?"

"Yeah, you're a big bad guy," his daughter said.

"That's right I am, and when I get home, I'm going to get you," he said as the children squealed with laughter.

"Robert, honey, we talked about scaring the children. It interferes with their therapy," his wife said.

"Sure thing honey, but they'd better watch it, or the big bad meanie is going to get them," Robert shouted into the camera.

"Robert, what are you doing?" his wife shouted.

"Oh, lighten up, Darlene. They could use a good scare. The way you coddle them is doing more harm than good, you know. Daddy's got to go do more work. I'll call you guys when I have some time. Love you," Robert said before he ended the call.

Letting out a sigh, he stripped off his red uniform. After showering and changing into a suit, he placed the inReal device on the ground and raised his hands over his head. As the orange orb rose into the air, he bowed low and waited for an answer.

"Rise, my dear Robert," Commander Holrathu said as his face came into focus.

"Greetings, Commander. It is always a pleasure to speak with you," Robert said.

"I hear you're having some difficulty. Is this anything we should be concerned about?"

"Not at all, sir. We've had a couple of hiccups, but as you well know, these kinds of things are to be expected. Everything is on schedule and under control. The portal opening tomorrow will go off without any problems. I assure you."

"The Emperor is counting on you to fulfill his wishes. Opening the portal on schedule and delivering our most sought after fugitive will grant you considerable favor with his Royal Highness, should you succeed. However, you are aware of the consequences of failure. The Emperor does not take kindly to those who displease him. It is in your best interest to do more than assure me everything will go well. From my perspective, your position doesn't bode well. It appears you have encountered a minor insurrection. The individuals in question must be apprehended and dealt with accordingly. This is no laughing matter. Even the most trivial insubordination must be dealt with severely, or there is no telling where it will end."

"Understood, sir. I will not let you down. The prisoner transfer will go ahead as scheduled, and our little problem will be dealt with accordingly."

"Very well. I've provided you with a new upgrade for your device. Master Sinisur used this development to squash a rebellion on a system in a different age, and we have continued to use it whenever we encounter resistance. May the 'Fists of Sinisur', grant you the strength to crush all who would stand in the way of the Emperor's will."

"I gratefully accept the Emperor's gift, and I am forever indebted to his Royal Highness. I will not let you down," Robert said before he bowed low before the commander.

"We have put our faith in you, Robert. Do not disappoint the Emperor. Contact us as soon as you are ready to open the portal," Commander Holrathu said to Robert and then ended the call.

"Thank you very much, Commander," Robert said. "'The Fists of Sinisur', I like the sound of that. I think I'm going to have some fun crushing this little insubordination."

38

"Do you think you can turn your thing off?" Mitch asked SoHee as they neared the exit to the cave. "They can track us and it's pretty bright. We don't want any undue attention."

"I can easily contain it," she said, making a few gestures with her hand. The orb fluttered for a moment before shuttering in on itself. As it packed down, it formed a thin ring and SoHee placed it around her neck, unobtrusive as a piece of jewelry.

"Not bad. That thing's pretty smart. What are you going to call it? Have you thought of a name?" Mitch asked.

"I didn't think about naming it. I haven't really had time."

"Yeah, it's been a little busy."

The cave opened up at the base of a hill shrouded in pine trees. Stepping out into the night air, they assessed their surroundings.

"We need to head this way," Mitch said, turning to the left. Bright moonbeams poured through the knotted limbs of the pine tress, lighting their way through the forest.

"If your map is correct, then I think I know exactly where we are. And if I'm right, the guys who are going to help us out should be hanging out nearby. It's Friday night in Kingsford, and there's only one place to go," Mitch said before he stepped under a clump of brush.

"Is there a nightclub nearby? It seems like we're in the middle of the forest, but I can hear music," SoHee asked.

"Well, it's the Kingsford equivalent of a nightclub," Mitch said while holding back a branch for SoHee. "Did you ever in your life think you would be doing something like this?"

"Stalking in the woods at night or taking on a massive corporation and their inter-dimensional overlords?" SoHee asked with a straight face.

"Ha, very true. I was thinking about something Drak told me before he left," Mitch said, stepping over a rock. "The generator runs on what he called 'dark energy.' To stop it, we needed to send a surge of 'positive energy' to its core. If we do that, we might cause a massive explosion that could destroy everything. I don't really understand it myself, but he said there is some kind of special material inside the generator that allows it to produce the wormhole. Apparently, the whole reason they came here was to tap into the energy field underneath Kingsford. I guess it's really strong, or they can get at it easily through the mines. Either way, there is enough energy here to power the generator, but once it is opened it's incredibly fragile, and any interference will cause it to collapse. If we can send a surge at the right moment, we'll be able to destroy it."

"Your friend may have been on to something, but I think your interpretation is a little off. As the theory goes, wormholes require some kind of exotic material to power them. This is only a theory. No scientist has ever found a wormhole in space, nor do we know what exactly the exotic material would be. The Masters may be using some type of matter we don't know about to power their generator. We could create a positive energy bomb using my 'thingy,' but there are two problems with this plan. One: How do we plant the bomb? Two: What do we do when it explodes?" SoHee asked.

"Well, it's a good thing you are along for the ride, Miss Science," Mitch said, stepping around a large tree. "If we know where to deliver the payload, I can sneak in and drop it as long as there is enough time to get out. This might sound a little crazy, but is it possible for you to do your little wormhole trick again and throw the generator inside? A wormhole for a wormhole."

"It's possible, but I've only ever done that once, and I don't even know how I did it. Even if I could, there's no telling where it will end up," SoHee said. "It almost seems suicidal."

"Perhaps, but at this point, I'm not sure if we have much of a choice. Get blown up or become slaves forever," Mitch said. "The one thing I do know about all of this inReal stuff is this: If you believe you can do it, then it becomes possible. If you believe you can create the wormhole and you believe you can send the generator to where it can't hurt anybody, then you can. Didn't you say that you saw images of what may come? What did those visions say about this?"

"From what I remember, there was a tremendous battle and a lot of destruction, but it's a little vague."

"Do we win, or are we sucked get sucked past the event horizon?"

"I only saw what I understood to be possibilities. In some situations, we survive. In others, we don't."

"Maybe we can ask your 'thing' when we get another chance. We're almost there."

Up ahead, a clearing was visible through the tree line, and firelight lit up the night sky. Voices shouted into the night, and music filled the air. As they approached the edge of the clearing, a wide pit of rocks and sand came into view. In the center, a crowd of kids gathered around a fire.

"Welcome to Kingsford pits," Mitch said with a laugh as he made his way down the steep bank. Half way down, he looked up to see SoHee standing motionless at the top of the cliff.

"Come on, it's ok, they won't bite, well not much anyway" Mitch said, holding out his hand to help her down. "You already took on the entire MindHIve security force. Don't tell me you're scared of a bunch of teenagers?"

Descending the steep bank, they caused enough of a commotion that gathering at the fire took notice. As Mitch walked up to the party, a deathly silence hung over the gravel pit.

"What are you doing here, Mythic?" came a familiar voice. The crowd parted to reveal Sage Rhinus standing beside Candace McAllister. For a moment, the only sound that could be heard was the fire crackling in the warm summer night.

"Everybody, the great and amazing Mitch Mythic has decided to grace us with his presence, and it looks he's brought a friend," Sage said with a sneer. "To what do we owe the honor?"

"I didn't come here to fight, Sage," Mitch said. "We need your help. We need all of your help."

"Oh, you need our help, do you?" Sage snapped back. "We all saw you on TV, Mister Superstar. Nice suit, by the way."

"I never wanted any of this," Mitch said. "The last few months of my life have been a living hell and the people I needed to have my back became my enemies. I wouldn't wish that on anybody. You guys all laughed about #epiccrotchshot, but I lived it and a lot more. That's not even the half of it. Because of that video, I've been dragged into something bigger than all of us, bigger than anything you could even imagine."

"Yeah, celebrity is a real drag isn't it?" Sage said. "This is the wrong place to come and complain about how hard it is being famous."

"That's not what I'm here for," Mitch said, so that all could hear. "Something terrible is about to happen. We're all in danger, but together, we can stop it."

"Oh, this is going to be rich. Let's all go help Mitch Mythic save the world. What is it, Mitch? Are aliens coming to get us," Sage taunted.

"It's more than that," Mitch snapped back. "I didn't expect you to believe me, but I've got proof. I can't show you here, but if you come with me, I'll show you all something that will blow your minds."

"No one's going anywhere with you, Mitch," Sage said. "Isn't that right, everybody?"

"Who says we have to listen to you, Sage?" a voice piped up from the back and Gareth 'Double-Cheese' Lishinski stepped out into the light of the fire. "I want to know what the hell Mitch is talking about. By the way, Mitch that was an awesome goal you scored in that game."

"Who's going to listen to you, Double Cheese?" Sage shot back.

"Shut up, Sage. Nobody made you captain. I'm with Mitch too," Darren Francis said, pushing past Sage.

"Who else wants to join these losers and run off with Mitch Mythic? What a joke," Sage spat out.

"This is no joke," Mitch said. "I wouldn't come to you guys and ask for your help unless I was deadly serious. We're all in danger, and I can prove it. They are hunting for SoHee and I right now. You might've heard about her. She's the girl that was in the accident everybody is talking about. That was no accident, and they made her a prisoner. MindHIve didn't come to Kingsford to have a convention. It's all just for show. They came here for an entirely different reason. You will not believe me if I tell you, but if you come with me, I can prove it to you. If you still don't believe me after I show you what I know, you can go back to believing whatever you want about me, but I doubt that will be the case once you see what's really going on."

"This sounds like some ridiculous conspiracy theory," Sage said. "You guys are all idiots if you go with him."

"I want to see what this is all about. I heard some crazy rumors on the Internet," Greg Curtis said, joining the others.

"Greg, if you go, I'll never invite you to swim in my pool again. Mitch, you said they are looking for you. I think it's time I phoned this in." Sage said before he reached into his pocket and pulled out his phone.

"Sage, I don't think you're getting it," Mitch shot back. "This isn't about you and me. You need to get over it. I know I have."

"What are you guys doing?" Sage shouted while more kids rushed over to join with Mitch.

"You do whatever you want, Sage, but I'm not going to let the past drag me down," Mitch said, looking Sage in the eye. "Come on, everybody. There's not much time. Follow me."

Turning to leave, Mitch led the group back from the way in which he and SoHee had come. They scrambled up the edge of the pit and filed into the forest, leaving Sage and Candace alone by the fire.

"We've got to go in here, but trust me it'll be all right," Mitch said as they approached the mouth of the cave. "Everybody follow SoHee, she's got a light. Once we're inside, she'll lead the way."

As his friends filed past him, he looked back through the moonlight streaming through the pine trees, and spotted two figures in the distance.

After a few more minutes of stumbling over rocks, they entered into the large cavern where Mitch and SoHee appeared a short time before. Walking at the front of the group, SoHee used her "thing" to light the way. To everybody, it just looked like a flashlight. As Mitch stepped to her side, SoHee held it in her hand while his friends gathered around them in a circle.

"Ok, so what I'm about to show you may seem insane, trust me, that's how I felt when I first heard all of this, but it will all make sense if you just hear me out," Mitch said while dozens of expectant faces looked back at him. "SoHee, show them what you've got."

SoHee nodded and held out the necklace in her hand. Everybody's jaw dropped in unison while it unpacked itself before their eyes.

"You've all heard about inReal and its capabilities, but this is nothing like anything anybody has ever seen before. I'm not going to try to explain the science. I'm not that smart, and we don't have time, but what I will do is try to show you everything I have learned in the last little while as quickly as possible. Now you might not believe what I've got to say, but a picture is worth a thousand words," Mitch said while he looked out at his audience. "SoHee, let's start at the beginning."

As the orb flashed images of the events leading up to the present circumstances, Mitch tried his best to explain his experience. After he finished, the onlookers sat in silence for a moment before a voice spoke up in the back.

"Do you really think we can stop these guys, Mitch?" Sage Rhinus said, stepping into the light.

"Yes, I do. With your help and everybody here, I think we can stop them," Mitch said.

"Well, then there's only one thing I want to know," Sage said. "When are you gonna shut up and show us how to use these things?"

The cavern erupted in cheers as everybody jumped to the feet and crowded around Mitch.

"Ok, settle down. If we're going to do this, we've got a lot of work to do, and we don't have much time. MindHIve is going to open up that portal anytime now, and we need to act fast. Does everybody have a MindHIve phone on them?" Mitch asked, and they all nodded their heads. "All right, I need everyone to line up single file in front of me. SoHee, get your thing ready. We're going to have an inReal crash course right here in this cavern."

Flashes of light lit up the cave as the orb altered each phone. Gathering around Mitch with their upgraded devices, Mitch explained to his friends how to activate inReal. There were a few hectic moments and near-crashes, but soon, everybody was hovering off the ground. After a few helpful pointers from Mitch, the whoops of laughter and joy echoed off the cavern walls while they became more confident with their new abilities.

"Motion is one thing, but weapons are a whole different level," Mitch explained as he brought the group together. "You can produce weapons and shields at will by focusing your mind on what you want to see. The most important thing is you've got to believe. You have to believe you can do it. Once you believe in yourself, you can do anything. Now, who wants to be the first volunteer for combat?"

"I do," Gareth said, floating toward Mitch.

"All right, Double-cheese. Let's do this," Mitch said with a grin.

39

"You're sure this is going to work? I cannot afford any mistakes. We've only got one shot at it."

"According to the specs you provided, everything is in place and ready. We've drill deep enough into the core to draw the appropriate amount of energy required for the procedure. Unless some unforeseen circumstances arise, the process should go according to plan," Gerald Tobero said while he and Robert stood in the vast cavern beneath the MindHIve complex observing engineers attending to the pulsing beam of energy shooting up into generator situated beneath the central dome.

"Well, I want all hands on deck for this one. Any interference should be handled with full force. Have you had any luck locating our little love birds? The fact that they are in the wild is pushing my blood pressure to dangerous levels," Robert said as two engineers measured the toxicity of the cavern.

"We've searched the data banks of the satellites, and we've combed over the CCTV footage throughout the area, but we haven't been able to uncover any clues of their whereabouts. It's the strangest thing I've ever seen. They simply disappeared."

"Regardless of what happened, they are on the loose as we speak and that is unacceptable. If those little punks think they're going to compromise all we've worked for, they're in for a big surprise. How about the procedure? Is everybody ready?"

"The security team has been briefed, and we drilled the scenario several times. We've also run a number of simulations, and the data assures us we have a high probability of success."

"Are you kidding me? 'A high probability?' I don't want to hear that phrase ever again. You tell me this going to go off without a hitch, and then you tell me we have 'a high probability' of success. So there is a chance this could blow up in my face? What kind of percentages are we talking about? You know what, cancel that. Don't tell me any numbers. You just make sure this thing works. If those two show their faces around here, I've got a surprise for them. How long until we're ready? I've got to go and prepare the package."

"The main dome has been sealed, but the convention is in full swing, and we don't want our attendants getting suspicious. Midnight seems like an appropriate time to begin the procedure."

"Well, it's 5 pm now. We've got a few hours more to get ready for this. I want all hands on deck for this one. I'll need Alpha team with me up top, and I want Beta team down here guarding the pipe," Robert said before he made his way to the elevator.

"Understood, sir," Gerald said while Robert disappeared into the blackness above.

Upon reaching the surface, Robert exited a hatch and stumbled upon Allan, laying on an ergonomic body chair.

"Working hard or playing DeathWorld, Allan?" Robert said with a grin.

"Working hard, as usual, sir," Allan said, jumping to his feet. "Your social media accounts are on fire at the moment. Me and the rest of the team are trying to stay ahead of all the reports coming out. There is wild speculation everywhere about what happened during the blackout."

"You just stick to the script, Allan," Robert said while he strode past. "I've got enough on my plate as it is. I don't want to have to go sort out any more PR messes."

"Understood, sir. But even with everybody onboard we're having a tough time keeping up," Allan said as he tailed Robert.

"At this point, the press is the least of my worries. If everything goes according to plan tonight, we'll be able to sing a different song tomorrow. Have you made certain everybody within the complex is aware the main dome will be completely off-limits for the next 24 hours?" Robert asked, approaching a door flanked by two security guards.

"We've issued warnings using every platform imaginable. Everyone understands the dome is being repaired after the power surge," Allan said as Robert stopped in front of the security guards.

"Good work, Allan. Keep your eyes and ears open. We cannot afford to have anybody drop the ball now. If we get out of this clean, there'll be a big promotion in the works for you, but if you blow it, you'll be out the door so fast it'll make your head spin," Robert said before the sliding door opened in front of him.

"Aren't you going to scan my pass?" Robert asked the guards standing before the doors.

"But you're him," one of the guards replied.

"I don't care who it is at the door. Everybody gets their badges scanned. Now I understand why we experienced such a massive breach yesterday. I've spent billions of dollars on security, but you just can't escape the fact that people are morons. Get your head in the game," Robert shouted at the guards while they scrambled to scan his pass.

Walking to the last door at the end of the hallway, he scanned his pass and walked into the observation room that looked in on Drak's cell.

"Get on your feet," Robert snapped at a guard who sat slumped over in his chair looking at his phone.

"Uh, yes, sir. Right away, sir," the guard said, jumping up.

"I swear I've been too easy on you guys. I'm not sure about the bonus situation the way things have gone over the last while," Robert said before he walked over to the window and looked in on his prisoner.

"Apologies, sir. Things haven't changed in the last while. He's just been sitting at the desk with his head down."

"Well, that's over now. It's time to prep him for transfer. Full shackles. Before you do that, I'll need the room for a moment. He and I are going to have a little chat before we wash our hands of him," Robert said as he stepped to the door of the cell.

"Understood, sir. We'll prep the gear while you go inside. Are you sure you don't want anybody to stand watch? Mr. Tobero said this guy is super dangerous."

"He won't give me any trouble," Robert said before he scanned his pass and walked into the cell. Drak didn't look up as Robert walked in. The room smelled like stale sweat and old urine. Robert scrunched his nose as he stood before his prisoner.

"Oh, you look pretty rough, but that's to be expected, I guess. It is jail and all. I'd offer you a final meal, but they say you haven't been eating," Robert said while he sat down at the table.

"You know what's coming next, right?" Robert asked as Drak sat up and leaned back.

"I understand you are selling out your people for a limited gain," Drak said.

"Ah, a freedom fighter to the end, how admirable," Robert said with a grin. "I told you I could help you if you cooperated and I'm still holding out that olive branch, but I'm pretty sure there isn't a fiber in your body willing to work with me."

"You are correct."

"Did you enjoy the game? Your friend Mitch is quite the talent. I look forward to making good use out of him. You may have had your paws on him, but I'm pretty persuasive myself. I'm sure he'll come around to my way of thinking once he understands the scope of the situation. You, on the other hand, have proven to be a tough nut to crack. I'll commend you for that, but look where it's gotten you: a one-way ticket to the absolute worst place in the Universe. Our big metal friends have got it bad for you. I'll bet they have all kinds of wonderful surprises waiting on the other side."

"I am not afraid of the Masters."

"Well, you should be. The way they talk, I'd be pissing in my pants, but by the smell of it, I'm guessing you already did. We're going to have to shower you up before we hand you over. I can't have my prize prisoner smelling like a urinal."

Robert rose out of his chair and looked down at Drak before he left.

"Don't think about trying anything when we wheel you out, or I'll make your last breathing moments the most painful experience of your short, miserable life."

"You will be defeated."

"You think your buddy Mitch is going to come and save you? He hightailed it out of here with his lady friend as soon as things got heavy. He's hiding out somewhere like the spineless little twerp he is. If he even thinks about showing his face around here, I will squash him like a bug," Robert said before he walked out.

40

"It's time. Gather everyone together," SoHee said as she looked at Mitch.

"Everybody come here. We need to go over the plan," he shouted to his friends, practicing their new-found skills in the darkness of the cavern.

Coming together as a group in front of the glowing orb, a hush came over everyone in anticipation of SoHee's plan.

"My 'thing' has suggested a two-pronged approach," SoHee said after she stood up. "The generator draws its power from an energy source beneath the MindHIve complex,"

A 3D image of the complex appeared within the orb as SoHee spoke. Rising from the core of the earth, a pillar of energy passed through a massive cavern beneath the facility before connecting to the generator in the main dome.

"One team will need to infiltrate this cavern and deliver the payload to this location," SoHee said while a light flashed where the column of energy connected to the ceiling of the cavern.

"After the agent is delivered, the second team and myself will be transferred using the orb's wormhole capabilities to the main dome where we will establish a perimeter around the generator while the orb creates a standing wormhole that will catch the blast. It's a risky plan that requires speed and execution rather than force. The first team must enter the cavern and drop off the bomb before the MindHIve forces can shut down the generator, and the second team must time their arrival precisely in order to have enough time for the orb to establish a standing wormhole while not being overwhelmed by security. The time to strike will be when the generator powers itself up to create the portal. The column of energy will swell substantially as the generator draws more power. This will be observable within the cavern. The first team must infiltrate the cavern at this point and wait for the generator to initiate the process," she said before a flashing indicator became visible on the cavern wall.

"Once the process begins, the team must deliver the payload before the generator is able to establish the portal. If the payload is delivered after the portal has been generated, the consequences will be disastrous. Does anybody have any questions?" she asked her audience.

"Why don't you just send in the orb and have it warp whistle that generator out by itself?" Greg Curtis asked.

"That may be possible, but the orb will need time to create the standing wormhole, and the generator is likely to be heavily guarded, so a team will be needed to keep the attention of the security team while the wormhole is established," SoHee said.

"Why do we need to blow it up? It seems really risky," Sage asked.

"The generator is connected to the Masters' network. By triggering an explosion within their system, we will cut them off from our world and prevent them from coming back," SoHee replied.

"What about this payload?" Double-Cheese asked. "What kind of bomb is it?"

"The orb will generate a concentrated ball of energy that can be handled and maneuvered using inReal. It must be manually inserted into the beam as close to the generator as possible. According to my calculations, the location indicated on the map the best possible location," SoHee said.

"So somebody has got to go over there and shove this thing in the hole?" Darren said, and everybody laughed.

"That's correct," SoHee replied. "Mitch will lead the first team into the cavern, and I will lead the second team into the dome. There is no doubt this is a high-risk plan, but it is our best chance given the conditions."

"How is the first team supposed to get into the cavern? It must be on lockdown," Candace McAllister asked.

"The orb has traced a path from this location to the cavern that will allow the first team to approach undetected," SoHee said before a twisting 3D map appeared in the orb. "I'm sending this map to everybody on the first team. You can use your device to follow the map so you won't get lost."

A flashing light caught everyone's attention as they pulled up their panels. Several tentacles of light extended out of the bulb and presented a small glowing cube. SoHee took the cube and held it in her hand.

"This is the payload," she said. "Inside is a condensed ball of positive energy. You can open the box using your inReal, like this."

Running her hand over the box, it unpacked itself to reveal an illuminated ball. As the group covered their eyes, she packed it down again and handed the cube over to Mitch.

"Open it when you are absolutely certain," she said, placing the cube in his hands "You'll only get one shot at this."

Mitch took the cube and ran his hand over the top as SoHee had shown him. Holding the ball of light before him, he felt intense vibrations moving up his arm. As he brushed his hand over the top, he closed it back down and placed the cube in the pocket of his blue uniform.

"There's no looking back " he said loud enough for all to hear. "We need to move. If you received the map, you are on the first team, and if not, you are with SoHee. Remember, we're not trying to beat these guys at their own game. Just keep them distracted and stay safe."

He engaged his inReal device and jumped into the air. Hovering for a moment before SoHee, he looked her in the eyes and nodded.

"First team follow me," he shouted as he broke his gaze and shot to the opposite end of the cavern.

Keeping his panel open, he followed a blip on the map. It was a twisting and curving trail, and they had to pause several times to make sure they hadn't lost anybody. After passing through another large cavern, they came to a narrow cave illuminated at the far end.

"We're here. Keep quiet. We don't want to blow our chance. Disengage your device now, or we'll be detected," he said before he lowered himself to the ground and crossed his arms over his chest.

Crouching low, he entered the narrow cave and made his way toward the light. It was only a short distance to the end of the tunnel, and he had to cover his eyes while he approached the opening. As he neared the end, he spotted a rocky ledge at the mouth of the cave.

Shading his eyes while he peered over the rock, he was awestruck by the sheer size of the pulsing column of energy illuminating the massive cavern. After he adjusted to the light, he spotted the heavy security presence surrounding the beam. He dropped back down below the rock and looked back at his friends. Anxious eyes looked out at him from the shadows.

"We're going to need a lot of luck to pull this thing off," Gareth whispered while he crawled over and sat next to Mitch.

"Someone once told me if you believe in yourself, anything is possible," Mitch said. "I didn't believe him at the time, but I've been through enough in the last while to know he was right."

Raising himself up, he peered over the rock again. The column was pulsing with energy, and it had expanded in size. The generator was powering up. As he pushed off the rock into a crouching position, Mitch indicated to his friends that it was time to act.

"Sage, take your guys and head to the left. Draw them to you. You don't need to engage them, just keep them busy. Darren, do the same on the left, but wait until Sage gets their attention. Double-Cheese, you stick with me," Mitch said before he engaged his inReal.

Bringing up the directory, he accessed his MindHIve account. He tapped the live video feed and pressed the record button.

"My name is Mitch Mythic. You may know me as #epiccrotchshot boy. I know people have been saying a lot of crazy things about what is happening at the MindHIve convention, but if you are watching this video, you are about the see the truth. I'm not going to say too much more, but just know we are here to put an end to this, and I'll let everybody out there be the judge of who is right and who is wrong," Mitch said into the camera before looking out at his friends.

"Just believe, and everything else will follow," Mitch said as he turned and leaped over the ledge. Pushing himself toward the ceiling of the cavern, he saw Sage and his team shoot to the left as they had been instructed. Gareth followed closely behind him, and he pulled up next to Mitch after they reached the top.

As Darren led the other team towards the right, he spotted some cover amongst a group of stalactites and shot toward them.

"Once both teams attract the attention of their new playmates, we'll be heading straight to the top of the column," Mitch whispered at Gareth while they pressed their backs against the rocks.

"Got it," Gareth said as he looked down and gulped.

In no time flat, the guards noticed the swathe of kids flying at them. Opening fire, the MindHIve forces pushed out of their defensive positions to intercept the intruders.

"Now's our chance. Time to move," Mitch said before he let go of the rock.

41

A small group of men and women dressed in dark suits looked down on Drak from a platform near the stage as he was led into the main dome. Allan could be seen standing among them. Aside from the group of onlookers, the stands were vacant, but a large contingent of the MindHIve security force was on hand, positioned in strategic locations overhead and on the ground.

All eyes were on Drak as he approached the stage. Two guards walked in front of him while two guards followed from behind. Bound at the wrists, an inReal collar hung around his neck and he floated off the ground. As he neared, he spotted Robert standing in front of the same generator he attempted to sabotage only a few days earlier.

"Ladies and Gentlemen of the board and our esteemed guests. Please allow me to introduce you to a very special person. He is the reason we are all gathered here in the lovely little town of Kingsford. You could say none of this would be possible without him, but that would be giving him a little too much credit. Please give a warm round of applause for Drakon Trendago! He's a long way from home, and we're about to send him off on a journey he won't forget." Robert said as he looked up at his audience.

"Before we get started, there are some safety precautions I want to warn you about. You've all been issued a special pair of glasses. Please don't take them off because it might get a little bright. We'll be sealing you inside an inReal protective bubble while the process takes place. This is for your safety. Once you are inside, you won't be able to get out, so if you need to go to the bathroom, I suggest you go now."

After several people made their way to the exits, Robert turned his attention to his engineering team, who were preparing the generator to open the portal.

"Are you eggheads ready for this, or do I need to remind you how easily I can take away your yearly bonuses?" Robert snapped while he watched several engineers stumbling over each other around the generator's control panel.

"We're almost ready, sir. You have to understand that this is an incredibly delicate procedure," Andrew said. "Even the slightest miscalculation could compromise the process. If we are off by even a fraction, the consequences will be severe."

"Yeah, yeah, we'll all get sucked into oblivion," Robert said, cutting him off. "Just get it done. The clock is ticking. We need to start the generator in the next five minutes, or we risk missing our window."

"Understood, sir. It won't be much longer," the engineer said.

"Get this sorry excuse for a prisoner in place before the generator," Robert commanded his security personnel while he glared at Drak.

Two guards came forward and grabbed Drak by his arms on either side and dragged him to the mark indicated by Robert in front of the generator.

"Keep a close eye on him as well. He is as dangerous as they come, but you wouldn't know it just by looking at him."

As he watched his underlings prepare, he received an alert in his inReal. Tapping the screen, the face of Gerald Tobero appeared before him.

"Sir, we've got action in the sub-level. I've deployed every available asset, but the situation is critical. We are under attack. I repeat. We are under attack."

"Just hold it together down there. We're about to kick-start things up here right now. Who is perpetrating the attack?"

"It appears to be a group of kids led by your protégé, Mitch Mythic."

"Mitch Mythic has returned. This is going to be fun. I'm pretty sure you can handle those little punks. If you happen to get overpowered by a bunch of hick kids, you'll lose more than your beach house, Gerald. Do you understand?"

"Understood, sir. We won't let you down," Gerald said before he ended the conversation.

"We're ready to begin the process, sir," the engineer shouted to Robert.

"Well, what are you waiting for? Let's get this party started. It looks like we're in for an interesting night," Robert said with a grin.

As he spoke, a blinding flash of light filled the auditorium, forcing him to cover his eyes. After he recovered, Robert looked up to see a glowing green orb with a petite female hovering at its center. Several youths flanked her on both sides, floating above the generator with their rogue devices engaged.

"Well, look at what we have here," Robert said, gazing up at his new guests. "I thought prom was next week, or did I get that wrong? Either way, if you came to dance, you came to the right place. Get 'em."

While the guards rushed out to engage the intruders, Robert walked over to Drak.

"Jackson, Baldwin, stand guard over this one. I'm going to show our new friends how we handle uninvited guests," he shouted before he stepped back. Crossing his arms over his chest, he raised himself into the air.

SoHee lobbed balls of fire down on to the security forces, but she took a defensive position as she saw Robert approaching.

"Is that all that you thought it would take?" Robert said as he shot toward Sohee. "You think you could just drop in here and do whatever you like and get away with it."

"I think I'm not afraid of you," SoHee said before she shot a ball of light at Robert.

"Well, you should be," Robert said while charging forward. Slamming his fists together, the field of energy around him expanded into a cloud of billowing red. Surges of energy pumped along his arms, forming two red clouds around his fists.

"Did you really think you could come here, to my house, and defeat me?" Robert said, hovering in front of SoHee as spires of energy crackled around his form.

"That's the plan," SoHee said as she commanded her orb to send several bombs of light at Robert.

"I love your enthusiasm, but your naivety is beyond explanation," Robert said while he blocked her attack. "Either way, I was hoping you guys would drop in. I've got an upgrade I have been itching to try out."

As he spoke several, pulses rippled over his body. Extending his arms overhead, he brought down his fists with a furious rage. The impact sent everyone in the vicinity sprawling backward, all except for SoHee, who held fast and locked eyes with her foe.

"Well, look at Miss Science," Robert said with a laugh. "Do you want to play, little girl? I've got a few moves I've been dying to try out."

"Let's see what you got, old man," SoHee said.

Paul Ormond

42

A firestorm blasted out at Mitch and Gareth as they shot toward the pulsing column.

"Shields up Double-Cheese. Things are going to get hot," Mitch shouted over the din. "They're coming at us. Let's duck under and come around. Follow me."

Changing course, Mitch dropped straight down with Gareth following close behind.

"They're on our tail now," Gareth shouted while the soldiers fired orbs in their direction.

"That's where we want them. Keep moving," Mitch shouted as he pushed ahead through the rocks strewn across the cavern floor.

Nearby, Sage was taking fire from all directions. Having drawn the attention of a swarm of security guards, he and his squad spread out across the cavern as the soldiers gave chase.

Beneath him, he spotted Mitch and Gareth rocketing along the floor of the cavern while he dodged shots from several incoming guards.

After he came out of a turn, he shot back a volley of his own and changed direction in one motion. Rising above his attackers, he watched Candace spike several balls of light at the soldiers charging toward her.

Stunned, they plummeted to the ground and Sage let out a whoop of encouragement. His joy vanished as he spotted Mitch shooting towards the base of the column with a group of guards in hot pursuit. Looking up to the apex of the pillar, he saw a slew of soldiers entering the cavern from the ceiling.

"Mitch is in trouble. We need to help him. More of 'em are coming in from the top," he shouted at Candace. "Up there. Let's move."

Nearing the base of the column, Mitch glanced back to see the security team closing in.

"Follow my lead. We're going up," Mitch shouted at Gareth before he changed course.

"Keep close to me. Let's try something out," Mitch said while he circled around the gigantic pillar. Behind him, the security guards closed the gap, but he and Gareth were able to avoid their fire by staying close to the surface of the column.

"Get ready to slam on the breaks," Mitch shouted as they shot up. "On the count of three, let's drop down. Three, two, one, go."

Dropping down the column several feet, they raced around the pillar and opened fire on the unsuspecting troops from below, clearing the way to the top.

"We're almost there. Cover me while I get the payload ready," Mitch shouted as he reached into his uniform.

"I'll shield you. Keep moving," Gareth hollered back.

After he pulled out the small black cube, Mitch dragged his hand over its surface and a ball of light hovered in his hand.

"We've got to get to the top. Keep pushing and don't let anyone sneak up on us from below," Mitch shrieked over the din.

"I'll see what I can do. But those guys up there might have other ideas," Gareth shouted as the soldiers guarding the top of the column took notice of their approach and opened fire.

With all of his energy focused on his shield, Mitch readied himself to shoot the payload into the energy source. Hammered by incoming blasts, he reached back and inhaled. Just before he was released the ball of energy, he felt something heavy and hard slam into his back. He screamed in horror as he watched the payload slip out of his hands. Spinning out of control away from the column, he looked back to see Davis rocketing after him.

"Where do you think you're going, Mythic?" Davis shouted after Mitch righted himself.

"I'm putting a stop to this," Mitch said as he dodged Davis's attack.

"You think you can stop this? Do you have any idea how ridiculous you sound?" Davis said while he spun to face his opponent. "You're the most wanted terrorist on the planet right now."

"Is that what they're saying?" Mitch said before he shot away from his opponent in search of any sign of the payload.

Racing toward the pillar, Sage watched a lone guard attack Mitch from behind before he could release the payload. As he rushed to help his friend, the ball of light shot past him.

"Is that what I think it is?" he shouted.

"It looks like it," Candace yelled back while she and a dozen of their friends kept pace with Sage.

"You guys keep them busy. We're going to go salvage this mission," he shouted over at his friends while he and Candace changed to retrieve the payload before it was lost into the wall of the cavern.

Despondent after loosing sight of the payload, Mitch ascended toward the ceiling of the cavern. As he saw his friends approaching the tower, a snarl formed on his lips.

"We can at least give them a fight they won't forget," Mitch said aloud. He hoped the live video was getting out there and somebody, somewhere, was watching it.

As swathes of fire shot out of from the top of the column, the attacking youths were forced to retreat or risk being incinerated. The soldiers had formed a wall of shields around the column, and it proved to be an impenetrable defense. In close quarters, the seasoned guards had the advantage, and from their covered positions, they were able to reduce the number of attackers rapidly.

Nearing the pillar, Mitch gritted his teeth and searched for any sign of an opening. As he circled the wall of shields, he spotted Davis join the ranks of soldiers and engage his shield.

A barrage of fire followed him as he raced around the pulsing column. Time was running out. If he didn't act fast all would be lost. Coming full circle, his heart soared when he saw Candace and Sage flying at him.

In his hand, Sage carried the payload, and he held it high as he raced toward the pillar. With his heart pound in his chest, Mitch charged forward to help his friends.

Reacting to Sage's attack, Davis and a swathe of guards rushed out from their positions to cut him off before he could deliver the payload. As the guards pushed out, Mitch watched Candace break away from Sage. Focused on the payload, a gap in the defenses formed as the guards advanced. Swinging to his right, Sage swatted the ball out in front of Candace, and she came down upon the ball with a furious strike, sending it rocketing toward the column.

Davis had anticipated the move, and he broke away from his formation to cut off the shot. As Davis blocked the ball of light on its way toward the column with his arm, Mitch rushed in from the right.

Deflecting off the Marine's limb, the ball bounced into the air and Mitch reached out and caught the orb. At full speed, Mitch pulled the ball to his side, and he saw the column in front of him.

Righting himself, Davis rushed toward him along with a swarm of MindHIve forces. Going full force, Mitch charged towards the column. As Davis was about to reach him, Mitch changed directions, evading his attacker and swatted the payload into the column.

For a brief moment, silence blanketed the battle before a tremendous wave of energy rippled down the pillar, and the entire cavern was filled with a blinding light.

The impact of the explosion sent everybody reeling in all directions, and Mitch lost any sense of bearing as he spun out of control. People and debris tumble around him, and he saw his own body stretched out before him, but he was powerless against the force of the explosion.

As he slammed into a steep bank, he tumbled to the floor of the cavern. Bodies were strewn across the ground, and both guards and kids groaned in pain as they recovered from the blast. Getting to his feet, Mitch looked up to the now ruptured column of energy. He tried to activate his inReal, but it didn't respond.

Knowing full well that things were far from over, he needed to find a way up to the central dome. SoHee was up there along with his friends, and they could use all the help they could get. He spotted a MindHIve guard nearby on the ground, and he appeared to be unconscious. Searching the body, he found the guard's inReal and stuffed it into his suit. According to the panel it was 60 percent charged, and the shields were still somewhat intact. It would have to do. Rising into the air, Mitch pushed up and rocketed toward the roof of the cavern again.

The pillar was still incredibly unstable, and explosions emitted from its membrane at random. As he closed in on the ceiling, he spotted a metallic catwalk leading to a stairwell that connected to an opening in the ceiling.

Hitting the platform at full speed, he charged for the stairs, but was cut off by a tall black man with a shaved head who dropped down onto the landing from out of nowhere.

"In a hurry, Mitch Mythic?"

"You could say that."

"Do you think you stand a chance here?"

"As a matter of fact, I do."

"Well, then I won't stand in your way. These stairs lead to the sub-level beneath the main dome. Turn to the left, and you will find another set of stairs that allow access to the ground level next to the stage. You must hurry. Things are escalating quickly up there," Gerald said.

"Why are you helping me?"

"Because I don't want to be on the wrong side of history," Gerald shouted at Mitch. "Now get out of here. This place is going to erupt at any moment, and I intend to save anyone I can before it does."

43

"How are you enjoying our little gathering now, Miss Science?" Robert shouted before he brought his fist down upon SoHee's shield and knocked her across the dome.

As she righted herself, a series of pulses burst from her core before several long limbs extended out of the surface of the sphere, thickening with each surge of energy. She raised her new arms into the air and smashed them together, sending a shock wave toward the center of the dome.

Robert saw the wave approaching and brought his fists down to counter her attack. Towering into the air, SoHee stalked toward the generator, and her limbs let loose a barrage of fire at Robert's hulking form. As the projectiles rained down upon him, Robert created a protective dome around the generator to deflect the onslaught.

"Something's happening. The readings are going nuts," Andrew shouted at him as an oval cloud of billowing energy hovered over the generator. A band of black appeared within the oval, widening by the second.

"You just hold this thing together," Robert shouted back. "I'll keep little Miss Science at bay."

"I think you're going to need to see this, sir," the engineer shouted again. "The energy field has been destabilized somehow. Something entered the stream, and it is disrupting the process. If things continue at this rate, we're going to have a meltdown on our hands."

"What do you mean by meltdown? This can't be happening," Robert shouted in a rage. "Open that goddamn portal right now."

"We're trying, sir, but we need a stable flow of energy to maintain the portal," the engineer said.

"This is just typical. If you want something done, you'll just have to go and do it yourself. Get out of the way and take some cover this might get messy," Robert ordered the engineers.

Rising up in front of the sputtering portal, he reached out with his massive arms and gripped the edge the ring before a beam of energy shot out of the energy cloud swirling around him. As the portal stabilized, he released his grip on its edges.

"I'm using my device to balance the energy field, but I'm not sure how long I can maintain it, so get to work," Robert shouted at his engineers again.

Keeping the beam of energy focused on the portal, he turned himself around.

"Haven't had enough?" Robert said as the multi-limbed orb bore down upon him.

"I need you guys up here now," Robert shouted at the guards surrounding the generator. "Defend this beam at all costs. I've got to teach somebody a lesson."

"Yes, sir," the guards responded before launching into the air.

Charging toward her adversary, SoHee lobbed a barrage of fire in his direction as she approached. Robert used his huge limbs to bat them aside with ease before pummeling her with his large fists. The impact knocked her backward, but she counter-attacked with one of her long green limbs, and locked onto Robert's left arm. He brought down his free fist onto SoHee's outstretched arm and was able to free himself. Raising his fist in the air, he struck at her again as SoHee locked onto him with several of her limbs.

As the battle raged, Drak remained on his knees, listening to the events unfolding in the dome through the hood covering his head. He heard shots fired nearby, and the surrounding guards scrambled for cover. Several more blasts went off, and one of the guards screamed. Footsteps approached him from behind before a hand grasped his hood and yanked it off. Drak looked up to see Mitch Mythic's face grinning back at him.

"Did you miss me?" Mitch said while helping Drak to his feet. "Now, how do you get these things off?"

"There on the guard. That square thing," Drak shouted.

Reaching for the device on the guard's belt, Mitch unlocked his friend and pulled him back behind a barrier. After checking to see if the coast was clear, Mitch returned to the guard. He searched his body and came back holding an inReal device.

"Wouldn't want you to miss out on all the fun," Mitch said before he tossed the unit to Drak.

"I'm happy you care about my feelings, Mitch Mythic, but what took you so long?" Drak said while he engaged his device and launched into the air.

"I was a little busy getting acquainted with my new friends," Mitch said as they moved toward the massive figures locked together in front of the portal.

"We've got to help her," Mitch said while they neared SoHee and Robert. "That beam is keeping the portal open. We need to knock it out. If we can find a way to shut it down, we should get that lunatic's attention long enough for SoHee to generate the wormhole. That sounds a little confusing when I say it out loud."

"Ha, you've been busy," Drak laughed as they moved in on the beam.

"That's right I have," Mitch said before he brought up his shield to deflect the shots unleashed on them by the guards defending the beam.

"You can tell me all later. Now, we finish what we started," Drak shouted while he sent a hail of fire down upon the soldiers.

"We need to get his attention," Mitch shouted. "She has powers that can stop all this, but she can't do anything while Robert has her locked down like that."

"I've got a plan. You keep him busy and wait for my signal," Drak said before he raced away.

"Another one of your plans? I'm not sure if I like the sound of that," Mitch shouted before Drak vanished from sight.

Below him, the generator pulsed at a phenomenal rate, growing more unstable by the second. The beam Robert generated blasted the portal, and the opening continued to grow, even though the generator was disintegrating beneath it. Overhead, Robert's hulking form held SoHee back from the mechanism.

"Hey Chapman, you having fun getting beat up by a girl?" Mitch shouted as he buzzed by Robert's head.

"Nice of you to join us, Mythic. It wouldn't be a party without #epiccrotchshot boy in attendance," Robert shouted at him before he smashed his fist into a long green limb. "Do you always send your girlfriend to fight your battles?"

"Ha, it looks like you've got your hands full," Mitch said while he circled the monstrous forms.

"When I'm done with her, it'll be your turn next," Robert shouted back. "Do you really think you can beat me?"

"It looks like we are. Your generator is falling apart. You'll never get the portal open in time. Just take a look around. You've lost. Give in, and we can stop this, or we'll all die here and now," Mitch shouted over the noise.

"You have no idea what you're messing with," Robert shouted.

In a rage, he grabbed SoHee's entire form and hurled her across the dome. As she left his grasp, Robert swung toward Mitch and caught him with his giant fist.

"Well, now look at how the tables have turned. I told you that you could never beat me," Robert said, locking eyes with Mitch.

"You're out of your mind. This whole thing is going to blow, and it's not just us that will die. The whole planet is at risk," Mitch shouted as Robert turned his form to face the portal.

"Oh, you kids are all so overdramatic. Once we open this portal, we'll be able to stabilize the generator and everything will calm down. After I send your friend Drak packing, you'll be on your way to prison for attempting a terrorist plot to destroy the work of MindHIve. I, on the other hand, will be praised as a hero for foiling your plot. Life goes on. Or you could accept my deal, and all of this goes away."

"What's the deal? What happens to me if I accept?"

"No one will ever know what happened here and you'll come work for me. That's a pretty good offer. You've got a natural talent with these devices, and we've already got big plans for inReal ball."

"What about the Masters? They're going to enslave us all."

"Don't worry about that. Those useless old tanks only need to feel like they are in charge. We're going to make the world a better place. With inReal, we'll be able to keep everybody in order. There will be no more wars and no more unnecessary suffering. We can control the population and reduce the impact humanity has on this planet. It's all for the best, Mitch," Robert said as he reached out with his other massive arm to steady the portal.

Drak managed to sneak underneath the chaos raging overhead by disengaging his device and crawling between the empty rows of seats to the left of the stage. As he edged to the backside of the generator, he spotted his target sitting near the stage. Two guards were positioned on either side of the chariot, and they were shooting at the kids swirling above them, oblivious to the fact that Drak lay in wait just a few feet away.

Re-engaging his device, he positioned himself between two chairs. He jumped, and up unloaded on the unsuspecting soldiers. As the guards crumbled to the ground, Drak didn't waste any time watching them fall. He leaped into the chariot and took cover. Moving fast, he brought up his panel and hit the self-destruct button while he attempted to turn on the chariot. As the seconds ticked down on his panel, the chariot came to life beneath his feet.

Rising into the air at the helm of the vehicle, he stumbled forward after a round of fire pummeled the vehicle. The ambushed guards had revived, and they were none too pleased he was about to take off in Robert Chapman's chariot. Dropping down, he felt more blasts hit the side of the craft. From his crouched position he made two gestures, and the chariot accelerated away. He popped up and fired back several shots at the guards as they dove for cover. With a grin on his face, he reached out and drove the chariot toward the expanding portal.

44

As the opening stabilized, several hulking figures appeared on the opposite side, looming silhouettes reaching forward.

"What happens if I accept? How do I know you'll keep your word?" Mitch shouted while glancing over his shoulder at the crackling portal.

"Why don't you trust me, Mitch? After all we've been through," Robert said as the gap widened. "You just let me take care of the mess you made, and then we'll talk about your future."

In the distance, Mitch spotted a green glow rising from the rubble. The portal neared its maximum width, and Robert greeted his guests with several hand signals. As he did, the ring stabilized, and the crackling pulses subsided.

"You see, Mitch. I told you everything would be all right. Just let the adults handle this for now," Robert said.

"You know, there's just one problem with your plan, Mr. Chapman," Mitch said. In the distance, a ball of fire careened toward the portal. A lone figure stood tall at the helm.

"What could I have possibly overlooked, Mitch?" Robert said.

"You may think you can control everybody, but you forgot one thing," Mitch shouted. "No matter how hard you plan it out and design it, it is kids like me who are gonna take your stuff and do whatever we want with it."

Robert caught Mitch's eye, and he turned to see his chariot charging toward the beam. Swinging his immense fist, he brought it down in a rage as the chariot made contact with the light. As Drak's device exploded, the beam reflected back into Robert's off of of the gleaming chariot before it burst into flames. He staggered backward and clutched his eyes, allowing Mitch the opportunity to break free.

Rocketing away from Robert's flailing limbs, Mitch looked back to see SoHee's green orb rise out of the rubble and extend itself toward the portal. While pulses of energy tore through the dome, the hulking metal figures moved toward the opening, but as they reached the crackling halo, the generator imploded upon itself drawing the open portal into a swirling vortex.

From across the dome, Mitch saw SoHee fall from the glowing orb as it rushed toward the spiral of energy rising into the air. While it charged forward, The orb expanded into a gigantic ball of white and green light.

As the gravitational pull of the negative mass grew in strength, the platform upon which Allan and the small audience of Robert's accomplices stood buckled over under the pull. Pounding on the bubble in a desperate attempt to escape, the riser gave way, and they were sucked in to the whirling maw.

Amidst the chaos, Robert swung away from the portal with his massive fists, and he managed to get a grip on the metal floor of the dome. He pulled with all his might against the forces dragging him in, but the power of the implosion was too strong. As the panel he held broke free, he fell into the swirling mass of energy.

Angling away from the explosion, Mitch pushed himself to find SoHee, but another wave of energy knocked him across the dome. He looked back as he sailed through the air and saw the green orb fully cover what remained of the generator before the core exploded. Jagged bolts of blue and green clashed against each other while pulses of light shot out of the swirling cloud of energy rising into the air.

As Mitch slammed into a row of seats, a blinding light engulfed the dome. Shaking his head as he regained consciousness, he rose to his feet and looked out at the scene before him. Smoldering wreckage covered the floor in every direction, and at the center of the dome where the generator had once stood, a massive crater smoldered in its place. From where Mitch stood, he saw was able to spot residual energy crackling within.

Mitch tried to activate his inReal, but when he crossed his arms over his chest, nothing happened. He reached into his suit and pulled out his device and saw it was smashed. Tossing it aside without any hesitation, he raced down the steps that led to the floor. As he climbed over the rubble and mayhem strewn across the dome, his eyes scanned for any sign of his companions. He came to the place where he thought he saw SoHee fall, and he tried to clear the debris in search of her body.

"Did you miss me?" a familiar voice said from behind. He whirled around to see SoHee sitting on top of a piece of crumpled staging.

"Don't scare me like that," Mitch said as he rushed over and embraced her. "Are you all right? What happened? I thought we were dead for sure. What happened to your thingy? Where is Drak?"

"Slow down. Your brain might explode," SoHee said. "I think we're ok, but I can't say for sure what exactly happened. Just before the explosion, I felt something grip my shoulder. I looked up, and I saw a face looking down at me. It smiled at me and then I knew everything was going to be ok. I can remember falling to the ground, but I wasn't afraid."

"Well, whatever it did, your thingy just saved our lives," Mitch said. His face darkened as he looked around. "Drak was right there. He must've gotten sucked in. Did you see him?"

"I didn't, but I haven't really had any time to look around," SoHee said while she got to her feet.

Mitch heard a commotion come from across the dome and he looked over to see Sage and his friends rushing towards them.

"You guys are alive. We're all alive," Mitch yelled as his teammates gathered around him, filling the dome with whoops of joy.

"Hey Mythic," Sage said, locking eyes with Mitch. "Nice shot."

"I couldn't have done it without you," Mitch said. "It was all of us, together."

"Hey look, it's that weird terrorist kid," Gareth shouted. Turning around, Mitch saw Drak limping over some debris. He broke away from the group and rushed to help his friend.

"You're ok," Mitch shouted while shoving broken chairs out of his way.

"You have not seen the last of me yet, Mitch Mythic," Drak said as a grin lit up his face.

"Well, it looks like I'm stuck with you now. Your window out of here seems to have closed. Come on. I need you to meet some people," Mitch said while he led Drak toward his friends. "Everybody, this is Drak. He's my friend, and he's the reason we are all alive right now. If not for him, there's no telling what would've happened to us."

"I remember you from the park," Sage said as he stepped towards Drak. "You need to teach me some of those moves."

"I'll see what I can do," Drak said before everybody laughed.

Another commotion caught their attention again, but this time, the mood in the dome grew grim. A swathe of heavily armed police officers and soldiers entered the room, and they closed in on the group of kids gathered around Mitch.

"It'll be all right. It's me they're here for," Mitch said while he stepped forward.

"Now, nobody move. We're here to contain this situation and bring you all in for questioning," One of the cops nearest to the group said: "Which one of you kids is Mitch Mythic?"

"That would be me, sir," Mitch said with his head down.

"You've got some nerve, son," the cop said while climbing over a pile of wreckage. "The whole world saw that video. You did the right thing by recording it. I don't think I've ever seen anything more incredible in my entire life. You kids are all heroes."

Everybody cheered again, and Mitch was showered with hugs on all sides.

"Now just settle down. This is a volatile situation. We need to get everybody to safety and lock this place down. Anybody with a MindHIve badge needs to be detained immediately, and where the hell is Robert Chapman? I've got a warrant for his arrest here in my hands. He is being charged with high treason and several other counts of conspiracy," the cop said.

"You can search, but I don't think you'll find him," Mitch said. "The last time I saw him, he was standing where that crater is."

"I see. You all need to get out of here. We're going to take statements from all of you and contact your parents. There is quite a crowd of media outside, and I'm pretty sure they're going to want to hear your story as well," the cop said. "Miller and Stephens, take these kids outside and see they get checked out by doctors. I want statements from all of them before we release them."

"Got it, sir," Stephens said as he and another ushered the group toward the exit. "Everybody, follow me."

After being checked out by the doctor in an adjacent dome, Mitch was led into a room and questioned by two detectives. He recounted his story to them, leaving out the parts about Drak. After several tense minutes, the cops seemed happy with his statement and released him. He was then told to sign a few documents, and a military officer told him not to talk to the press. It was still dark when Mitch walked outside, but the first inklings of dawn showed on the horizon.

A crowd of reporters rushed him after he pushed the door open, and he had to bat away cameras and microphones from his face as he tried to move forward. A commotion from behind startled everyone, and the crowd parted to reveal a heaving Mike Mythic striding toward his son while his mother and his little brother followed close behind. "We're so happy you're ok, son," his father said as he hugged him.

"We love you so much, Mitch. We were so scared," his mother wailed before she clutched him on the opposite side.

"I love you guys too," Mitch said with tears in his eyes. "Let's get out of here. I really just want to go home."

As he embraced his family, Mitch watched SoHee run into her mother's arms. They embraced amidst a shower of tears, before an older Asian man wrapped his arms around them both. She looked over at Mitch as she hugged her parents and made a small wave. Mitch waved back while he was led away by his family. He searched the crowd for Drak, but he was nowhere to be found.

45

The MindHIve logo spun clockwise while video chat loaded. The screen went blank for a second before a forehead appeared.

"Let me adjust the camera," SoHee said while her hand covered the screen. "There, that's better."

"You made it home," Mitch said as SoHee's face came into focus.

"Yes, it's so hot here, but I was really happy to sleep in my own bed," she said while she yawned. "Is everything ok in Kingsford? I'm sorry I didn't get to say goodbye. The Korean government officials took us right away, and we were flown out almost immediately. I got to meet the president though," SoHee said with a laugh. "Well, the Korean president anyway."

"Ha, look at you climbing up in the world," Mitch said. "Everything is still a little hectic around here. The government seized control of the site right after, and I keep getting calls from different agencies asking me to make statements about what happened. It's kind of a pain because the media is hounding me as well, but I have been forbidden to speak until the president makes an official statement about what happened."

"Well, your video kind of speaks for itself. I can't believe it's already had over a billion views."

"Yeah, it's a bit nuts, but you'd think after I saved the world they'd stop calling me #epiccrotchshot boy."

"Oh '#epiccrotchshot boy' saved the world, is that right? I seem to remember a certain someone dropping an unknown substance on an impending disaster in the nick of time."

"Well, congratulations. Why don't you go write a blog post about it, Miss Science?"

"Maybe I just will, but it will be tough to beat #epiccrotchshot boy for the media attention. They say they haven't found any sign of Robert Chapman. Apparently, he is the most wanted man on the planet right now."

"They can search all they want. I saw him get sucked into that thing. There is no way he survived. Speaking of Robert Chapman, any plans to delete your MindHIve account? I hear that's all the rage right now."

"I thought about it, but it'll only mean more work, and you know what they say: the devil you know is better than the devil you don't."

"That's pretty deep, Miss Science. Maybe you should try your hand at philosophy. I kinda feel the same way though, plus all of my friends are already there, so what am I supposed to do?"

"What happened to your friend? The one they were calling a terrorist,"

"Oh, Drak? I have no idea. He disappeared while the cops were questioning us and I haven't seen him since."

"Do you think the government took him, or did he escape?"

"That's a good question, and I wish I could give you an honest answer. The thing I know about Drak is he is pretty resourceful. I'm sure I haven't seen the last of him. Hey, I've got to get going. I'm meeting some friends, but let's stay in touch, ok."

"Yeah, I think I need some more sleep. It's actually early in the morning over here, but I'm still not over the jet lag."

"Yeah, I slept for like two days after I was finally able to get to bed."

"Ok, Mitch, thanks for showing me a good time in Kingsford. When are you going to come to Korea?"

"I'm glad you had fun while you were here. I'll come to Korea for sure, maybe you could whip up a wormhole, and I'll pop over for some bibimbap."

"Ha, that's not a bad idea. I'll get back to you on that one. Annyeong-ee-gasaeyeo, Mitch Mythic."

"What does that mean?"

"It means 'go in peace,' but you can just say 'annyeong' because we're friends."

"Well, annyeong, and let me know when you get that wormhole going."

"I will," SoHee said with a laugh and then waved goodbye before the screen went black.

Sunbeams broke through the tree branches, slicing across the path while Mitch walked through the greenbelt near his house on his way to meet up with his friends. The sounds of birds and the babbling brook filled the ravine. Making his way up the hill, he heard a strange whistle in the forest. As he turned around, he saw a familiar hooded figure walking up the path.

"The terrorist has returned," Mitch said before Drak removed his hood and grinned. "You vanished while I was talking to the cops. What happened?"

"Homeland security took me to a special place."

"I bet they did."

"You would be surprised. They wanted to know everything about me. I told my story over and over again to different people. Told them everything. I told them truth."

"You told them your story. Everything?"

"Yes, everything. I am a refugee in this country. I have no family. I came here because my home is too dangerous. I took a volunteer job at MindHIve convention for immigration credit. That night I tried to make a delivery, but I got lost. The guards captured me, and they called me a terrorist. It's a simple case of mistaken identity. Now that they know who real the bad guy is, they brought me back here and let me go."

"Well, welcome home. What are you going to do?"

"What do you do for fun here? Play hockey? No ice?"

"Don't worry. It'll get cold soon. Let's just enjoy the rest of this summer. I'm going to my friend's house. He has a pool. Do you want to come?"

"Uh, another time. I've got to go on a secret mission. The Masters are coming soon."

"I don't like the sound of that."

"You fool easily, Mitch Mythic. You should see the look on your face. Like you've seen a ghost," Drak said with a laugh. "I'll come, but I don't swim so good. You'll save me if drown, right?"

"Man, don't scare me like that," Mitch said as they walked up the hill together.

46

He opened his eyes to nothing. Reaching out, he strained to find anything in the black emptiness pressing against his form. He scanned every direction for a hint of light or a landmark of some kind. Crying out, he couldn't tell if he even made a noise.

After what felt like an eternity, a speck of light appeared before him, faint as a distant star. He covered his eyes with his hands to make sure he wasn't hallucinating. When he removed his hands, he saw the point of light again, but this time it was much larger than when he had first noticed it. It appeared to be gaining speed, and he had the sudden realization that the light wasn't growing larger, it was actually him that was rushing toward it.

As he accelerated, the streaks of light closed around him and formed a narrow tube. Moving at an immeasurable velocity, he raced headlong into oblivion. The light ahead grew at an alarming rate before a tremendous flash consumed the cylindrical passage and he felt himself flattening out, drawn into the void.

He hit something hard. Laying still for a moment, his heart raced in his chest. A wet, gray mass started back at him.

"How was your trip?" a familiar voice said from above. Looking back, he found himself lying on a stone slab.

"Rise, my dear sweet Robert," the voice of Commander Holrathu said before his hulking frame stepped forward from the shadows.

"Oh, thank god. You saved me," Robert said while a wave of relief flashed over him. "I thought I was going to be lost out there forever."

"Oh, my dear sweet Robert, how funny you are. Do you really think you have been saved?" Commander Holrathu said with a chuckle. "After we get through with you, you'll wish you had been obliterated

251

in that explosion. I warned you about what happens to those who disappoint our Royal Emperor. Guards, take this wretch to his holding cell while he awaits his punishment."

Two fearsome metal guards stepped out of the darkness, clutching gigantic staffs.

"You don't understand. It's not my fault. I did everything you asked me to do," Robert screamed as the guards pointed their staffs in his direction. Two red beams of energy seized him around each wrist.

"Oh, I understand very well, my dear Robert," Commander Holrathu said while the guards dragged Robert away. "I understand you made a mess, and now I have to go and clean it up."

Made in the USA
Middletown, DE
30 September 2020

20283199R00151